"I have a

"Until I get you off this hot hillside, why not let me splash you with some water," Blair suggested, lifting the canteen.

Justine half closed her eyes in anticipated ecstasy. "Splash away."

He trickled it onto her temples, and it ran down her neck and into her shirt, giving her a deliciously cool sensation.

She caught the look on his face and was startled to discover that the thin fabric of her damp shirt now clearly revealed her lacy bra and the outline of her full breasts. Then, to her horror, she felt her nipples harden. His eyes smoldered as he dragged his gaze away from her breasts and looked back at her face.

"Something's having a powerful effect on you. Is it the water?" He leaned closer. "Or is it me?"

Dear Reader,

Spellbinders! That's what we're striving for. The editors at Silhouette are determined to capture your imagination and win your heart with every single book we publish. Each month, six Special Editions are chosen with *you* in mind.

Our authors are our inspiration. Writers such as Nora Roberts, Tracy Sinclair, Kathleen Eagle, Carole Halston and Linda Howard—to name but a few—are masters at creating endearing characters and heartrending love stories. Their characters are everyday people—just like you and me—whose lives have been touched by love, whose dreams and desires suddenly come true!

So find a cozy, quiet place to read, and create your own special moment with a Silhouette Special Edition.

Sincerely,

The Editors
SILHOUETTE BOOKS

REBECCA SWAN
Chase the Wind

Silhouette Special Edition

Published by Silhouette Books New York

America's Publisher of Contemporary Romance

To Grandpa and Grandma Nelson,
and to my dad, Joe Rogers, in loving memory.
They rest where the meadowlarks sing.

SILHOUETTE BOOKS
300 East 42nd St., New York, N.Y. 10017

Copyright © 1987 by Elizabeth J. Rogers

ISBN: 0-373-09393-4

First Silhouette Books printing July 1987

America's Publisher of Contemporary Romance

Printed in the U.S.A.

Books by Rebecca Swan

Silhouette Special Edition

Love's Perfect Island #281
Chase the Wind #393

REBECCA SWAN

is happiest when she's writing, traveling or reading, and her life reflects her favorite pursuits. She grew up in a career navy family and has traveled extensively throughout the world. She's currently teaching language arts and is a free-lance writer in her spare time. Her articles have appeared in many national magazines. She lives with her husband, Karl, and her cat, Beatrix, near Mount Rainer in Washington State.

CANADA

Shelby
•

Reardon
•

Seattle
•

Colockum

Olympia
★

CASCADE MOUNTAINS

WASHINGTON

IDAHO

OREGON

Underlined places are fictitious.

Chapter One

A covey of gray partridges burst into the air, shattering the peace of the silent field. With frantic wing beats the startled birds flew off in a dozen directions. The source of their sudden panic, a peregrine falcon, landed where the partridges had been gleaning seeds among the furrows. The falcon blinked its shiny black eyes and looked around in apparent confusion. Gawky and inexperienced, the young hunter had rocketed from the sky and missed its mark. Instead of grasping a plump bird, the peregrine's talons rested on clods of earth. A few feathers from the escaping partridges floated to the ground on the still, warm air.

"What the hell!" a deep male voice bellowed.

Moments before, Justine Fleming had felt a surge of pleasure and excitement as she'd watched her falcon's first hunting stoop, a swift, dramatic arrowing to earth on folded wings. Now she stared in surprised dismay as the man who'd shouted the epithet appeared from behind an outcropping of rocks. Justine had thought she was alone in the upland field, high above Lake Shelby. What was this stranger doing up here in these deserted hills so soon after dawn?

She didn't get a chance for further speculation. With growing alarm Justine watched as the man strode toward her falcon. His brisk pace and agitated manner contrasted with the serenity of the August morning. Clad in snug, faded jeans and a plaid shirt with the sleeves rolled up, he emanated restless energy as he stalked across the calm backdrop of milky blue sky and distant pine groves.

Suddenly fearing for the peregrine's safety, Justine sprinted over the uneven ground, stumbling in her haste to reach her falcon before the man did.

"Hey!" she shouted. "Stop! Don't touch her!"

The stranger halted a few yards away from the peregrine and turned to look at Justine, apparently noticing her for the first time. A little cloud of dust, kicked up by his feet, settled to earth. Justine saw that his handsome face was a mask of impatience and surprise.

The falcon eyed the man with obvious alarm as it prepared to fly away. Its leg bells jingled, and it spread its wings. Justine reached it a moment later and prevented its escape by planting one booted foot on its jesses, the short leather straps that trailed from the bird's ankles. In spite of her trembling fingers and pounding heart, she was able to hood the nervous falcon. As soon as it could no longer see its surroundings, the bird calmed down and allowed Justine to lift it onto her leather-gloved fist. With a deftness born of practice, Justine snapped the short lead that was attached to a ring on her glove to the jesses. Only then did she allow herself the luxury of a ragged sigh of relief; her falcon wasn't going to disappear over the horizon, after all.

"There now," she soothed the peregrine in a shaky voice. "It's all right."

With her bare free hand she swatted dust from the jeans that hugged her long legs and swept some tendrils of ebony hair off her hot forehead. Trying to calm her agitated breathing now that the crisis was over, she faced the stranger, who'd watched her capture the falcon without a word. She knew that her green eyes were sparkling with indignation as she met his cool gaze.

"Exactly what do you think you're doing?" she demanded in a tone that conveyed more courage than she felt.

In the heavy silence that followed, Justine got the distinct impression that this man was more used to asking the questions than answering them. The fluting of a meadowlark pierced the quiet, its song a lighthearted counterpoint to the mood of tension building between Justine and the stranger.

"I was minding my own business until the interruption," the man finally drawled in a voice that returned her challenge.

Emotion churned in the depths of his gray eyes, reminding Justine of storm clouds gathering over forbidding mountains. The powerful image, though fleeting, made her pulse race, and she fought to maintain her facade of composure.

"Why were you going after my falcon?" Justine wanted to know.

"I wasn't going after her," the man corrected. "I was trying to get a closer look, that's all." He shrugged, but Justine could tell that his nonchalance was a thin veneer over tense watchfulness. "It isn't every day that a hawk almost lands in my lap," he added in a dry understatement.

"You scared her," said Justine. "If you'd gone any closer, she would've flown away. I'm not sure I could've called her back." Her tone carried a mixture of accusation and relief that the worst hadn't happened.

"Hey, look, I'm sorry," he responded as he raised his hands, palms toward her, then lowered them. "But I had no idea there was someone up here with her." He tilted a quick half smile at Justine. The expression cooled her irritation a few degrees, and she regarded him more closely.

He stood with his scuffed boots slightly apart, his thumbs hooked inside his back pockets. A shock of hair the color of dark, wild honey fell across his wide brow. Justine noticed that his tanned skin carried a faint sheen of perspiration. It reminded her that the clear sky and rising temperature promised to deliver another typically hot day.

The stranger appeared to be in his mid-thirties. Justine noted his square jaw, wide mouth and full lips. A pale scar cut through one eyebrow. Rather than marring his good looks, the scar added a dash of character. She wondered how he'd gotten it. A few moments earlier, his brows had been drawn together into a frown of annoyance. Now one of them quirked upward, which gave his face an amused expression, as if he were savoring a secret joke. He shifted his tall, solidly built frame as he addressed Justine.

"You know, it seems to me that you're the one who owes me an explanation. I thought I had this place to myself until your bird startled the living daylights out of me." He shook his head slowly from side to side. "Not even in the wilds of eastern Washington can a person find a little peace and quiet." He rolled his eyes with a look of disgust.

"I thought I was alone!" Justine tossed back. "How could I know that someone was hiding up here?"

The falcon stirred on her arm, its bells tinkling softly. Justine reached up to smooth its breast feathers with a calming hand. As always the touch of the bird's soft warmth reassured her.

"I wasn't hiding," the man said. An edge had crept back into his voice, and his gray eyes lanced a warning at Justine. "My pickup's parked down in that gulch." He jerked a thumb over his shoulder. "I was sitting on the other side of those rocks. I'd just poured myself a cup of coffee and was admiring the great view." He nodded toward the landscape below.

Justine looked where he was indicating and felt a familiar wave of pleasure wash over her. In all of her twenty-eight years, she had never found a scene that delighted her more than this one. Lake Shelby gleamed like a polished slab of lapis lazuli. The small summer resort town of Shelby lay at its east end. Gullies sprouting sagebrush and pine trees creased the fawn-colored hills that surrounded the lake. Neat rows of apple and cherry orchards marched along the plateaus, and a window in a white farmhouse mirrored the sun's fire. To the northwest the long lake curved out of sight into the wild Cascades, the mountain range that separates rainy western Washington from its dry eastern counterpart.

The cooing of a mourning dove purled on the still air as Justine again regarded the stranger. An unexpected blush warmed her cheeks when she realized that he'd been staring at her. It was probably her imagination, Justine thought, but the expression on his face seemed to convey more than idle curiosity. Suddenly she felt flustered and self-conscious under his intense appraisal. She tossed her mane of curly black hair in an attempt to shake off the unsettling effect he was having on her.

"So . . . uh," she said, "you like our scenery."

"That's right," he said. "I'm visiting from Seattle. Naturally, I thought I was alone up here at this early hour. I didn't even know those quail were around until they came at me like feathered cannonballs." He paused, giving special emphasis to his next words. "Thanks to your pet bird." He glanced pointedly toward the falcon perched in regal repose on Justine's arm.

His words nettled Justine. "Those weren't quail," she corrected him in a manner that sounded more patronizing than she'd intended. "They were gray partridges. And," she added, "Aldora is not a pet."

The man shook his head and gave a dry chuckle that revealed his disbelief. "Right," he scoffed. "A hawk that wears a little hood and a leash and has a name isn't a pet."

His mocking tone caught Justine off guard, and she felt goaded into correcting his false impression. She hated to seem defensive, and she knew she shouldn't even bother to explain her situation with Aldora to this prickly stranger. But her back was up, and that was as good a reason as any to clarify her position, she told herself.

"Pets are animals you get attached to and plan to keep," she replied. "I'm sure it looks like Aldora's a pet, but in fact, I'm training her for release. If I thought of her as a pet, I wouldn't be able to part with her." She paused. "Al-

dora's a peregrine falcon, by the way," she added. When he
made no response, she continued. "She's still quite young
and couldn't possibly take care of herself." She looked at the
falcon, and a wistful feeling tugged at her heart, but she
shook it off. "She's made wonderful progress since I got
her, and it won't be long before I can let her go." She raised
her chin a fraction. "It's the right thing to do with wild
creatures, don't you agree?"

"Yes, I do," he answered. Interest showed on his face as
he changed the subject with a smoothness that again threw
Justine off balance. "My name's Blair Sutherland." He
paused. "And yours?"

Justine wasn't sure if she wanted to give him her name,
but she was unable to think of a polite way to get out of it,
so she answered, "Justine Fleming."

Blair's attractive mouth curved into a smile as he studied
her. "Justine," he repeated, and his voice was a caress,
warm and honeyed. "It fits you," he added.

Her cheeks again felt suffused with heat. She fought to
suppress the blush that was revealing how much of an impact his close observation was having upon her.

"Wh-why do you say that?" she stammered.

"Justine sounds like the name of a medieval princess," he
responded. "And that's what you remind me of, with that
beautiful falcon on your arm—a tall, elegant medieval
princess." An appreciative expression gleamed in his gray
eyes.

At that moment a soft breeze from the lake ruffled Justine's thick, shoulder-length hair and lifted it off her neck.
She welcomed the cool, silky touch against her fevered skin.
Hmm, a medieval princess. No one had ever said that about
her before. The image intrigued her; the fact that this man
had made such a comment intrigued her even more.

Blair continued his assessment. "You're even sort of
dressed for the part, with that fancy comb in your hair and
that blouse. If I didn't know better, I'd say that you'd just
stepped out of an ancient tapestry."

Justine had found the silver filigree comb in an antique shop several years ago. She could feel that it had worked loose during her sprint across the field and, at the moment, was doing little to keep her heavy hair from billowing around her face.

She'd bought her blouse during a vacation in Mexico. Made of cool white cotton, it was the perfect garment to wear in the desertlike climate of eastern Washington. Embroidery in colors inspired by butterflies' wings decorated its neck and bodice, and the long sleeves were full and loose.

She was relieved when Blair steered them away from his scrutiny of her looks and back to their previous topic.

"How do you happen to have a peregrine falcon, Justine?"

His attractive eyes bored into her. Suddenly she felt exposed, as if he could read her mind or see beneath her clothes. His gaze swept down her trim figure, lingering momentarily on her full breasts and narrow waist, and she fought the impulse to draw together the open throat of her thin blouse. The gesture would've seemed ridiculous, and anyway, what could his curious eyes see besides the outline of her body? She felt the need to press ahead, to use words to distract him from his warm appraisal. The scene in the high field had taken an unexpected turn, one which she wasn't sure how to handle.

"I... I was up in the hills a few weeks ago," she hastened to say, trying to conceal her discomfort. "I came across some kids who said they'd found this falcon and didn't know what to do with her. They were tourists who were heading home that night, and they couldn't take her with them. Even if they had, they wouldn't have known how to care for her and train her to hunt. They were actually trying to feed her potato chips." She sighed and shook her head at the memory. "So I took her, of course."

"Where did you learn falconry?" There was a look of genuine interest on his face. She could also tell that he was aware of the effect he was having on her and was amused by it. She struggled to gain control of the situation.

"My grandfather had a falcon when I was a child," she answered in a tone that was as composed as she could make it. "Grandpa Fleming taught my sister and me how to fly it and take care of it one summer when we were here on vacation." She looked at Aldora with fondness and smoothed the feathers of one wing. "When I got Aldora, she was half starved. The poor thing was so weak she could hardly hold her head up. As you can see, she's come a long way since then."

"Yes," agreed Blair, "she's magnificent. Tell me, how did you come up with her name? It's kind of unusual."

"I happened across it in a book. Aldora is Greek—it means 'winged gift.'" She paused, then sighed with chagrin. "I actually wasn't going to name her, at first. When you name animals, they do seem more like pets," she admitted. "I didn't want to start feeling attached because I knew that I'd eventually be releasing her." She smiled. "But the name seemed so perfect I couldn't resist."

Talking about the majestic falcon had calmed Justine's jangled nerves. She'd kept her possession of the bird a secret for so long she hadn't realized how eager she was to share the story with someone else. But secrecy had seemed her only recourse, she reflected. She was well aware that the inhabitants of this valley held strong, protectionist views regarding the abundant wildlife that roamed these hills. If the conservation-minded people of Shelby knew that Justine was keeping a wild falcon captive, surely there would be a loud public outcry against her project. Caught in the cross fire of protest would be Aldora, a foundling whose recovery depended on careful handling, without a surrounding storm of controversy. No, the people there wouldn't have understood Justine's motives at all, she'd concluded.

Studying Blair, she dismissed the thought that she was telling him too much. After all, he'd said that he was only visiting. He'd no doubt be returning to Seattle in a few days, so there seemed no harm in answering his questions about her falcon.

"Aldora *has* been like a gift because she's brought me so much pleasure," she continued. "When I'm working with her, I forget all about myself and about the problems of the world."

"You're lucky you've got that kind of escape," said Blair, a thoughtful look in his eyes. "I have a business that keeps me hopping, and I rarely have time for anything else." He paused. "Which reminds me," he added half to himself as he glanced at his watch, "I've got to call my manager later this morning."

His suddenly brisk demeanor and the crisp, efficient way in which he looked at the time contrasted sharply with the peaceful atmosphere of their surroundings. Justine mused to herself that this city type seemed out of sync there in the country. His manner made her feel a little jumpy.

He nodded toward Aldora. "Was it much of a hassle getting the permit for your falcon?"

His unexpected question caught Justine by surprise, and her nervousness intensified. "The . . . the permit?" she repeated. It was hard to keep up with his fast conversational shifts.

"Yeah, you know, the government permit." A slight frown creased his forehead. "Aren't there some pretty stiff fines for keeping a peregrine without a permit? I mean, these birds are endangered, right? Correct me if I'm wrong."

"Um, yes, you're right," she said. "They're endangered."

She felt her eyes widen as she took a step backward. The urge was strong to turn and run to her Jeep, which she'd parked among some pines at the edge of the field. Somehow she must avoid letting this man find out what she'd sworn to tell no one. If she wasn't careful, this smooth operator would work it out of her.

Hoping to throw up a smoke screen to distract him from the subject of the permit, she added, "You were lucky to have seen a peregrine's hunting stoop. It's one of the most dramatic sights in the whole world, and most people never get to witness it." As she talked, she edged away from Blair, planning her escape.

To her dismay he followed her, which made Justine wonder if she'd be able to shake him. Her heart pounded. He was now acting like a predator on a strong scent trail.

"I didn't actually see her stoop," Blair corrected her, "just the startling results of it." His intelligent eyes narrowed as he folded his arms across his broad chest and leveled a curious gaze at her. "Why are you suddenly so nervous?" he drawled. A knowing smile played at the corners of his mouth. "It's something about the permit, isn't it?" There was a long pause. "You don't have one, do you?"

"I didn't say that," she said, her voice rising, her answer too hastily given.

"You didn't have to."

His statement rang in Justine's ears. She wished with all her heart that she were a million miles away from those perceptive eyes. It was obvious from his next remarks that her silence had told him much.

"Ah, yes," he said with a satisfied nod. "Now let's see if I can put this together. You have conveniently neglected to obtain a permit to keep this endangered species. That way, no one will know you have it, and you can enjoy a private taste of falconry without any of the red tape."

"No!" she exclaimed. Her throat tightened; he'd made her sound selfish and dishonest. "You've got it all wrong. Aldora was almost dead when I got her. I felt so sorry for her I just had to see if I could nurse her back to health. I was afraid that if I reported I had a peregrine, I'd be forced to give her up. If an impersonal, bureaucratic agency took her, it might not have been able to give her the proper care. I couldn't let that happen." Aldora twittered softly, as if she comprehended the distress in her mistress's voice. "You tricked me into telling you all this," Justine added, her tone angry and bitter.

"Not really," he said, shrugging off her accusation. "I'm just good at putting two and two together, that's all." He regarded her, his head tilted to one side. "You know, I'll bet you'd have a very good chance of getting a permit. I mean, you obviously know how to care for a falcon."

"Maybe you're right," she responded with a sigh, her tension easing somewhat, "and maybe I'll still apply for one. I don't know." She paused. "I just keep putting it off and putting it off.... In the meantime, I decided it was best not to tell anyone about Aldora. What a shame that my little secret is out." She frowned at him and felt a pang of regret whip through her.

Unexpectedly Blair laughed. The pleasant sound rang across the empty field. His eyes sparkled with humor, and his teeth flashed white and even in the bright sunshine.

The remaining strands of tension that had gripped Justine broke apart and scattered in the pine- and sage-scented air. She was charmed by the throaty sound of Blair's laughter. There was something appealing about the man. Even though she felt wary of him, she couldn't deny that he was attractive and that he piqued her interest. This reaction disturbed her, and she shook it off.

"What's so funny?" she demanded.

Blair's mirth faded to a smile, and he shook his head. "This whole crazy thing," he responded as he rubbed the back of his neck. "I can't get over it, it's so unreal. I mean, I come to a little town out in the sticks. I drive up to an empty field, never dreaming I'll run into anyone, let alone a woman with a falcon, the two of them looking like a . . . a fantasy out of the Middle Ages. Then to top it off, the woman has a secret—"

"It *is* a secret," Justine interrupted. Her voice was pleading.

"Relax, Justine." Blair held out one hand in a gesture of reassurance. "Don't worry. Your secret is safe with me. I believe Aldora's with the right person, and I don't intend to tell anyone you have her. You've got my word on that."

Hardly believing her ears, Justine sighed with relief, then returned his smile. "Thank you," she breathed. This seemed like a good time to make her escape. "And now I really must go."

She turned and began walking away from him. Her boots kicked up little puffs of dust with each rapid step. She wasn't sure she could trust Blair. All she could do was get away from him fast and hope that he'd keep his word about Aldora.

"Hey, wait a minute," he called out behind her.

Then she heard his footfalls as he caught up with her. He took her by the arm, halting her progress across the field. The touch of his firm hand on her forearm felt like an icy-hot brand through the thin cotton of her blouse. In spite of the morning heat, a shiver raced down Justine's spine. She caught her breath and turned to look up into Blair's face.

"Do you live around here, Justine?" he asked.

His gaze was unwavering as his eyes fastened on hers. It unnerved Justine to be regarded with such intensity, and she fought to calm her suddenly leaping pulse.

"Yes, I guess I do," she answered.

"Ah, she's a coy one."

"Not really," she said. "I don't mean to sound mysterious. It's just that I haven't been in Shelby for very long, and I'm not quite used to the idea yet."

"Oh? I guess I assumed that you'd lived here your whole life."

She laughed. "Oh, no. I grew up in a little town called Reardan, about a hundred miles east of here, but I've been living in Los Angeles for the past several years. A friend and I own a bookstore down there. Recently I decided to sell my share in the business and move to Shelby. Sandra—my friend—hasn't found a new partner yet, but I expect she will soon. Anyway, I've been here for about a month now...." Her voice trailed off on a note of hesitation. She wasn't sure how much she wanted to reveal to Blair.

"If you don't mind my asking," said Blair, "was your store losing money, or did you simply get tired of it?"

"Neither," replied Justine. "Our profits are the highest they've ever been, and I love the retail book business."

A puzzled frown creased Blair's brow. "Then why would an attractive woman—who owns part of a successful business—decide to sell out and move to a little town that's in the middle of nowhere?" He waved his hand at the lake and the golden, summer-dry hills. "This is a gorgeous place, I grant you, but it's about as different from Los Angeles as you can get. I can see why tourists flock here to get away from it all. But you're no tourist." He paused, regarding her with perceptive eyes that gleamed with interest. "You're running away from a man, is that it?"

Her brief laughter sounded brittle. "I wish it were that simple," she said. "Would you believe I'm running away from an entire city?"

His frown deepened. "I don't understand."

Justine shook her head. "I may not be a tourist, but I have definitely come to Shelby to get away from it all. More than anyone will ever know," she added half to herself.

"Go on," prompted Blair.

"Look, it's a long story, and I don't want to bore you with the gory details. Let's simply say that I've given up on life in the big city."

"And you've found a better lifestyle in Shelby?"

Justine smiled. "I can't begin to tell you how much better. It's clean and quiet here, I'm more relaxed than I've been in years and I don't even have to lock my door at night. I've regained my health, my happiness and my sanity." She ground out her next words. "I will *never* live in a city again."

"Never's a long time." His gray eyes twinkled with curiosity. "Would you ever visit a city?"

She shook her head. "Frankly, I can't even picture myself doing that, I feel so burned out on the subject. Ask me again in about ten years."

The sound of their easy laughter floated on the warm air. Then Justine tilted her smiling face up at Blair.

"And what about you?" she asked. "Are you a confirmed city dweller?"

"Yep," he said with a grin, "I sure am. Of course," he added, "I haven't had the bad experiences it sounds like you've had, or I might feel differently about it. I grew up in San Francisco, but about six months ago I moved to Seattle. I love it there—Seattle's a wonderful city." He nodded in the direction of Lake Shelby. "Oh, sure, it's great to escape to the wide open spaces now and then for a little peace and quiet, but I'd never move to a small town. I like to be where the action is, and that means living in a city."

"Cities have too much action to suit me," said Justine. "But it sounds like you thrive on that lifestyle."

"Oh, I do," he said with a smile that lit up his handsome face. "Give me the fast lane in the rat race any day. I'd die of boredom if I lived out in the sticks."

"You and I are poles apart," murmured Justine. All of this talk about cities had given her a sinking feeling in the pit of her stomach. Suddenly she again wanted to make her escape.

"I'm sorry, what did you say?" asked Blair.

"Oh, nothing important. I'm just muttering to myself. Our different opinions about lifestyle remind me of a story I read when I was a kid—about a country mouse and a city mouse." She paused, then continued in a brisk manner. "Well, it's been nice talking to you, but I really should go now. I hope you enjoy your stay in Shelby." She turned away and began walking toward her Jeep.

He called after her. "Hey, country mouse, I'd enjoy it a lot more if I could see you again."

"I don't think that's a good idea," she tossed over her shoulder without breaking stride.

"Wait, Justine."

Blair caught up with her as she reached her Jeep. She settled Aldora on her perch in the back, flung off her heavy glove and began searching for her key. Then she chuckled and removed her hand from her pocket.

"Force of habit from the bad old days," she said. "My key is right where I always leave it now—in the ignition. Try doing *that* in the city."

Blair was not to be sidetracked. "I want to see you again, Justine," he repeated. She got the impression that he never took no for an answer.

"There's no point in seeing me again," she said.

She started to slide behind the steering wheel, but the teasing expression in Blair's eyes held her back. He was leaning against the Jeep with his arms crossed over his broad chest. His trim, athletic body, even in that relaxed pose, projected the raw strength of a predator. Justine found the image fascinating, as well as a trifle unsettling.

"No point in seeing you again?" he echoed. "Ah, but there is." An ingenuous smile curled his lips as he added, "You can help me."

"Help you?" she asked in a wary tone. "What do you mean? What kind of help?"

She was enjoying her solitary existence at Lilac House, the lake property left to her by her deceased grandparents. The last thing she needed was the demands of another person complicating the sane and simple lifestyle she'd adopted. Her instincts told her that whatever it was that Mr. Fast Lane Sutherland had in mind, it would complicate her life, all right. And she'd had enough of that, thank you, in Los Angeles.

"I need a guide," said Blair.

Justine shook her head and opened her mouth to turn down his strange request. Before she could utter a word, however, he held up one hand and continued talking.

"Wait, before you say no, let me explain. I arrived in Shelby yesterday. As I said before, I recently moved to Seattle, where I've opened a new store. This is my first trip to eastern Washington. I'm working on a special project, and I need someone to show me around."

"You don't need someone to show you around," replied Justine. "What you need is a guidebook. I'm sure the Shelby Tourist Bureau would be happy to help you. Now if you'll excuse me—"

"A guidebook," interrupted Blair. "Precisely! Oh, you've played right into my hands, Justine."

Now she was suspicious. And confused. "What is that supposed to mean?"

"Let me back up a little. I'm in the recreational equipment business. Sutherland Outdoors carries everything from hiking boots to canoe racks."

"You're *that* Sutherland?" asked Justine.

"At your service." He smiled as he sketched a salute in the air.

"What a coincidence. I saw one of your ads in a magazine just last night." She tilted her head back and gazed upward as she searched her mind. "Let's see... 'Eight stores to serve you on the West Coast—let Sutherland Outdoors outfit you for your next adventure.'"

"You've got a good memory," said Blair. "Have you ever been one of our satisfied customers?"

"As a matter of fact, yes," replied Justine, nodding. "I ordered a down vest through your catalog last fall."

"We do a brisk business through the mail. In fact, we've barely been able to keep up with the orders ever since we outfitted the last Mount Everest climb. That gave us lots of great publicity."

Justine could tell from Blair's animated way of talking— hands gesturing and excitement gleaming in his eyes—that he loved his work and took pride in offering quality products.

He continued with a smile, "Now back to how you can help me." His expression was so appealing Justine felt herself waver. But a little voice inside her whispered that she'd heard this line before.

"Sorry, but I'm not available."

"Do you have a job in Shelby?"

"Not at the moment."

"Then you *are* available," he said. "Besides, you'd be the perfect person to show me around. You grew up near here, and you've spent summers in Shelby, right?"

"Well, yes, but—"

"So you must be really familiar with this area."

She sighed with impatience. "Yes, I'm familiar with this part of the state, but I don't think—"

"You haven't heard me out," he interjected. Justine felt as if she were trying to swim against a riptide. Didn't this man ever give up?

"You mentioned a guidebook, remember?" he asked.

She nodded and tried to quell her feeling of restlessness. His persistence was getting under her skin.

"That's why I'm in Shelby," explained Blair. "The kind of guidebook I'd like to see on this area doesn't exist yet. I'm adding a whole new line of outdoor guidebooks to our merchandise. Each book will focus on a different region in the western states. They'll cover just about every kind of outdoor recreation you can think of, with emphasis on hiking and camping.

"I think the Shelby area has great potential for people who love open spaces and warm summers." He waved a hand toward the golden hills that encircled the sparkling lake. "I can imagine hikers walking along those ridgelines. With our book as a guide, of course. So," he continued, "I'm combining business with pleasure. Before I commission some writers for the project, I'm checking out this area myself. I was long overdue for a vacation, anyway. I want to get a feel for the place, see what's here, take a few notes. But I'll need a guide." He dipped his honey-blond head toward her. "And that's where you come in."

"No, that is not where I come in. As I suggested before, go to the Tourist Bureau. They may not have the kind of guidebook you're talking about, but I'm sure they can put you in touch with someone who can show you around."

"But I want you to show me around."

His voice was soft, its tone compelling. Justine felt caressed by the velvety sound, and her knees abruptly turned weak and watery as the intense gray eyes continued to regard her. If she was going to resist Blair's entreaties, it was now or never. She took a deep breath.

"Look," she began, "I don't want to complicate my life right now with new relationships, either business or social. Good luck with your project. I'm sorry I can't help you."

"Are you sure you won't reconsider?" asked Blair, his masculine voice deep and confident-sounding.

"Absolutely," replied Justine. She started to climb into the Jeep.

"Then you leave me no choice."

That stopped her. What was he implying with such a cryptic remark? She turned to look at him.

"Just what is that supposed to mean?" she demanded, keeping her voice cool and steady.

No longer leaning against the Jeep, Blair now stood with his hands resting on his hips. Justine thought she saw a roguish twinkle in his eyes, but his tone was all business. Something told her that the bastion of her resistance was about to come tumbling down.

"I hate to resort to such tactics," said Blair, humor tugging at the corners of his handsome mouth. "But since I apparently can't enlist your help with charm alone, I guess I'll have to impress you with my connections."

"What are you driving at?"

"Remember, Justine," he began, "I know that you're keeping an endangered species without a permit. Your little secret is out."

"But you said it was safe with you!" exclaimed Justine.

She was aghast at this unexpected turn of events. Was he going to blackmail her? Would he threaten to tell Fish and Game about Aldora if she refused to be his guide? A rising tide of panic welled up inside her. What rotten luck to have blundered into the kind of man she never wanted to see again, the aggressive city type who ruthlessly manipulated people the same way he did his business.

Blair lifted a hand as if to halt the flow of words that was about to tumble from her mouth. "Hold on," he said. "Before you get all steamed up, let me explain. Your secret's safe with me, but there is one person I think I should tell. He's a friend of mine who works for the state government in Olympia. I'll bet if I called him this afternoon, he could cut through a lot of red tape and get you a permit for your falcon. That way, you wouldn't have to keep her a secret anymore. You'd be all nice and legal. How would that be?''

Justine suddenly felt sorry that she'd suspected Blair of something as devious as blackmail and was glad that she hadn't voiced her doubts. So he had a friend in Olympia who could help her get a permit for Aldora. Hmm, the idea appealed to her. Gaining legal status for her possession of the falcon would solve the many problems that had been created by the need for subterfuge. To ensure that Aldora's training sessions would go undetected, Justine had risen every day at dawn, long before the rest of the valley was stirring, and driven far up into the secluded hills. Returning home was trickier because of the chance that, at the later hour, she might run into someone. Fortunately, Shelby had plenty of back roads. Lilac House itself was private. It was surrounded by its own overgrown park and towering lilac hedges, which prevented prying eyes from seeing the transfer of the peregrine back to her enclosed pen.

Blair's voice broke into her thoughts. "I can see that you're tempted," he commented.

"Yes," she conceded, "I admit it. Having a permit for Aldora would definitely make life simpler."

"You must be quite the artful dodger to have kept her a secret in such a small town. I mean, she's not exactly the size of a canary." He paused. "Hasn't anyone figured out yet that you're training a falcon?"

"Not that I know of," answered Justine, shaking her head. "A couple of people have seen her but only briefly, and I'll bet they didn't believe their eyes."

She chuckled as she recalled their looks of openmouthed astonishment. Then her mood sobered as she again thought about the permit. Yes, she could save herself a lot of trouble by accepting Blair's offer. Of course, doing so would put her in his debt. She sighed. Complications. Oh, well, it would be worth it for peace of mind.

"Are you sure your friend can get a permit for me?"

"Oh, yeah, he owes me a favor. A couple of years back I gave him a big discount on some camping gear he needed for a rafting trip. Besides, when I describe how you've saved the life of a member of an endangered species, I'm sure he'll agree that you deserve to have a permit. There shouldn't be any problem." He paused. "So let's strike a bargain."

Oh-oh, here it comes—the hook. Justine held her breath; she knew what he'd say next.

Blair continued, "In exchange for a permit for Aldora, you'll be my guide while I'm in Shelby." An engaging smile spread across his face. "Such a deal. How can you refuse?"

Justine stared at him as she considered his proposition. She had to admit that she was impressed with the way Blair was using the situation to suit his own designs. He was probably a born opportunist, which no doubt explained how he'd built a business empire before he was forty.

She glanced at Aldora. Justine had been coming to these upland fields for weeks, training the falcon and watching with satisfaction as the bird progressed toward independence. Those sessions had helped take her mind off the disturbing reasons for her having fled Los Angeles. And now a chance confrontation with a stranger had reminded her that her project could've ended on an unpleasant note.

Blair was right; how could she refuse his offer? The crux of the matter, however, was probably the fact that his ego couldn't take no for an answer. She should've applied for the permit long ago and taken her chances. But it was too late now; he had her. The deal he was offering was too good to pass up.

"All right," she said, "you win."

"We both win."

"Okay, we both win. I'll show you around, but I give you fair warning, Blair. This is strictly a business arrangement."

He flashed her a winning smile, his attractive eyes creasing at their outer corners. "I prefer to leave all doors open.

I suggest that you do the same," he added smoothly. "Now when can we start? My stay here is rather limited, so I'd like to get going as soon as possible—today, if you're free. Every minute counts."

Justine was not about to submit to his pressure and put aside her plans for the day simply because he was in such a big hurry. Surely he could wait twenty-four hours before collecting on her debt.

"Look, I have some things I need to take care of today. How about tomorrow morning? Eight o'clock would be all right."

"Yeah, okay. Where do you live? I'll pick you up."

She described how to get to Lilac House, then Blair said, "I'll see you tomorrow." He glanced at his watch again and turned to leave, then stopped and faced her once more. "Oh, and I'll let you decide where we'll go. After all, I'm entirely in your hands now." He smiled, then strode briskly back across the field.

Justine wasn't sure what disturbed her more—Blair's provocative-sounding final comment, or the fact that he seemed to be in charge of the situation and not the other way around. With an explosive exhalation of breath, she slid behind the wheel. What had she gotten herself into? she wondered. She started the engine, slammed the Jeep into gear, then turned around and began driving along the dirt road. She was halfway down the hill before she realized that she was acting like a woman possessed. Not since she'd left the Los Angeles freeways had she careered along at this reckless speed. She glanced in the rearview mirror and saw a huge cloud of dust boiling out behind her. Aldora swayed on her perch, her talons digging into the padded crossbar.

Justine forced herself to slow down and take a couple of deep breaths. She shook her head as an irony dawned on her; although her relaxing weeks in Shelby had eased away the frenetic pace that she'd acquired in L.A., all it took was a few minutes in the company of a keyed-up city man to put her right back into high gear. She needed to assess her situation calmly. There was no point in getting upset just because she'd made a harmless bargain with Blair Sutherland.

Harmless? She wondered about that. At the very least, her agreement with him was a complication, and she'd wanted to avoid new relationships for the time being. Maybe he'd let her off the hook after a day or two. No, that didn't seem likely.

What a smooth operator he was, exactly the type of man she wanted to leave behind forever. First he'd confused her with a barrage of questions and figured out that she didn't have a permit for Aldora. Then he'd capitalized on that information and maneuvered her into a corner, where she felt forced to yield to his demands. Now she'd have to keep company with him—and submit to the pressure of his aggressive, fast-lane approach to living—for the entire week or so that he'd be there.

Damn! Again she floored the accelerator, this time leaving an even bigger dust storm in her wake.

Chapter Two

By the next morning Justine had assumed a philosophical outlook about her agreement with Blair Sutherland. As usual, she arose at dawn and took Aldora up into the hills for her workout. As she watched the magnificent falcon in flight, she analyzed her feelings from the day before. Her annoyance with Blair had cooled, and she actually welcomed the chance to be diverted by him from her worries. He was certainly attractive and charming. How terrible could it be to spend a few days in his company? Her mood was optimistic as she drove back to Lilac House.

Later Justine took a few extra pains with her appearance as she prepared for Blair's arrival. She laughed at herself as she bathed and changed into clean clothes. She couldn't understand why she was making these special efforts, especially after having stated so clearly to Blair that theirs would be a "business only" relationship. Shrugging, she let the question rest for the time being.

Besides being charming, Blair was also punctual, Justine mused when his truck pulled up promptly at eight. She hurriedly pushed a couple of combs into her hair, pulling the curly mass away from her temples. A quick dash of rose-colored lipstick and a pair of small, silver hoop earrings completed her appearance. She smoothed her fitted corduroy slacks over her slim hips and flicked an imaginary speck of dust from the collar of her open-necked shirt. There, she was ready.

She ran down the stairs just as Blair rapped on the door. Feeling like a nervous schoolgirl, Justine paused before answering his knock. She took a deep breath and composed herself.

When she opened the door, she found Blair standing on the wide old porch, his feet slightly apart.

"Good morning, Blair."

"Hello, Justine."

Her pulse leaped as she registered his good looks. He wore a faded, blue work shirt rolled up at the sleeves, revealing tanned forearms. A small triangle of curly chest hair showed above his open collar. His jeans and dusty desert boots had obviously seen much wear. On him, the casual attire was attractive, even sexy, Justine noted. A faint spicy fragrance wafted from him, causing her to breathe more deeply to savor the scent. It was pleasant, a clean masculine smell that made her want to move closer. Her interest must've shown on her face.

"Hmm, are you that happy to see me?" asked Blair. There was a note of teasing good humor in his voice.

She hedged. "Oh, let's just say that I've decided to take our arrangement in stride."

"That's the spirit," he said warmly. He scanned her quickly from head to toe and back again. "You look very nice, Justine, but you didn't have to fuss for me." His deep voice carried a seductive undertone.

Justine suddenly felt a warm flush begin to creep up her neck and into her cheeks. So that Blair wouldn't notice her discomfiture, she turned back into the hall. She grabbed her canteen and day pack from a chair.

"What makes you think I fussed?" she said. "You must be used to having women drop at your feet like flies."

His chuckle was throaty as he returned her light banter. "Fine, I'll play along. This is just an ordinary day. Shall we go?" He was already moving off the porch.

Closing the door behind her, Justine followed him out to his truck. She tossed her pack onto the floor and settled herself on the passenger seat. Immediately she rolled down the window. Although the day was young, the sun blazing in the clear blue sky was already making the temperature climb. Another scorcher was on the way. The inviting waters of Lake Shelby gleamed at the end of the expansive lawn that sloped away from the house. Justine was already looking forward to an afternoon swim.

"So where are we going first?" asked Blair. He smiled at her, his hand on the ignition key.

Being this close to his broad shoulders and lean thighs made Justine feel a little light-headed. Surprised at the effect he was having on her, she pulled her gaze away from him and said the first thing that popped into her mind.

"Um, drive up to the Shelby Mountain Lookout," she said, trying not to sound as flustered as she felt.

There was a long moment of silence in the truck. A powerboat hummed in the distance.

"You're forgetting that I'm a stranger here," said Blair, laughter in his voice. "You'll have to give me some directions."

"Oh, yes, of course. I had forgotten. Turn left at the road."

Slowly Blair steered the truck down the curved driveway. Ancient, gnarled cherry trees lined one side, and a vast lawn studded with evergreens spread out on the other. A couple of immense maples grew near the cream-colored house. Their broad limbs reached out over the grass, creating blessed shade on hot summer days. A dense hedge of tall lilac bushes encircled the grounds, except on the lake side.

Blair paused at the road and glanced back over his shoulder. The two-story, Victorian-style building known as Lilac

House was no longer visible. "I can see how you've kept Aldora a secret. This is a very private place. Beautiful, too. It must be nice to have your own park right on the lake."

"Yes," agreed Justine, "it's very pleasant. My grandparents bought this property about sixty years ago." She paused. "Of course, it's been terribly neglected since their deaths, but I'm changing that."

"In what way?"

"I've recently hired an older fellow to come in and clean up the grounds. A high school girl helps him. Leonard and Ellen have already cleared away the blackberry jungles that were strangling the lilac hedges, and they've weeded some of the flower beds. Of course, they've barely started, and it's going to be a huge job, but I'm determined to restore this place to the way it was before my grandparents died."

"It must've been quite a showcase." He turned left onto the quiet road and shifted into a higher gear.

"Oh, it was," she breathed. "You should've seen it. Grandpa and Grandma worked for years to assemble a collection of native conifers. They also planted some oldfashioned rose varieties that will be lost forever if the weeds aren't cleared away." She laughed. "I think I've begun the restoration project in the nick of time."

"From the looks of it, restoring the park will take years." He shot her a glance.

She nodded. "Oh, I'm sure it will, but that's fine with me. I like to keep busy, and now, thank goodness, I have that wonderful commodity known as time—something I never had enough of in L.A." She paused. "Go straight here."

They drove in silence for a few minutes. The road wound beside the lake. Between the summer cabins that perched on its shore, Justine could see cool blue water. Pieces of driftwood bobbed on the gentle swells, and a man puttered with an outboard boat that was tied up at a private dock. Green unripened apples hung from trees in an orchard on the other side of the road.

"There's the sign to the lookout," said Justine, pointing.

Shortly the dirt road they turned onto left the lake and cabins behind. It climbed steadily; Blair eased the truck into a lower gear. The track was dry and dusty with many rough spots. Justine held on to the armrest and gazed at the view. Twisting and turning, the road snaked high up into the hills. On either side were sage lands and scattered pine trees. Fat brown cones littered the ground beneath the trees. Meadowlarks caroled from fence posts, sunlight gleaming on their butter-yellow breasts. Several mourning doves flew across the road in front of the slowly moving truck. In the air was a mixed fragrance of dry dust and pungent sage.

Blair broke their silence. "Why are we going up here, Justine?"

"For the view."

"But won't it be the same one we had yesterday?"

"Yes and no," she answered cryptically.

"Now you're being mysterious again," he said, taking his eyes off the road to glance over at her. His mouth was curled up at one corner. He seemed to feel easy in her presence.

"I suppose I should explain," she said. "Yes, we'll get almost the same view. But we'll be higher up and will be able to look in more directions. We'll see the Columbia River and the beginning of Douglas County south of here. That's why there's a fire lookout on this ridge. It gives you a great overview of this part of the state."

He nodded. "Sounds like a good place to start." Looking around at the empty hills and lonely road, he commented, "This is a pretty isolated spot. I wonder if the lookout worker ever feels scared to be up here all alone."

Justine laughed. "I can't imagine anyone being afraid to be up here. The crime rate in this area is so low it's not even worth discussing."

There was silence as Blair negotiated a rough spot. Then he asked, "Is that why you left Los Angeles—to get away from crime and violence?"

"That was part of it...." She paused. "Are you sure you want to hear about that?"

He smiled over at her. "You've got me curious, Justine. Fill me in unless you think I'm being too nosy."

"No, not at all," she assured him. She took a deep breath and began. "While I was growing up in Reardan, I couldn't wait to leave. My one dream was to live in a big city someday and have my own business. After college I moved to Los Angeles, where my friend Sandra and I opened our bookstore. Everything went fine the first two or three years, then things began to go sour for me." She paused as the distressing memories played back in her mind.

"In what way?" prompted Blair.

Justine continued, "The city started to...to wear me down in a lot of different ways. I dreaded commuting on those crazy, crowded freeways, where everyone drives like they're racing in the Grand Prix. And the smog began to bother me. On really bad days my eyes would burn terribly. My car was stolen, and then the break-ins started." She shook her head. "My apartment was hit three times in two months. It got so bad I was afraid to go home at night. My stereo and TV were taken, along with a lot of other stuff. Later my couch and chairs were slashed. There wasn't anything valuable left to steal, so the creeps took their frustration out on my furniture. They also broke a favorite vase of mine that had belonged to my grandmother."

"You didn't have an alarm system, apparently," said Blair.

"That's right." Justine sighed. "I finally installed one and put bars on the ground-floor windows, but the damage had already been done by that time. All of this cost me a small fortune, and I ended up feeling like I was living in an armed camp. I was upset and worried all the time, and I couldn't sleep. I'd always been such a healthy person, and suddenly I was unhealthy, unhappy and a nervous wreck. That is no way to live," she said with emphasis. "Mind you, I think Los Angeles is a wonderful city in many ways, but it's obviously not the place for me." She hesitated as she struggled with another memory.

As if sensing how difficult it was for her to continue, Blair prodded her in a gentle voice. "There's more, isn't there?"

Justine moistened her suddenly dry lips. "My...my younger sister, Myra, also lived in L.A. She had a wonderful job as a reporter for the *Los Angeles Globe*, and her whole career was ahead of her. She was happy and full of fun, and then..." Tears stung Justine's eyes as she fought back the pain. She cleared her tightening throat and rushed on. "Then she had a terrible experience that forced her to quit her job and move back to Reardan. That was about six weeks ago. She's being counseled, but I sometimes wonder if Myra will ever be her old self again."

"Was Myra a crime victim, too?"

Justine sighed heavily. "Yes, she was, all because she happened to be in the wrong place at the wrong time. She was making a deposit at her bank when some jerk decided to rob the place. I guess he panicked and bungled the job. Anyway, he took my sister hostage and held her in the bank—it was just the two of them—all night and most of the next day."

"That must've been terrible for her." Blair's voice was sympathetic.

"Yes, it was. Oh, he didn't really hurt her, thank goodness. He just waved a gun in her face and scared the living daylights out of her, that's all." Her tone was bitter. Then her voice became quiet. "The worst part came at the end. The guy tried to make a run for it, and the police shot him. I'm sure they did it to save Myra's life. He died on the way to the hospital. Myra saw the whole ugly scene, of course. On top of the hours she'd already spent in terror, being a witness to such awful violence was too much for her. She went into a kind of emotional shock, which forced her to leave her job and move up here."

"I can tell that it's hard for you to talk about all this." There was an unmistakable note of empathy in Blair's voice, for which Justine was grateful.

"Yes," she said, "it is." There was a heavy pause. "You see, I was there, too. I also saw that man shot down in the street." The repugnant memory flickered in her mind like a grainy, old-fashioned movie. "The police had called me the day before to let me know that Myra was being held. I'll never forget how shocked I was to hear such incredible news—my heart started pounding, and I couldn't seem to get my breath all of a sudden." She bit her bottom lip. "Anyway, I spent the next twenty-four hours in the street, as close to the bank as I could get, where the police had set up their barricades."

Justine's eyes narrowed as she stared into the distance, and her memories turned especially sour. "You know, in thinking back about it, I'm not sure which was worse— being worried sick about what was going to happen to Myra, or having to stand around in the crowd that gathered to watch. Crime scenes in the city seem to attract the very worst element of curiosity seekers. My sister's life was being threatened, but to the gawkers outside the whole thing was no more than a piece of cheap entertainment. God, it was like a carnival." She shuddered, rubbing her eyes to dispel the images.

Blair's voice broke the silence that followed. "I'm sorry." He paused. "It sounds as if you and your sister are very close."

"Oh, yes, we're best friends," said Justine. "Our parents died when she and I were in high school, and we've had to depend on each other. We got lots of help from our godparents and from Grandma and Grandpa Fleming, of course."

"How's Myra doing now?"

"She seems to be improving. Her counselor is Dr. Anderson, our godfather. Uncle Bob, we call him. If anyone can help Myra put her ordeal behind her, it'll be Uncle Bob. Myra and I talk on the phone almost every day. I've noticed lately that her spirit is definitely returning." She paused and gazed at the glittering blue lake that was now far below them.

As Blair rounded a hairpin curve, he said, "If Myra's anything like you, I'll bet she'll eventually bounce back. You're one of the most spirited women I've ever met."

Justine felt pleased by his comment. She turned away from the view and stared across at him. His well-proportioned features created a striking profile, especially when seen that way against a backdrop of golden, sun-drenched hills.

She glanced away, afraid that he might catch her staring at him. Suddenly a wave of self-consciousness swept through her. She'd revealed a lot about herself, much more than she'd ordinarily tell a stranger. She realized that something in Blair's manner had encouraged her to share her private thoughts and feelings. There was a reassuring quality about him that inspired her trust. Nevertheless, she had the impulse to pull back.

"I . . . I'm so embarrassed," she stammered. "Why am I telling you all this?"

"There's no reason to be embarrassed, Justine" was his soft reply. "I think you need to talk about these things. They certainly explain why you retreated to a small town. What happened to Myra must've been the last straw, on top of everything else you'd already been through."

"Yes, it was," replied Justine. "But what actually made up my mind was a trip I took with an L.A. outdoor club. I spent an incredible week at one of their cabins in the mountains. It was such a shock going back to my apartment in the city; I could see that I had to break away. I'd taken all I was going to. Besides—" she shrugged "—I figured that it was only a matter of time before what happened to Myra—or something worse—might happen to me." She looked over at Blair and raised her chin with conviction. "So I escaped, too, while I still could and fled to a calm life in the country." She waved her hand to indicate the sage lands and vast blue sky.

"I had saved quite a lot of money—enough to keep me comfortable for a number of years. I told Sandra that I wanted to sell my share in the store," she continued, "then

I moved to Shelby. When Myra and I were growing up, we spent every summer vacation here with our grandparents. Their house has stood empty for years, and it needs a lot of work. But as soon as I decided to leave Los Angeles, I knew there was only one place I wanted to be—in Shelby, living in Lilac House, where I'd spent some of the happiest times of my life. It truly felt like coming home."

"City mouse becomes country mouse," said Blair, smiling easily over at her.

"Yes," she said with emphasis, "and loving every minute of it." She looked around. "Here we are."

The truck had arrived at the top of the ridgeline. A few tall pines and some weathered silver snags thrust skyward among the sagebrush. Blair parked the truck, then he and Justine got out and stretched their legs in the bright sunshine.

Blair shielded his eyes with his hand and gazed at the fire lookout. "I don't think anyone's home up there."

"Maybe they're out getting groceries," said Justine. She strolled to the edge of the ridge and looked around. "It sure is quiet up here on top of the world."

On one side, as she'd promised, they could see the lake and town. Off in the distance loomed the jagged peaks of the Cascade Mountains. Thick evergreen forests covered their flanks. On the other side of the ridge, to the south, the land stretched away to a hazy horizon. Sage lands were intermixed with cultivated fields. Orchards grew close to the source of their irrigation, the mighty Columbia River. The river flowed far below, a blue-gray ribbon with occasional patches of white water. A breeze blew up from the Columbia, its touch cool and silky on Justine's skin. She sighed with contentment.

Blair took a pen and a small notebook from his pocket. Justine began pointing things out to him. She got her binoculars from her pack so that he could look more closely at several canyons across from the lake where there were good camping sites. She drew his attention to particular ridges where, as children, she and her sister had hiked. Reeve

Orchards, far below them, was an interesting place to visit, she told him. Washington State apples were famous. A visitor would enjoy touring the apple sheds in the fall when the harvest was in full swing.

Blair fired off a barrage of questions and took several pages of notes. Then he returned the binoculars to Justine, and she stowed them in the truck. She strolled back toward him and sat down on a log.

Blair finished writing in his notebook, then closed it with a snap. "Well," he said, "time to be off to our next stop."

The abruptness of his remark caught her off guard. "But . . . we just got here," she said.

He looked at his watch, flicking his wrist with that same clipped, economical movement that Justine had noticed the day before. He'd told her that every minute counted; he obviously lived by the clock, trying to pack every hour to capacity. In contrast Justine had stopped wearing a watch soon after her arrival in Shelby and was perfectly content with her new, relaxed nonschedule.

"Don't you want to sit for a while and enjoy the view?" she asked. She was surprised that Blair seemed unmoved by the grandeur of their surroundings.

"No," he said with a shrug as he glanced around, "I've pretty much seen what there is to see up here, and now I'd like to move along. Let's go."

Justine felt herself becoming annoyed by his haste. How anyone could take this magnificent view so casually was beyond her. "Wait a minute," she said. "Is this the pace you mean to keep the whole time I'm showing you around? Because if it is . . ." She hesitated, unsure of what his reaction might be to her protest.

He narrowed his eyes and gazed steadily at her. His unwavering glance made her feel nervous. He said, "If it is what, Justine?" He jammed his notebook and pen into his breast pocket and continued staring at her. He was waiting for her answer. She took a deep breath and plunged ahead.

"If this is going to be your normal pace, then I won't be able to accompany you."

"Look," he said, hands gesturing with forced patience, "I have just so much time in this area before I have to return to Seattle. I came over here on a short vacation, but I also want to get this project completed as soon as possible. Now I don't have time to sit and stare at the landscape as much as you apparently think I should. Let's go." He began striding toward the truck.

"You call this a vacation?" she called after him as she stood. "Rushing from one place to another, scribbling a few notes, then dashing on to the next stop? That's how you relax? I realize that you also have work to do while you're here, but don't you ever slow down?" She paused. "It looks like city living has taken its toll on you, too."

Her words had been flung at his retreating form. Then he turned and stalked back toward her. Shards of storm-gray glass seemed to glint from beneath his lowered brows. Justine could tell that she'd angered him. Her challenge had put him into a dangerous mood, and she wondered how far she could go in defying him. Here was a man who was used to doing exactly what he wanted, when and how he wanted. There probably were not many people who dared to cross him.

He spoke slowly, his voice low and commanding. "Whether or not the city has taken its toll on me is none of your concern, Justine. As I told you yesterday, I love living in the city, and I wouldn't want to live anywhere else. Just because I happen to be on a tight schedule, don't jump to any conclusions about the state of my mental health." He paused, hands on hips. "Now are you coming or not?"

Justine surprised herself by giving a cool, one-word response. "Not." Silence followed, broken only by a sudden breeze rattling the sagebrush.

"What did you say?" His tone was disbelieving.

She gathered her courage. "I said I'm not coming with you. I moved here to get away from the pressures and fast pace of living that I coped with for so many years in the city. I'll be damned if I let you or anyone else rush me or put me into high gear again. I'm through with all that." She shook her head. "I knew this wouldn't work."

"What wouldn't work?"

"This arrangement of ours—my acting as your guide. You're on your own, Blair. Goodbye and good luck." She turned and began hiking down the dirt road, her boots kicking up little puffs of dust that settled on her pant legs.

Blair's voice roared after her. "Come back up here, Justine. You can't walk all the way to town. It's miles. You'll get sunstroke. Don't be so damned stubborn."

Turning to look back, she spoke slowly, making the words slice through the air toward him. "I would rather walk from here to the coast than spend another minute in the company of someone who is so firmly caught up in the rat race. You said you like traveling in the fast lane, Blair. How convenient that you carry it right along with you." Then she turned away and resumed her march.

As soon as she was around the first curve, she expelled a sob of frustration and anger. Tears stung her eyes. She brushed them away with an impatient swipe of her hand. It felt good to tell Blair what she really thought. Rushing through life simply wasn't her style anymore. She'd had her fill of that in the city. How incredible that when she took him to the most fantastic view in the county, he'd acted as if it were no more remarkable than a postcard. What a casual attitude. She almost felt sorry for him.

As she walked, she wondered about their bargain. Now that she'd backed out of it, would she still receive a permit for Aldora? Upon reflection it seemed likely that she would. Blair didn't impress her as a man who would renege once he'd given his word. Then she felt guilty for not honoring her part of their agreement. There must be some way she could repay Blair's favor besides acting as his guide. She wasn't sure what form that repayment would take, but she'd think of something....

Maybe she'd been rash to challenge Blair. Then again she'd really had no other choice. She would simply have to live with the consequences now, she thought grimly. What a mess. She trudged on in the heat and dust.

An hour went by, during which Justine put a lot of distance between her and the lookout. She wondered why Blair hadn't driven by her yet. The road was the only way down. Bitterly she speculated that he was purposely letting her get plenty hot and thirsty before he pulled up behind her. He probably assumed that she'd be so relieved to see him she'd jump obediently into the shady cab of his truck. Well, she'd do no such thing, she told herself, gritting her teeth. If it took her the rest of the day, she'd walk to the bottom of the hill, then she'd call for a taxi.

Damn, she wondered, do towns as small as Shelby have taxis? Oh, well, she'd worry about that when she got to the road.

The August sun blazed down on Justine's bare head. Her boots kicked up powdery dust with each step, and her mouth felt parched and cottony. In her haste to get away from Blair, she'd left her canteen of cool water in his truck. He was probably enjoying the water now himself. The mental picture of him gulping long, refreshing drafts from her canteen made her kick peevishly at some rocks in the road.

"Ouch!" she cried out, wincing in pain from her stubbed toe.

She stood still for a moment, biting her lower lip and wondering what she should do. She unfastened the top button of her thin shirt, hoping that the slight breeze would cool her heated skin. Her legs baked in the heavy corduroys. She bent and rolled her pants up to her knees. Thank goodness she'd worn her hiking boots; the road seemed even rougher on foot than it had in the truck.

She licked her lips. Near her was an eroded streambed. In the spring, water from melting snow had poured down this gully. Now the bed was as dry and dusty as the road. Far below her gleamed the lake. The sight of all that beckoning water taunted her and made her throat ache. Sighing, she pushed some sweaty tangles of hair off her brow and trudged on.

A few minutes later Justine heard Blair's truck behind her. Not deigning to look around, she moved to the side of the track. She wanted him to drive past her as she did her best to appear unconcerned that several miles still lay ahead. Lifting her chin, she assumed an "I don't care" demeanor. She dug her fingernails into her palms and stared straight ahead.

The truck edged by her and drove on a few yards, then stopped. Blair got out and looked up the road at her. There was no way Justine could get past him without a confrontation. She took a deep breath to steady her nerves.

His eyes swept the length of her, glancing at her rolled-up pant legs, boots coated with talcum-fine dust and partially unbuttoned shirt. She knew that her face must be flushed from the heat. She felt hot and sticky. Her thick hair clung to her neck in damp coils. One of her combs had slipped out along the way, allowing part of her hair to fall forward onto her sweaty brow. She knew that she looked a mess, but she didn't care.

"Had enough?" His tone was as dry as the surrounding desert.

Justine wasn't about to let him know how uncomfortable she felt. And she certainly wouldn't admit that she regretted her decision to walk back to town. The remainder of her self-imposed ordeal loomed ahead of her; she'd be plenty hot and tired by the time she arrived at the main road. She gathered the shreds of her composure.

"You're forgetting, Blair," she said lightly, "that I grew up in eastern Washington. I'm used to the heat." She tried to ignore the dry, croaky quality of her voice.

An amused look crossed his face. "And are you also used to going without water?" He held up her canteen. "Come on, Justine. Stop being stubborn and calling it strong, and have some water. Judging from the gravelly sound of your voice, you need a long, cool drink." He stepped forward and tried to hand her the container.

Justine stared at the canteen and licked her lips. She yearned to grab it, wrench off the top and quaff great gulps of water. But she was reluctant to let Blair know how eager she felt.

Blair must've sensed her inner conflict. His expression softened, and he spoke without a trace of his earlier amused satisfaction.

"Look, I'm sorry, Justine."

His words were so unexpected Justine wasn't sure if she'd heard him correctly. "What?" she rasped, the water momentarily forgotten.

He laughed. "My apology seems to have taken you by surprise." He reached into his pocket and pulled out a small silver object. "Oh, before I forget, you dropped this about a mile back."

"Thank you," she said softly. She took the comb from his hand and reset it in her hair. "But I don't understand...."

"Here, drink up, and I'll explain."

When Justine took the cap off the canteen, she was startled to find that the container was still full. She looked up at Blair. "You haven't had any water, either," she said in a puzzled tone.

He shrugged. "Oh, don't think I wasn't tempted," he said with a chuckle. "But every time I thought about taking a nice cool sip, I pictured you walking in all this heat." He waved off her reaction and added melodramatically, "I couldn't have taken the guilt."

Justine took a long drink, reveling in the relief that the moisture brought to her parched mouth and throat. She pressed the back of her hand against her wet lips and returned the canteen to Blair, who also took a drink.

He continued, "Like I said, I'm sorry for what happened at the lookout, Justine. For the past hour I've been sitting up there, looking off into the distance. I thought a lot about what you said."

He handed the canteen back to her, and she again drank from it, relishing the reviving effect the water was having on her entire body. She brushed some hair from her forehead.

"It's true," said Blair, "that I'm caught up in the rat race. Oh, not that Seattle is like Los Angeles, mind you. The rat race I'm referring to is of my own making. I push myself in my business, sometimes working sixteen hours a day, making every minute count. It's been so long since I've taken a real break from my work that I've sort of forgotten how to take it easy. I was trying to relax yesterday when Aldora flew down into those partridges." He chuckled ruefully. "Only a man whose nerves are wound as tightly as mine are would react the way I did, shouting and running from behind those rocks. No wonder Aldora almost flew away." He paused. "I love my work, Justine, but I need to learn how to slow down and smell the roses, as someone once said." He looked deeply into her eyes and held up his right hand. "I hereby vow to let you set the pace. I need a good teacher along that line. Will you continue to be my guide, country mouse?"

His mouth and eyes were smiling at Justine, who'd stood listening with great interest. Could she trust him? she wondered. Would he really be able to put aside his fast city pace and slow down? She didn't know, but she wanted to believe that he'd at least try.

"Okay," she said, "I'll keep showing you around." She hesitated. "Why do you push yourself so hard, Blair?"

His expression became guarded, and it occurred to Justine that she might be pressing into sensitive territory. Thoughtfully he rubbed a thumb across his bottom lip before answering her.

"That's a long story, and someday I may tell you the whole thing. For now, let's simply say that I've got a strong aversion to poverty."

Although he spoke in a light manner, as if this were his standard response, Justine had the distinct impression that he'd just revealed a key point about himself. Wondering what made Blair Sutherland tick, Justine decided to let him keep his secrets for the time being. She was curious, though, about what lay behind his veiled remark.

He broke into her thoughts. "Say, you look refreshed. Feeling better?"

She laughed. "Much . . . I also feel a little embarrassed. That was pretty silly of me to go stomping off like that."

"Forget it," he said with a smile that lit up his handsome face. "You're a spirited woman, remember?"

His comment erased Justine's feelings of chagrin and made her smile in turn. "What I really need now is a cool shower or a dip in the lake," she said.

Blair reached for the canteen, which she still held. "I have an idea," he said. "Until I can get you off this hot hillside, why not let me splash you with some of this water? There's a lot left. Does that appeal to you?"

Justine half closed her eyes in anticipated ecstasy. "Does it ever." She held her hair away from her face and tilted her head back. "Splash away."

First Blair trickled some of the water onto her temples. The streams ran down her neck and into the fabric of her shirt, giving her a delicious sensation of coolness. The silky moisture flowing between her heated breasts felt especially wonderful.

"More," she murmured languorously, turning her head slowly from side to side. "Mmm . . . that's fantastic. Don't stop."

Blair poured a large stream at the base of her throat. Then he filled his hand with water several times and splashed her face and neck with the refreshing liquid.

"That's fine," Justine finally said, laughing as she wiped water from her cheeks. "Thank you."

Then she caught the look on Blair's face. He was standing so close to her she could hear him breathing. His eyes were appreciative, their gray depths revealing flickers of keen interest as he stared at her. He held the canteen loosely in one hand. His lips were slightly parted, the corners turned up into a half smile.

Justine followed his gaze and was startled to discover that the thin fabric of her damp shirt now clearly revealed her lacy bra and the outline of her full breasts. The look on Blair's face sent shivers racing through her. Then to her horror she felt her nipples harden. Blair's eyes smoldered wolfishly as he dragged his gaze away from her breasts and looked back at her face. He drawled his comment.

"Something's having a powerful effect on you. Is it the water?" He leaned closer. "Or is it me?"

Suddenly there was so much erotic tension sizzling in the pine-scented air that Justine felt light-headed. She inhaled sharply and fought to keep her hands still at her sides. Blair certainly did have a strong impact on her, but she didn't want him to know it.

"Now...now remember, Blair," she stammered, "I'll be your guide and nothing more. You know, I really think we should—"

Before she could finish her sentence and move toward the truck, Blair dropped the canteen to the ground. A last trickle of water drained out of it and stained the dust. Blair grasped Justine's shoulders in his firm hands and drew her to him.

Chapter Three

The faint spicy fragrance of Blair's after-shave filled Justine's senses, and her legs suddenly felt weak and unsteady. Blair's grip on her was powerful, a drawing force that pulled her into the circle of his strength. His smooth, tanned skin, parted lips and penetrating eyes were mere inches from her face.

"Sweet Justine," he murmured, his warm breath a caress on her skin.

She felt dizzy and knew that it would be pointless to struggle against the emotions that were coursing through her.

He continued, "I'm interested in you as more than a guide. You must know that. Oh, I need a guide, all right, but I need a—" he hesitated, as if searching for the right word "—I need a companion more than I need someone to show me around. Be my sweet companion, Justine."

He dipped his face toward her until their lips met. Pressing her slender form against his hard chest and thighs, he encircled her with his strong arms. Justine's impulse to resist vanished as her five senses took over and pushed the objections from her mind. Blair's lips felt smooth and firm. Their slow, studied caress implied that a wanton eagerness lurked beneath the surface. Justine slid her arms around his neck and returned his kiss with a fervor that surprised her. Responding to her encouragement, Blair nuzzled her mouth with greater insistence. His lips parted, and his silky tongue touched the corners of her mouth.

Unable to resist, once she'd answered the initial challenge of his sensual demand, Justine parted her own lips and reveled in the sweet, flaring intimacy that followed. Her awareness of time vanished. She clung to Blair in the middle of the road, her body cleaving to his hard frame as if it had a will of its own. Blair's hands grasped her waist and hips, pulling her even closer to him. Justine felt her pulse race, and colors swirled crazily behind her closed eyelids.

Then unbidden thoughts intruded on her ecstasy. She drew away from Blair, pushing against his solid chest with the flats of her hands, even though she wanted to cling to him for an unmeasured time. No one had ever kissed her as expertly or with such ardor as Blair had, and Justine longed for more.

"No, wait," she gasped from between lips that felt erotically swollen.

He tried to pull her back to him, his mouth partially open and questing. His voice was husky, his breathing ragged. "What do you mean no, sweetheart? I've never had a woman react like that to my kiss. Come here. You were made for loving, Justine."

"But I don't want to get involved," she said, a note of panic entering her voice.

Blair immediately responded to her distress, and his hands loosened on her body. He gazed down at her with gentle eyes in whose depths the fires of ardor still flared.

"What do you mean?" he asked.

She broke out of the circle of his arms and backed away from him, trying to catch her breath. Her heart was still racing from the intensity of their embrace.

"I moved here to get away from complications and all of those other things that weighed me down in the city," she said. "What I need now is peace and quiet so that I can think things through and find myself again. The last thing I need is a relationship that I can't do justice to. Please try to understand that, Blair." There was a pleading quality in her voice. She desperately hoped that he would comprehend what she was trying to explain to him: she needed time to think and the uncrowded space in which to do that thinking.

He placed his hands loosely on his hips and dipped his head toward her. "Justine, I respect your right to live your life the way you want to." He took a step in her direction. "But you have to admit there's a powerful chemistry between us, and we can't simply ignore that. At least leave the door open."

She shook her head, feeling very much at a loss. "Blair, I don't think that I should leave that particular door open. At least not right now. I'll admit that I'm attracted to you...."

He grinned. "Well, it's a relief to know that I wasn't imagining things."

She smiled in spite of herself. He was so charming, so confident. "No, you weren't imagining things." She hesitated. "But you caught me off guard. I don't want that to happen again. You've got me as your guide—we should leave our relationship at that." She paused to think. "In fact, maybe you ought to let me off the hook...."

"Oh, no." He smiled, one side of his mouth quirked in wry amusement. "I'm not about to fire you from your job. At the moment that's my only hold on you." He shifted his weight from one leg to the other. "I'll try not to pressure you about any other kind of relationship, for now. But I give you fair warning, Justine. I can't keep my distance indefinitely. I'm very attracted to you, and these strong urges of ours can't be shelved forever. Sooner or later we'll have to give in to them." He lowered his voice to a near whisper that caressed her ears. "And I can hardly wait until we do, sweet lady."

His intense gaze so unnerved Justine that for a moment she could do nothing but stare speechlessly into his eyes. Then she found her voice and began walking briskly toward the truck.

"Yes, well, I suppose it's time we left." She forced a laugh to lighten the mood. "I'm really going to appreciate being out of the sun during the ride back."

"Look," he said as he followed her, "why don't I drop you at your place for the rest of the day. That'll give you a chance to recover from your little trek in the desert." He slid behind the wheel as she settled herself on the passenger side. He flung the canteen, which he'd retrieved, onto the floor. "I have some things to take care of, then I'll fix us a little barbecue dinner at my place. How about it?"

She began to protest, but he quickly continued, "Now, before you turn me down, let me plead my case. You have to eat anyway, right? It may as well be with me. Besides—" he flashed her a roguish grin "—I'm a terrific cook, if I say so myself, and I do."

"I really don't think we should see each other socially." Justine, who already felt herself wavering, sighed. She wanted to ignore the warning bells that were clanging in her head. For too many days she'd been alone and silently thinking since she'd come to Shelby. She realized that she'd been out of touch with people for too long. Yes, she definitely needed Blair's company that night.

He started the engine and began easing the truck down the hill. "Tell you what," he said, his eyes on a curve they were approaching, "let's plan our itinerary tonight. You can bring a map and show me where you'll be taking me. That way, you can justify coming to my place." He glanced across the cab at her. "You do like barbecues, don't you?"

His apparent concern over her culinary preferences was so unexpected she burst into laughter. "Yes," she said, "I love barbecues. I'll come."

"Great."

"Where are you staying?"

He was living in the borrowed houseboat of a Seattle friend of his named Noel, he told her. The houseboat had a deck, where they'd eat their meal and watch the sun go down. He described how to find the place and told her they'd eat around eight.

They drove in silence for a few minutes. Then, as if sensing the doubts that were churning in Justine's mind, Blair said, "Hey, relax. I'm not setting you up for a seduction." He grinned. "Not that the idea doesn't appeal to me. I hate to eat alone, and I can't think of anyone I'd rather eat with than you. Thanks for agreeing to come over."

Justine felt some of the tension drain from her body. Blair's kiss had revved her nerves into high gear. His comment that he would probably press home his romantic demands on her at some future time had made her wonder what she was getting into that night. His words of reassurance helped ease some of her doubts.

As she watched the cobalt-blue lake get closer and closer, her thoughts turned inward. When was life ever going to be simple for her? She'd moved to the country to escape from the pressures and complications of city life, only to find a new and most unexpected complication.

With an impatient sweep of her hand, she brushed hair off her forehead and stared out the window. This was the last thing she should be doing, she chided herself—getting involved with a man at this sensitive juncture of her life. With a great effort she tried to force her thoughts away from Blair and onto safer topics. But she was unsuccessful, and her mind kept returning to the disturbing male presence on the seat beside her.

When Blair dropped Justine at her house, she hurried inside and quickly changed into her swimsuit. Grabbing a beach towel, she was out the door again within fifteen minutes. She walked across the lawn to the edge of the lake, dropped her towel onto the ground and waded into the calm, clear water. She spent the next hour floating lazily and stroking to and from a small diving platform. The cool water thoroughly revived her and erased the effects of her hot hike on the lookout road. The sky was a pale, hazy blue without a cloud anywhere. An occasional seaplane buzzed overhead, then landed near the state park on the opposite shore. The dry hills shimmered in the distance. Justine felt more at peace than she had since meeting Blair.

Completely refreshed, she toweled herself dry and strolled back to the house. She changed into a T-shirt and shorts, then entered Aldora's pen to tidy up the roomy enclosure. As she was pouring fresh water for the peregrine, a sharp killy-killy-killy caught her attention. The sound had attracted Aldora, too, who stopped preening her feathers and turned her keen-eyed gaze skyward. Justine looked up and saw a kestrel perched on a limb above the open-air pen. About half the size of Aldora, this smallest member of the falcon family had apparently spotted the peregrine and was calling excitedly about its find. Aldora responded with a series of slurred whistles and stirred restlessly on her block.

Aldora's reaction to the wild, free kestrel reminded Justine that she would soon be releasing the peregrine. A pang of sadness passed through her. She dreaded letting go of Aldora but knew that it was something she couldn't avoid. Keeping this splendid bird captive after she was capable of fending for herself appealed to Justine even less than the idea of parting with her.

Shrugging off her mixed emotions, Justine finished her chores and went inside. As she poured herself a glass of iced tea, her thoughts returned to Blair. She knew that she didn't want to become his summer fling. And judging from the possessive way he'd kissed her that day, he was used to moving up fast on women. She was sure that he'd find it convenient for her to be his sexual partner during his brief stay there. He'd already implied as much. Afterward he'd return to Seattle, and she'd probably never hear from him again. She felt her anger rise.

She sipped her tea and tried to calm herself. She was still smarting, she realized, from the two unhappy romances that she'd had in Los Angeles. The affairs had turned out to be

shallow, leading nowhere. Unfortunately, too many of the
men she'd met in the city had believed that relationships
were disposable. Aggressive and preoccupied with making
money, the men had been incapable of deep commitment.
Blair was no doubt just like them. As she stared out the
kitchen window, Justine vowed to proceed with caution
where he was concerned. There would be no more transi-
tory, throw-away relationships for her.

Later she was sorting through some family pictures upstairs when the telephone rang. She set the old album down
and went into her bedroom to lift the receiver.

"Hello?" she said. For a moment she thought that it
might be Blair calling and was surprised to feel her pulse
quicken.

"Hello," said the unfamiliar voice of an older woman.
"My name is Ursula Pennington. I'm the curator of the
historical museum here. Are you Justine Fleming?"

"Yes, I am." Justine sat down on the edge of her bed. She
brushed aside a twinge of disappointment that the caller
wasn't Blair, after all. "What can I do for you, Mrs. Pennington?"

"Well, my dear, I'm calling to ask if I may stop by Lilac
House later on today to discuss a special project. I knew
your grandparents for many years. Since both of them were
from pioneer families who helped settle the Shelby Valley,
I'd like to include something about them in a new display
we're putting together at the museum." She paused. "Are
you free this afternoon?"

Justine quickly thought about her plans for the rest of the
day. "I'm working in the house, so please drop by anytime,
Mrs. Pennington. I'll be here."

"Very well, my dear. I'll see you around three, then."

They rang off, and Justine returned to her project. She sat
back down on the floor in the midst of several old photo albums. Besides the albums there were a couple of shoe boxes,
crammed with loose photos. She dug into one of these and
pulled out a picture that had been taken on her grandparents' wedding day. Andrew Fleming sat rigidly on a

straight-backed chair and stared soberly into the camera.
His suit was dark, his high white collar stiff and uncom-
fortable-looking. A handsome handlebar mustache curved
down to frame his most prominent feature, a slightly jut-
ting lower jaw. In his early twenties Andrew Fleming gazed
at the world with eyes that shone with hope and curiosity.
It was an expression that he'd carried his entire life, Justine
reflected fondly.

Behind Andrew stood Margaret, a young woman of
barely eighteen. Her right hand rested on her husband's
shoulder. A simple veil fell from the luxuriance of hair that
was arranged on her head in tidy coils. Margaret's sweet eyes
looked the same to Justine as the last time she'd seen them,
still sparkling in a face lined with age.

Justine held the photo for a long time, staring at the two
dear people in it. Sunlight streamed through the windows of
the silent room, which was piled high with boxes and trunks
and furniture covered with sheets. Although Grandma had
died fifteen years ago, Justine remembered the old lady very
well. Grandpa had lived another nine years. Right up until
his death he'd often mentioned Grandma, referring to her
as "my sweetheart."

Justine marveled at the deep love that those two had
shared. It must've been difficult for Grandpa to live alone
at Lilac House, surrounded by memories of his departed
wife.

She laid down the photo and stood. Through the open
window she could see the overgrown park, encircled by the
sweet lilac hedge that her grandmother had planted so long
ago. Their enduring love for each other...that was what
she'd always remember best about her grandparents.
Thinking about their many happy years together caused a
wave of longing to wash over Justine. She wondered if such
a love were possible in this modern age. Everything moved
so swiftly, and people seemed to be in such a big hurry. Did
anyone pause in today's busy pace to savor a relationship
and nurture love? Such a love would certainly endure time
and the aging process.

Justine sighed. She yearned for that kind of commitment. Part of her believed that it was possible in today's world, but another part wondered if she would ever find it for herself. Where was her sweet companion in life? Oh, she'd been around, even done the singles' bar route. But the men she'd dated in Los Angeles had proven disappointing. Sure, there probably were wonderful men there. But before she could find one, the negative aspects of city life had driven her away.

She turned from the window. There was no sense in dwelling on those unsettling thoughts, she chided herself. On with this project. It had slowly dawned on her when she'd returned to Shelby that she'd been rejecting her past when she'd adopted city ways years ago. Her roots were there in the wide open spaces of eastern Washington and particularly at Lilac House. Going home had reawakened her interest in her rural past, and she was eager to know more about it. Digging into her family history would satisfy that urge.

She gathered up some of the albums and carried them down the hall to a room that she was using as an office. She spent the next couple of hours recording information about the photos on the disk in her computer. Her work was so absorbing that she was surprised when she heard the doorbell ring. She glanced at a clock as she went downstairs—those two hours had flown by.

Justine opened the door and greeted the older woman standing on the porch. "Hello. You must be Mrs. Pennington."

"Yes, my dear," said the woman, extending her hand. "I'm so happy to see you."

Justine shook Mrs. Pennington's hand, which felt cool and dry. The woman appeared to be in her mid-seventies, and her grip was firm and confident.

"Please come in," said Justine, stepping back.

The older woman entered, and Justine closed the door behind her. Mrs. Pennington was dressed in a navy-blue suit and low-heeled shoes. In spite of the August heat, her appearance was crisp and well-groomed. She wore a carved brooch at her neck, nestled in the ruffles of a cream-colored blouse. A small straw hat decorated with artificial cherries sat on top of her gray hair. Justine could smell a faint lemony scent as Mrs. Pennington walked by her.

"Let's go through the kitchen and sit out under the trees," suggested Justine. "Would you like some iced tea?"

"That would be splendid," said Mrs. Pennington and followed the younger woman down the hall to the huge, old-fashioned kitchen.

A few minutes later they were sitting on wicker lawn chairs in the shade beneath the maple trees.

"This is lovely," said Mrs. Pennington, gazing around her. "What a cool haven in all this heat. Many's the time I've sat here with Maggie, your dear grandmother."

Justine had been studying the woman. "You look so familiar to me, Mrs. Pennington. Have we met before?"

Mrs. Pennington's lined face broke into a smile that lit up her pale-blue eyes. "Yes, it was a long time ago. You and your sister were little girls and were visiting your grandparents for the summer." She took a sip of her iced tea. "I was so surprised the other day when Bev, our postmistress, told me that you were up here from Los Angeles. How nice to know that Lilac House is being lived in again, if only temporarily." Before Justine could explain that her move to Shelby was permanent, the older woman continued. "Well, I'll get right to the point of my visit and not take up too much of your afternoon. You're probably very busy."

Justine smiled. "I used to be too busy to sit and chat under a shade tree, Mrs. Pennington, but not now. Please take all the time you need to tell me about your project."

The older woman smiled in return. "Thank you, Justine." She paused. "May I call you by your first name?"

"Of course."

"And you must call me Ursula." She rested her glass on the chair arm and settled back. "As I told you on the phone, I'm the curator of the Shelby Historical Museum. The Historical Society wants to set aside one room at the museum to commemorate Shelby's pioneer families. We need some display items loaned to us for that purpose."

Justine sipped her tea, savoring the refreshing liquid and the feel of the cool glass in her hand. She asked, "What kinds of things are you looking for?"

"We're hoping for variety. Your grandmother had quite a collection of antique dolls, if I remember correctly. Would you be willing to let us borrow some of those?"

"Yes, I would," said Justine. "Your project's a great idea." She paused, thinking. "Grandpa had an old gold pan, and there's a doll buggy with isinglass windows here somewhere. It's made of wicker and has real rubber wheels. My sister and I used to play with it. Would those things interest you?"

"Yes, indeed."

Justine gazed at the lake, lying like a smooth counterpane of blue silk at the foot of the lawn. Slowly she swirled her glass, causing the ice cubes to tinkle softly. "Hmm," she said, half to herself, "I wonder where that buggy is."

Ursula fixed her with a thoughtful look. "Are you sure that my request won't cause you a lot of trouble, my dear? Maybe you don't have time to search for those things. I'd hate to inconvenience you."

Justine shook her head. "It'll be no trouble at all, Ursula," she replied. "As a matter of fact, I've taken on a big project here. I'm sorting everything in the house and recording the family history on a computer I brought with me. I'm going through each room systematically, so putting things aside for the museum will be no problem at all." She smiled. "Besides, I'm happy to help."

A look of surprise appeared on Ursula's face. "You're recording the family history on a computer?" she asked. "My, that will take a long time, and summer's almost over. How will you finish such a big project before you have to return to Los Angeles?"

"Well, actually, I'm not going back."

Ursula's eyebrows rose. "You're not? You . . . you mean, you're going to live here from now on?"

"That's right."

"Oh, my goodness." Ursula raised her ring-encrusted left hand and fingered her brooch. She regarded the younger woman with a sober expression. "My dear, I've no business asking this, but are you sure you want to live in Shelby?"

Justine felt a moment of confusion. Why would her decision to move there cause such a curious reaction in the older woman? She answered Ursula's question.

"Why, yes, of course. I spent all of my summers here as a child. Shelby holds many happy memories for me. I feel completely at home, and I love Lilac House." She paused. "Why do you ask?"

Ursula hesitated before responding. "Well, it's just that Shelby doesn't seem quite the place for a young and attractive woman like you, Justine. What I mean is, childhood summers are one thing, but to live here as a single adult who's gotten used to city life . . . well, this can be a frightfully dull place, especially in the winter."

"But you live here," objected Justine.

Ursula shook her head slowly and pressed her lips together into a thin line. "That's a long story, my dear, and has caused me much heartache." She paused, then sighed lightly and continued, "When I was a young bride back east in Baltimore, my husband James—may he rest in peace— had a serious falling out with his father. Mr. Pennington wanted James to take over the family business, but he insisted that James do it *his* way, Mr. Pennington's way. James couldn't bear the thought of living under his father's thumb, so he decided that we would go west."

"And you ended up in the Shelby Valley?" prompted Justine.

"That's right," said Ursula. "In those days there were even fewer people here than there are now. There was wide open space as far as you could see. James took one look and fell in love with the valley. He decided that we would live here, and Pennington Orchards is the result of that decision." She sighed. "And yes, we were happy." She paused and fixed Justine with an intense expression. "But, my dear, I never stopped wanting to return to Baltimore."

"How do you mean?"

"I must have cried myself to sleep every night that first year," confessed Ursula. "I missed the society of the big city, the parties, the lights, the circle of friends I'd grown up with. Poor James. He knew how much I missed those things, but he kept telling me that I'd get used to it here." She looked at the shimmering lake. "He was right. I did get used to it, and in my own way I grew to love it, too. But to this day I still think about Baltimore." She chuckled. "I must be a city person, through and through."

"Couldn't you go back now?" asked Justine.

Ursula gave a bleak smile. "Oh, no, my dear, it's too late. My sons live here, and they all have children. My boys run Pennington Orchards now, and they love the Shelby Valley as much as their father did. I couldn't leave my family." She paused and shook her head. "No, I'll live out my life here in the valley, even though part of my heart never left Baltimore." She leaned toward the younger woman. "That's why I reacted the way I did when you told me that you're going to live here, Justine. I at least had a husband when I arrived. A woman like you—someone creative and attractive—would have no husband prospects in this little community. Why, you'd be bored silly."

"Oh, I won't be bored," insisted Justine. "I'm going to open a bookstore in Shelby, and that'll keep me busy."

Ursula shook her head. "A bookstore in this little place may or may not do well—I have no idea. But I hope you'll give your plan very serious thought before committing yourself to it. I'm too old now to break away, but you're young. Don't bury yourself in a small town, Justine. Go back to the city where you can meet a nice man and get married. You'll have no such opportunities here."

Justine became increasingly anxious as she listened to Ursula's words of warning. She knew that the town rolled up its sidewalks when the tourists left in the fall. She was also aware that Shelby winters were bleak and frigid. The locals probably didn't venture outside except when absolutely necessary, dodging snowdrifts and turning up their collars against the cold. The skies over the valley were no doubt a dreary lead-gray for weeks on end. Justine could imagine the quiet days and empty nights slowly rolling by one by one. Perhaps reading and watching television would become her main sources of entertainment. In spite of the warm weather, she shivered as she pondered Ursula's words. Life in this small town suddenly seemed less attractive to her.

Later, as she cleared away the tea things after Ursula had left, Justine continued mulling over her decision to live in Shelby. Maybe she was making a mistake to move there. Perhaps she should give the whole subject more thought.

Nonsense, she scolded herself. She was simply feeling anxious because her share of the L.A. bookstore hadn't sold yet. As soon as she received the money from that sale, she could forge ahead with her plan to open a new store in Shelby. As she rinsed out the glasses, she made a mental note to call the real-estate agent who was looking for business property for her.

Drying her hands, she glanced out the kitchen window and felt a twinge of apprehension. Were the leaves on the maple trees already beginning to show the first signs of approaching fall? Or was it just a trick of the light? And why should a hint of autumn bother her, anyway? Fall had always brought a resurgence of activity to her life. It was a happy, busy time of year, when she and Sandra planned their Christmas sales campaign. Justine knew that fall in Shelby, after the apple harvest, would mean drawing in as people hunkered down for the long winter. Suddenly she knew that she'd miss the festive crowds that thronged to her Los Angeles store each holiday season. The realization gave her a chill. Would Ursula's words come back to haunt her someday?

Blair's houseboat was a rustic A-frame with a shake roof, floating beside its own dock in a small cove. Hiding the cove from the road was a screen of gently whispering pine trees. Justine parked her Jeep and paused to admire the secluded spot. A brass wind chime tinkled cheerily beneath the eaves.

She got out of her Jeep and walked along the dock. Before rapping on the door, she quickly looked down to check her clothes. She was wearing a sundress in a shade of pink that contrasted dramatically with her black hair. The dress had narrow straps and a drawn-in waist. The fluttering of the thin cotton fabric against her bare, tanned legs had a cooling effect on her. Silver hoop earrings and white espadrilles, whose straps crisscrossed up her ankles, completed her outfit.

A flood of nervousness abruptly washed over Justine. She turned around and began walking back toward her Jeep. She'd made a mistake accepting Blair's invitation that night. Going there would only encourage him and make him think that their relationship might evolve into something more....

"Hey, where are you going?" a deep, masculine voice called out behind her.

Chapter Four

Justine turned and saw Blair standing on the dock looking at her. A barbecue fork dangled from one hand. Feeling caught off guard and embarrassed, she stammered out an excuse.

"I...I think I forgot something in my Jeep." She fumbled in her purse. "Oh, no, I guess I didn't." She laughed nervously.

"I thought I heard you drive up," he said, walking toward her. He looked wonderfully handsome in blue jeans and a plaid shirt with the sleeves rolled up. "You took awhile, so I figured I'd better come around and check on you." He stopped and gave her a long, leisurely glance from head to foot, then he whistled softly. "You are one good-looking woman, Justine. I thought we'd watch the sunset tonight, but I'm not sure if I'll be able to take my eyes off you." His face creased with amusement. "You've certainly transformed yourself from the dry and dusty lady I found on a certain road this morning."

Justine felt her pulse quicken at his reference to the scene that she would rather forget. "Did you have to remind me about that?" she demanded, trying to keep her tone light.

He chuckled. "I'm only teasing, sweetheart."

The unexpected term of endearment caught her by surprise. It pleased her, yet mentally she drew back. He would get nowhere if he was counting on more than conversation tonight, she vowed to herself.

Blair interrupted her thoughts by taking her hand and leading her along the dock. "Come this way," he said.

They crossed a ramp to a spacious wooden deck that was on the back of the houseboat. Boulders and pine trees edged the shore. The temperature had cooled, leaving the air balmy and lightly scented with sagebrush and pine. Small waves gently splashed against the dock pilings. Some mallard ducks dabbled nearby, upending for food in the shallows.

The wide expanse of the lake was beginning to change from sunlit blue to a deep shade of periwinkle as the sun crept lower toward the Cascade Mountains. Dusky shadows had already pooled among the foothills, and here and there a farm light flickered. Twilight would soon be upon them, bringing the early stars with it.

"Have a seat," said Blair, "while I finish up."

He walked over to a portable barbecue, from which delicious smells were wafting. Justine sank onto a padded deck chair near a picnic table. She watched Blair as he bent over the pieces of chicken, a look of concentration on his handsome face. She found herself admiring his profile—the clean blade of his nose, the strong jawline. His tanned skin glowed with the reflected rays of the lowering sun. Quickly she looked away, afraid that he'd catch her staring shamelessly at him.

Blair brushed the chicken with sauce, causing the coals to hiss and smoke when the drippings hit them. The fragrance of the cooking food made Justine realize how hungry she was. Her mouth watered as she resumed watching him. He straightened and smiled at her.

"Your food smells marvelous," said Justine.

"Why, thank you, kind lady," he said, dipping in a shallow bow. "I'm using my own secret sauce. But I'm willing to share the recipe with beautiful women wearing sexy pink dresses."

"Blair," she said, a note of warning in her voice, "we agreed that this would be a working date. I brought along a county map that we can look at later. I don't see how we can stick to business if you keep complimenting me." Then she added, "As nice as it is for my ego."

He raised an eyebrow and flashed her a half smile. "All work and no play will make us very dull indeed." Then, apparently catching the look on her face, he added, "Don't worry, we'll study your map." He laid down his basting brush. "But in the meantime, would you like a glass of wine?"

"That sounds wonderful."

"I'll be right back," he said and went inside.

The entire rear wall of the houseboat was glass. Justine could see a comfortable sitting area with a plaid sofa and matching chairs on a hardwood floor. Thick, fluffy rugs and lamps with polished driftwood bases completed the casual decor. Above this area, toward the back of the A-frame, was a sleeping loft, where Justine could see the outline of a huge bed. The small kitchen was off to one side of the living room. It was from there that Blair was now emerging, carrying a bottle of wine and two glasses. He came out and set the glasses down on the picnic table. Condensation began forming on the wine bottle as the warm evening air met its cool surface. Blair poured wine into the glasses and handed one of them to Justine, who'd stood. He raised his glass in salute.

"Here's to success," he said and took a sip.

She followed suit, enjoying the crisp, cool taste of the Chablis. Curious about his toast, she lowered her glass and asked, "Success in general, or with something in particular?"

He smiled at her. "Success with both of our projects, my guidebooks and your falcon—" he paused, then added "—and with people."

Wondering if his comment was in reference to their relationship, Justine felt her cheeks grow warm. She tried to hide her discomfort as Blair continued.

"Now it's your turn, Justine. What would you like to drink to?"

She laughed. "Oh, that's easy. Whenever I'm asked to make a toast, I always think of Grandpa Fleming's favorite one." She shook her head at the fond memory.

"How does it go?" prompted Blair.

Justine raised her glass and looked up into Blair's gray eyes. "Here's to you, and here's to me, and here's—" She stopped abruptly.

"Yes? How does it end?"

"Well, I...I..." she faltered. "Maybe I don't want to give that toast, after all," she said in a soft voice.

Mentally she chided herself. Blair had made her so nervous with his comment about success in relationships that she'd jumped ahead without thinking. Grandpa's toast wasn't appropriate in this situation, and she should've seen that before mentioning it. Within the family it had always been given amidst playful banter. Surely Blair would think that she was openly flirting with him if she finished it now. Maybe he'd let her off the hook.

"Oh, no," he drawled, as if reading her mind. Keen interest gleamed in his eyes. "Now you've got me curious. Come on, Justine, finish the toast."

Feeling foolish and embarrassed, her heart fluttering, Justine took a deep breath. She gathered her courage and plunged ahead.

"Here's to you, and here's to me, and here's to the space between us," she said. "One of us has to go—not you, not me...but the space between us." She finished in a voice that had dwindled to a whisper.

"I will most definitely drink to that," murmured Blair as he raised his glass to his lips.

Both of them drank, Blair continuing to regard Justine closely. "I think I would've liked your grandfather," he commented. His voice had become husky.

"Oh, you would have," agreed Justine. She was searching her mind for a quick change of subject.

Her toast, and its seductive implication, however, continued to envelop the two of them like a perfumed vapor. The twilight air suddenly crackled with erotic tension. Blair put his glass down and took a step toward her.

"Oh, look," she cried, pointing over his shoulder, "the first star."

She neatly skirted around him, then walked to the railing and leaned on it, trying to catch her breath. She'd have to be more careful, she mused. It didn't seem to take much for her and Blair to become sidetracked into dangerous territory. She heard him walk over to the barbecue and pick up the sauce bowl. In the silence that followed, broken only by the hiss of the coals, she wondered if he, too, was struggling to compose his aroused feelings.

After a few minutes Blair said, "This is ready, Justine. Let's eat."

Justine helped him carry the food to the table. Besides the chicken, Blair had prepared sweet corn on the cob, crusty French rolls with a spicy butter spread and a big bowl of crisp coleslaw. Fresh local peaches floating in a simple brandy sauce completed the meal.

Afterward they took their coffee and sat near the railing to watch the rest of the sunset. During their meal the sky over Lake Shelby had changed from watermelon-pink to tangerine. Now it was soft mauve. The edges of the Cascades were dramatically backlit by the vanishing sun. A breeze had picked up, blowing a cool current of air over the deck. Justine leaned back in her chair and luxuriated in the whisper of the breeze on her bare arms and shoulders. She sighed with contentment.

"That was wonderful, Blair," she said. "You're a very good cook."

"Thank you," he responded from the chair close to hers. "The way I look at it, as long as we have to eat, anyway, why not make the most of it?" He added with a chuckle, "Yes, I suppose I'd make someone a good husband."

She turned sharply to look at him. His face was near hers, the intense gray eyes gleaming with humor. Justine felt a jolt of desire as his gaze pierced her. Never before had she known a man with this much charisma. Even in a relaxed pose he exuded an aura of potent male strength. She quickly turned from him and looked back at the lake.

"Don't you think I'd make a good husband?" His voice was low and teasing.

She decided that the safest response would be light, as well. Surely he didn't expect her to take this conversation seriously. Blair obviously loved his bachelor status and, for reasons of his own, was simply trying to throw her off balance.

"I have no idea," she hedged.

Before he could pursue this uncomfortably personal line of talk, Justine steered them toward a different topic. She reached for her purse.

"Let me show you the map before it gets so dark we can't see it," she said. "I've hiked in some canyons south of here, and toward the east are some ice caves. They're not really caves, they're actually rock slides over an old glacier. In the summer—" She was talking fast to cover up her nervousness.

Blair smoothly interrupted her by laying a warm hand on her arm. "It's already too dark, Justine," he said with a smile. "Let's relax. We can look at the map inside later, or even tomorrow. I've taken the vow to slow down and enjoy life, remember? Well, I'm enjoying it right now, can't you tell?"

Yes, she could. And she'd enjoy it, too, she told herself, if she could only calm down. But that was easier said than done. This man had an impact on her that was more than a little unsettling. She took a deep breath to steady her nerves and was relieved when Blair removed his hand from her arm. He leaned back in his chair and looked out at the darkened lake. Somewhere a night bird called. The peace and quiet were complete. Justine sipped her coffee.

"Tell me more about yourself," said Blair. "What are your plans now that you've moved to Shelby?"

Happy to converse on a safe topic, Justine told him about the bookstore she hoped to open soon in the little town.

"Here?" He sounded surprised. "From what I've heard, this place practically goes into hibernation once the summer tourists leave. Are you sure you'd have enough business to keep a bookstore afloat all year?" He looked over at her. "You may have to scale down your lifestyle."

She shrugged. "I won't mind. I came here to simplify my life, remember?"

"Sweetheart, your plan has two major flaws." His tone had become brisk and businesslike.

It rankled her that he would presume to give her advice. He was delving into very sensitive territory now, and she suddenly hated herself for feeling defensive about her plan.

"First of all," he continued, "starting up a business here might be a risky proposition."

"All right, and what else?"

"Second, you're too sharp of a woman to drop out of the mainstream and hole up in a small town." He held up one hand. "I'm not knocking Shelby. This is a very nice community, from what I can tell. All I'm saying is that I don't think your talent and experience as a successful businesswoman will be put to full use here. I think you'd miss the challenges of the city, Justine."

It was completely dark by then. There wasn't a cloud in the blackened sky, and the stars glittered like clusters of ice crystals. The Milky Way arced across the heavens, reminding Justine of the train of a sequined ball gown. She spoke with feeling as she remembered why she'd left Los Angeles.

"So you think I'd miss the challenges of the city, do you?" A sarcastic edge had crept into her voice. "Let me see... which particular challenges would I miss the most? Trying to avoid getting mugged, or being smashed on the freeway, or maybe I'd miss barricading my apartment against burglars and rapists." She shook her head. "No, thanks, Blair. I believe I'll leave those challenges to you people who thrive in the city."

"You'd be burying yourself here, Justine," he pressed on. "And don't paint all cities with the same brush. Between Los Angeles and Shelby, there are many shades of gray. Take Seattle, for example. I love that place. It has the advantages of a city, but the flavor and friendliness of a smaller town. It isn't so huge that you feel overwhelmed by crime and pollution. But it isn't so small, either, that you can't eat in an interesting restaurant or see a good show. For me, it combines the best of both worlds." He spoke with such feeling Justine could tell that he was sincere.

"Well, that's twice in one day," she murmured ruefully.

"What do you mean?"

"You're the second person today who's tried to convince me that I shouldn't live here." She was recalling her conversation with Ursula. "I think I know what's best for me. Besides, even Seattle sounds too big."

"It really isn't. Now that's where your bookstore would do well. Say, that's not a bad idea," he added in a teasing voice. "If you moved to Seattle, I could take you around."

She laughed softly into the darkness. "You'd like to show me the lights of the city, is that it?"

There was a pause as Blair leaned toward her. His breath was warm on her bare shoulder. "Yes, I would," he said in a low voice that thrummed pleasantly in her ears. There was an awkward little silence as his words sank in.

Then Justine stood up, feeling that the mood of the evening had once again become too personal for comfort. Better back off now and call it a night, she thought to herself.

"Well, it's time I left," she said, setting her coffee cup on the railing. "This has been very pleasant, thank you." She reached for her purse as Blair also stood.

"Wait," he said, "what about tomorrow? There's a place in town I'd like to visit. It's a restaurant called Parker's Apple Inn. I hear it has a terrific brunch. I want my guidebooks to include suggestions on good places to eat. What do you say, shall we give Parker's a try? I could pick you up around nine."

Not for the first time, Justine felt herself being pulled in two directions. Her instincts told her that she should avoid further contact with this disturbing man. Then she remembered her bargain with him. For as long as he was there, she was obligated to show him around. Her so-called guide service, however, was definitely taking on the flavor of a series of dates. She felt her stomach knot with apprehension as she wondered where such a course would lead her. Reluctantly she gave him her answer.

"Nine would be all right." She stepped onto the dock and began walking toward her Jeep. "Thanks again for the dinner. It was delicious."

Blair fell in beside her and took her arm. Together they walked along the dock. When they paused at her Jeep, which was parked in the deep shadows of the sheltering pines, Blair gently drew her toward him. Justine's heart leaped with excitement at being pulled close to his strong, broad chest. She was potently aware that they were hidden from the rest of the world, standing alone on the planet as it spun through the Milky Way. Her knees suddenly felt weak. She reached out to steady herself, pressing her hands against Blair's chest. Her touch registered a solid warmth, and she could feel his heart beating strongly beneath the smooth fabric of his shirt.

Before she could draw away, as an inner voice cautioned her to do, Blair dipped his head and captured her lips. As she'd done earlier on the dusty road to the lookout, Justine felt herself melt against Blair. Her mouth became soft and yielding beneath his persuasive kiss. His lips were wonderfully warm and provocative, and she knew that she was again falling under the spell of his seductive charms. Encircling her with his strong arms, Blair's hands caressed her waist and the sensitive place at the small of her back.

He finally dragged his mouth away from hers and whispered against her hair, "It's still early, Justine. Can I talk you into staying with me a little longer?"

Justine knew what accepting his invitation would surely lead to. She had to admit to herself that she was hungry for male attention. Blair kindled a fire in her, a burning need to touch and be touched. She hadn't felt such eagerness in years, perhaps not ever. But she mustn't allow herself to become involved with a man whose goals in life were so different from hers. It simply wouldn't work, and it would be folly to pursue such a course, she warned herself.

Justine stepped outside the circle of Blair's arms, firmly pushing his hands away from her body. She gazed up at him in the darkness. His eyes reflected the starlight, and she could hear his breathing, warm and urgent-sounding on the peaceful air.

She laughed briefly. "So much for keeping romance at bay." Struggling to control the tremor in her voice, she went on, "It's not a good idea for me to stay any longer."

"I think it's a wonderful idea, Justine," replied Blair. His deep voice was a potent caress on her senses. "I can tell that you'd like to stay."

"Yes," she admitted, "part of me would like to. But as I've already explained, I'm simply not going to complicate my life right now. Besides, I told you that you should expect nothing from me beyond guide service. Have you forgotten?"

"I remember, sweetheart," said Blair. "Do you remember my asking you to leave other doors open?"

Again he reached for her, but she stepped back, eluding the contact that she found herself wanting more and more as the moments passed. She knew that she'd have to make her break now or live with the consequences of not being able to tear herself away from him. She slid into her Jeep.

"Good night, Blair," she told him in a voice that still quavered with emotion. "I'll see you tomorrow."

He leaned into the open doorway and grazed her cheek with his lips. "Okay," he murmured against her fevered skin. "Escape back to your castle, princess. But you'd better raise the bridge over the moat because that's the only way you're going to be safe from me tonight."

Justine felt a moment of panic. Her eyes widened with alarm as she looked at Blair. "You...you wouldn't..." she stammered.

His laughter was rich and reassuring. "No, Justine, I wouldn't come calling at midnight, when you least expect me. I'm just revealing my fantasies, that's all." He backed away from her Jeep. "Good night, sweetheart. Drive carefully. I'll see you in the morning."

Later that night Justine turned off her bedside lamp and sank down onto her pillow. She gazed through the open French doors that led to the second-story balcony outside her room. A full moon had risen. It cast a quicksilver swath across the embroidered counterpane that covered the old four-poster bed. Justine closed her eyes against the mellow light and listened to the soft wind whispering in the trees. How would she ever fall asleep after the evening she'd just spent with Blair? Every instinct told her that she was sailing into dangerous waters by associating with a man who had such persuasive charm.

She turned onto her side and resolutely buried her face in the pillow. It was pointless to lie there and worry about the future. She had too much on her mind as it was. She would simply fulfill her commitment to Blair, he'd return to Seattle and that would be that. Even as these thoughts churned in her mind, a little voice murmured that it wouldn't be easy to keep Blair at arm's length. With a tired sigh Justine finally felt herself drifting off to sleep.

She dreamed. She was running in slow motion across a field, high above Lake Shelby. Near her flew Aldora, her jesses dangling tantalizingly close to Justine's eager, outstretched hands. Justine lunged forward and felt the leather straps trail against her fingertips. Then the falcon arrowed away again, calling to Justine, teasing her to follow. Instead, Justine laughed and fell to her knees on the soft,

warm earth. She looked up to see Blair standing above her.
The rising sun cast a golden mantle across his shoulders. He
smiled down at her, and she felt her heart race as she saw the
molten gleam of desire in his eyes. He reached one hand toward her. Aldora flew around and around them, her leg
bells ringing, ringing, ringing....

Justine awoke with reluctance and fumbled with the
switch on her lamp. The telephone rang again, insisting that
she drag herself away from the richly sensual dream that had
left her feeling hot and breathless.

"Hello," she said as she pressed the receiver to her ear.
Sinking back onto the pillow, she closed her eyes against the
lamp's glare.

"Hello, Justine. It's me, Myra."

Justine glanced at the clock. It was two in the morning.
A gust of panic swept through her.

"What's wrong, Myra?"

"I...I'm sorry to call you so late." Myra's voice broke
and she began to cry. "But I had a terrible nightmare, and
I just had to get up and call you. I hope you don't mind too
much." She sobbed quietly.

"Of course I don't mind," said Justine. "You know that.
Tell me about it."

She again closed her eyes and concentrated on what Myra
was saying. She could picture her slight, fair-haired sister
huddled in a chair, her tear-streaked face bent over the receiver.

There was a long pause as Myra continued crying. Then
she sniffed and said, "I was...I was back in the bank
and..." She hesitated and Justine urged her to resume her
story.

"Go ahead, Myra. Get it off your chest."

"I...I saw it all happen again, but it was much worse.
When the police shot him, he screamed and screamed. His
voice kept echoing, and it got louder and louder. It was
horrible—"

She broke off, and Justine heard more sobs. Myra had
been plagued by nightmares ever since the hostage inci-

dent. From the sound of it, that night's bad dream had upset her more than usual. Justine bit her bottom lip to keep from crying in sympathy for her sister.

"Tell me the rest, if you can, Myra. Get it all out."

"The worst part was how scared I was. And then I felt so terrible because I wasn't the least bit worried about him. I was only concerned about my own safety."

Justine opened her eyes and propped herself up on one elbow. "Myra, listen to me. We've already been through that. You have no reason whatsoever to feel guilty about what happened. That man was a criminal. He had a record as long as my arm. He carried a gun, and he used it to hold you against your will. The police did their job and got you out of that situation. You were not responsible for that man's death."

"I know." Myra's voice sounded thin and strained. "But I can't seem to make my emotions accept that. I keep wondering if I could've talked him into giving himself up."

"You tried to do that, but he decided to make a run for it instead. That wasn't your fault."

"No, I suppose not," said Myra. "I just keep asking myself it there wasn't something else I could've done or said to prevent what happened...." Her voice trailed off and Justine could hear her sniffling. "If only these terrible nightmares would stop."

"They will, Myra. You need time to sort out your feelings, that's all." She paused. "How are your sessions going with Uncle Bob?"

"Oh, fine. We talk at least a couple of hours every day." Justine could tell that her sister was no longer crying. Myra continued, "Except for the nightmares, I actually think I'm doing pretty well. It makes me so angry that I can't go to sleep without being afraid of reliving the whole damned thing again. It's frustrating not to be in control of what my mind does while I'm asleep."

"I know," Justine soothed. "But I'm sure that if you give yourself a little more time, the bad dreams will stop."

"I hope you're right," Myra sighed.

"Believe it, Myra. Be patient, if you can."

"Okay."

Justine could hear the smile in Myra's voice, and she felt relieved that the crisis was over. "Have you done any work yet?" Justine asked and held her breath.

Ever since the bank incident her journalist sister hadn't written a thing, claiming that she couldn't concentrate on forming sentences and paragraphs. Visions of her hostage ordeal kept interfering, she said. Her answer surprised Justine.

"I have, as a matter of fact," said Myra. Although her voice sounded tentative, it was tinged with joy.

Justine breathed out with happiness. Writing would be one of Myra's best healers, she believed.

"That's wonderful," she said. "What did you write?"

"Oh, a profile on one of the ranchers over here. The local newspaper is going to print it next week." She paused. "Of course, it's just something small and not very important...." Her words ended on a note of uncertainty.

Justine could picture her sister shrugging as she dismissed her accomplishment as insignificant. She hastened to reinforce Myra's attempt to return to a normal life.

"Now listen here, little sister. It's not unimportant. It's like learning how to walk again. First you do small articles, then the longer pieces for a bigger newspaper. Don't worry—it'll come back to you."

"Do you really think so?"

"Of course I do. Remember, it wasn't all that long ago that you were writing regular features for the *Los Angeles Globe*, no less. Maybe your editor would let you send in a few pieces from Reardan."

"Oh, I don't think so. Paul would want me down there in the city, not stuck out here in the tules. There's not a lot of news in Reardan, Justine." Both sisters giggled.

"I know what you mean," said Justine. "It's even smaller than Shelby, and I can't imagine you finding much to write about among the sagebrush and cattle fences over there. After you've profiled all of the ranchers, I suppose you could interview a badger and find out how it spends the winter.''

Again the two sisters laughed together, their shared warmth spreading through Justine. It pleased her that she could help Myra forget her troubles, even if it was only for the moment.

"Well," said Myra, "I'd better hang up and let you get some sleep. Thanks a million for listening to my troubles— again."

"No problem. Say, when are you going to come and visit me?"

They discussed some possible dates for Myra to drive to Shelby for a day or two, then they said their good-nights. Justine turned out her light and stared into the darkness for a long time, her mind whirling. The feelings that she'd kept in check while talking to Myra now surged through her. Hot tears leaped to her eyes and spilled down her cheeks to soak her pillow. What rotten luck that her only sister—and good friend—was still suffering from the desperate actions of a criminal who'd sprung from the overcrowded, uncaring city. It wasn't fair that a few should prey on the innocent, scarring them for life.

With painful clarity the hostage scene played back in Justine's mind. Instead of pushing those memories back into a dark corner of her brain as she usually did, she let them slowly unfold like the rotting pages in an old book. Perhaps by reliving the unpleasantness she could finally cast it out of her mind forever. She recalled that it had turned cold the night she'd stood watch at the police barricade. Tense and dry-eyed, she must've shivered, for a solicitous police officer had fetched a blanket from his patrol car and draped it over her shoulders. Turning her head, she'd automatically thanked him in a voice that sounded dull and disembodied.

Later, as she sipped some vile-tasting coffee from a Styrofoam cup, another policeman talked to her about Myra. The crowd behind them suddenly pressed forward, knocking Justine's coffee out of her hand and splashing her legs with the hot liquid. A reporter from one of the local radio stations had apparently overheard their conversation and realized that Justine was the sister of the hostage. Sporting a modified punk hairstyle and a leather jacket, the reporter aggressively thrust a microphone into Justine's face and began barking questions at her.

Stunned by the abrupt onslaught, Justine shrank back as the police hustled the reporter away. She caught her breath and faced back toward the bank. The building was drenched in the cold illumination pouring from floodlights that had been brought in for the vigil. Adding to the distressing carnival atmosphere were the pulsing red and blue lights that flashed rhythmically from at least two dozen police cars.

As the long night wore on, Justine noticed that the character of the crowd seemed to change. Many of the rubberneckers who'd arrived early reluctantly gave up their places in the front rows and wandered off, muttering things like, "Not enough's happening, man. Let's go get a beer." Taking their places were the hard-core gawkers, the voyeurs who live on every city's underbelly. Their insensitive comments and crude jokes made Justine sick. More than once she heard someone express the hope that they'd get to see someone being shot. Justine pulled her blanket more closely around her and concentrated on the flashing lights until she felt almost nauseated.

Just then a soft-drink vendor appeared from nowhere and began working the crowd. That someone would even consider profiting from a life-and-death situation involving her sister caused Justine to feel such intense fury that she began stalking toward the man. Punishing rebukes bubbled in her throat. Before Justine could reach him, however, a policewoman had steered the vendor out of the area, and the boisterous onlookers once more swallowed him up.

By then many of the local bars had disgorged their drunken patrons into the street, and the crowd became more rowdy. The sound of coarse laughter made tears spring to Justine's eyes. She'd never realized that people could be so cruel. Those people must be the same ones who congregate below whenever a tortured soul steps out onto a high ledge. Yes, Justine had reflected grimly, those are the onlookers who yell, "Jump! Jump!"

The police had their hands full keeping the crowd behind the barricades. Justine feared that the thrill seekers would make the already desperate situation even more dangerous for Myra. Somewhere a bottle shattered. Her increased anguish must've shown on her face, for a policeman walked over and offered her a seat inside one of the patrol cars. Gratefully she accepted. Sinking back into the shadowed interior and relative quiet, she sat out the worst night of her life.

Now, lying in her bed at Lilac House, Justine wasn't surprised that Myra still felt partly responsible for what had happened to her captor. Memories of his pointless death would probably haunt her for the rest of her days. Sensitive, caring Myra. Justine pictured her sister: the small, almost elfin woman, so childlike and yet so strong—at least before the bank incident. Myra had always worn her blond hair short in a fluffy cap that accentuated her delicate bone structure. Her eyes gazed at the world with curiosity and trust. That her trust had been so thoroughly shattered pained Justine, and more tears coursed down her face. She pounded the bed with her fist. The whole damned city of Los Angeles was to blame, she swore. Only a city could've spawned the kind of monster that had held her sister captive, then run out to face certain death in a mindless escape attempt.

A tremor shook Justine, and she reached to pull a light blanket up around her chin. She yearned for someone to comfort her now that she'd expended so much emotion on her sister's troubles. Her thoughts turned to Blair. His strong, warm arms around her would feel heavenly, she mused to herself as she dried her eyes.

Then she remembered her dream and the sensual impulses that it had created in her. Her body suddenly felt hot. She took a deep breath as her pulse quickened. Blair's parting comment about the bridge over the moat echoed in her memory. What a prophetic thing for him to have said. He *had* stormed her castle that night, just as surely as if he'd climbed the outside stairs to her balcony and entered her room through the French doors. As she imagined him standing there in the moonlight, she again felt her heart race. Her hands clutched at the bedclothes. . . .

Impatiently throwing off the blanket, Justine rolled over onto one side and squeezed her eyes shut. But it was a long, long time before she fell at last into a troubled sleep.

When loud bird songs finally awoke Justine, she looked at the clock and groaned when she saw that it was a quarter to nine. She'd overslept! Maybe she could catch Blair before he left his houseboat and ask him to pick her up a little bit later. She dialed his number and lay back on the bed, rubbing the tiredness from her eyes. Blair's telephone rang several times, its dull buzz an annoyance in Justine's ear. Her disturbed night of powerful dreams, plus Myra's distressing call, had left her feeling tired and jittery. Now she'd missed her usual early-morning workout with Aldora and had botched her date with Blair, as well. Not a very good start to another beautiful day, she fretted to herself.

She finally hung up the receiver. Blair was probably on his way already. Sighing with fatigue and frustration, she threw on her robe and slippers and went downstairs. In the kitchen she made herself a cup of coffee and was about to carry it upstairs when the doorbell rang. She set her cup on the counter and walked down the long hall.

Taking a deep breath to steady her suddenly leaping nerves, Justine opened the door and gazed up at Blair. She felt a tremor of pleasure ripple through her. He looked wonderfully handsome as he smiled in greeting. He wore slacks, an open-necked shirt and a sports jacket. It was obvious that he hadn't spent the night tossing and turning as she had, for his face appeared rested and composed. He also seemed pleased to see her.

His gaze quickly swept down her robed figure to her slippered feet. A teasing glimmer lit up his eyes as he again regarded her face.

"Is Parker's a come-as-you-are restaurant, or am I here too early?"

Justine suddenly felt self-conscious, standing there in her nightclothes. She must look a sight, with her hair wild and uncombed and her face pale from sleep and bare of makeup. She tried to conceal her embarrassment.

"I . . . I'm sorry, Blair," she said, pulling her robe more closely around her. "You're not early. I tried to call you a few minutes ago."

"You're not sick, are you?" His eyes searched her face, his expression puzzled and concerned. "Because if you are, we can do this some other time."

She shook her head. "No, I'm not sick. I overslept, that's all. You see, my sister called late last night, and afterward I couldn't get back to sleep."

A look of solicitude crossed his face. "Nothing serious, I hope."

Justine again shook her head and gave him a bleak smile. "Oh, it was the usual thing. Myra had another one of her nightmares about that bank robber, and she needed me to calm her down."

"Poor kid."

"Yes," Justine agreed. "This has really been rough on her. But I honestly believe that she'll get better someday."

"Well, look, I'm happy to wait while you get ready."

"Are you sure? I mean, I might not be the greatest company in the world today."

He put his hands in his pockets, his pose relaxed and reassuring. "It's no problem. Besides, what you need after your upsetting night are Parker's gourmet brunch and some sparkling conversation—with me, of course." He grinned. "I guarantee that your outlook will improve."

Justine felt her mood lighten as she considered the attractive prospect of again enjoying Blair's companionship.

She returned his smile. "Can't I at least offer you a cup of coffee while you wait?"

He waved off her suggestion. "No, that's all right." He glanced at the park. "It's such a beautiful morning, I think I'll wander around outside, if you don't mind."

"Of course not. Go right ahead."

Back in the kitchen Justine discovered that her coffee had grown cold. As she waited for more water to boil, she thought about Blair. He'd been very understanding about her failure to be on time for their date. She was grateful for that and was looking forward to spending a leisurely morning at Parker's.

Then a warning bell went off in her brain. How easy it was to fall in with Blair's plans. She certainly was beginning to feel more like his companion than his guide, she reflected ruefully, and that could only lead to problems. Well, she wouldn't worry about that now, she decided as she rubbed her forehead. She picked up her fresh cup of coffee and headed back upstairs.

As she entered her bedroom, she stopped and stared in surprise at the balcony. Blair stood there, leaning on the railing with his back toward her. Her heart skipped a beat.

He must've heard her because he turned around. The sight of him on the balcony was so like the way Justine had imagined it during the night that her hands began to shake. She spilled a few drops of coffee on the floor before she was able to set her cup down.

Blair took a step toward the open French doors. "Oh-oh, I think I startled you. Sorry."

"That's okay," she said, rubbing her hands together.

He nodded in the direction of the lake. "I saw the stairs and wondered if the view was any better up here." He smiled. "It is. I can see why you love Shelby and especially this house. It really must feel like a haven to you, tucked away like this far from the madding crowd." His tone was thoughtful.

"Yes," she breathed, "it does." She hesitated, trying to pretend to herself that finding devastatingly attractive men on her balcony was an everyday occurrence. In a tone that sounded more confident than the way she felt, she added, "If you've seen enough out there, please feel free to wait inside while I get ready. It won't take me long."

"Don't hurry on my account, Justine. Parker's serves brunch until noon."

He glanced in the direction of the sitting room that adjoined the bedroom. Furnished with white wicker and flowered chintz, the cozy room was one of Justine's favorites. Magazines littered the low coffee table. Sun poured in through the many windows, casting cheerful patterns on the striped wallpaper.

"Mind if I sit in there?" Blair asked.

She'd assumed that he'd go downstairs to wait. But there was no harm, she supposed, in letting him wait up there.

She shrugged and tried to sound casual. "No, I guess not."

"Great. Take your time."

He stepped through the French doors and walked over to the sitting room. He sank into a chair and began leafing through a magazine.

Justine felt a little nervous as she went to her closet and dresser to get her clothes. She was keenly aware of Blair's presence in the next room as she dug around in her lingerie drawer and listened to him turning pages. Gathering up her clothes, she scurried into the bathroom and shut the door. She stood still for a few moments, feeling breathless and terribly self-conscious. Although Blair was two rooms away, his nearness pressed close to her, as if he could see through the walls while she undressed. She hung her robe and nightgown on a hook, then stepped out of her dainty pink slippers. A quick bath would feel lovely. She began drawing water in the tub. It stood on clawed feet and was the biggest bathtub Justine had ever seen. When she and Myra were children, they'd been bathed together there by their mother. The tub could just as easily hold two adults, she mused.

She poured some white crystals under the tap, and a cloud of fragrant foam puffed up on the water. Stepping into the

tub, she eased back, sighing with contentment as the bath
melted away the fatigue from her restless, troubled night.
She closed her eyes and breathed in the delicate perfume that
was rising in a steamy cloud. It felt heavenly to relax and let
the warm, scented water sluice around her naked arms and
legs and caress her breasts and flat belly. She turned off the
tap and sank back down, again closing her eyes as she savored the moment.

Suddenly her eyes snapped open. She sat up abruptly,
causing some water to slosh over the edge of the tub onto the
tiles. Had she heard a noise right outside the room? Lilac
House needed many repairs. The lock on the bathroom door
was broken, for example. In the back of her mind, Justine
had been feeling a vague uneasiness about this with Blair
just a few feet away. Was he now standing near the bathroom door, about to walk in on her?

She froze for several long moments, straining to listen.
Then she let out her held breath and relaxed in the soothing
water. She must've imagined the noise, she told herself.
Wiggling her toes, she felt ashamed to have thought that
Blair might intrude on her privacy. He didn't seem like a
man who would do that.

She soaped her arms and breasts, luxuriating in the slip-
pery, silky feel of the rose-scented lather on her skin. The
image of Blair entering the bathroom persisted, and she gave
in to her fantasy. In her mind's eye she pictured him kneel-
ing beside the tub and rolling up his sleeves. She could see
him taking the soap from her to suds her back. As she lath-
ered up a washcloth, she imagined how Blair's wet, soapy
hands would feel on her back and shoulders. He would then
pay equally careful attention to her arms, her neck, her
breasts. Her sensitive nipples hardened as the pleasantly
rough texture of the cloth rubbed against them.

A surge of heat suddenly fanned throughout Justine's
body, caused not by the temperature of her bath but by the
flaming images that were cavorting in her mind. Hastily she
swept the cloth across her face, trying to cool the burning of

her cheeks. If Blair were a mind reader, he'd be having quite a show in the other room, she chuckled to herself.

She pulled the plug and stepped out onto the soft rug beside the tub. With a fluffy, peach-colored towel she rubbed herself dry. She brushed her teeth, then used a large, soft puff to powder her body with scented talc from an elegant container. As she fluffed the deliciously fragrant powder onto her breasts and into the tender hollow of her throat, she wondered if she should start rationing this luxury item. She'd been buying it for years at the best department store in Los Angeles. The price was exorbitant, but she'd always been able to justify the purchase. It's worthy of me, she'd laugh. She worked hard and felt that she'd earned—and could afford—a few luxuries. When the powder was gone, she might have to learn to do without that particular pleasure, for she was sure that this brand wasn't available in Shelby.

She put the container of cinnabar-red trimmed in gold back onto the shelf. Oh, well, she'd cross that bridge when she came to it, she supposed. Maybe she could order the powder through the mail. But then she'd miss the fun of going to the elegant toiletries counter to buy it in person. Yes, there definitely were some disadvantages to moving to a small town, she mused to herself.

So she'd give up a few luxuries, she mentally shrugged. It was worth it to have peace of mind. Feeling pampered and slightly decadent, she smelled the bath powder on her wrist. She knew that she'd be reminded of life's trade-offs every time she used dime-store talc when this was all gone.

She put on a soft lacy bra and some matching bikini panties. Fine lingerie was another luxury that she'd grown accustomed to in the past several years. She loved the rich feel of silk on her naked body and the way the cool-warm fabric molded to her curves like a second skin. No matter what outer garments she wore—business suit, party dress or blue jeans—she always donned fine underwear first. It gave her spirits a lift whenever she thought about the sexy wisps of silk hidden beneath her clothes. She supposed that she'd have to order her underwear by mail now, too. Bother. It simply wouldn't be the same.

She slipped a summery cotton dress over her head and discovered that the zipper was broken. Taking the dress off again, she wondered how she'd ever get it mended. She was all thumbs when it came to sewing and for years had used the services of a wonderful seamstress in Los Angeles. There was nothing that Pearl couldn't do with those clever fingers of hers, and Justine had come to depend on the woman's skill with needle and thread. Now what would she do? Justine Fleming replace a zipper? Absurd, she laughed to herself. She could still remember the D she'd received on an apron project in an eighth grade home economics class. What should've been a simple assignment had left her feeling thoroughly frustrated, and she'd sworn off sewing forever.

Yes, getting clothes mended had been easy with a seamstress close at hand. Pearl's expert services were one more thing that she'd miss about living in the big city, Justine thought with an impatient toss of her head. Wait a minute. Surely there was a seamstress in Shelby. She'd ask around and find one, and that problem would be solved. She suddenly caught her frowning expression in the mirror. What was wrong with her this morning? Her restless night must've put her into a mood to find fault, she concluded as she put on her robe and slippers. Then she left the bathroom to get another dress.

On her way back from the closet, Justine paused at the sitting room door and glanced in at Blair. He was still relaxing in the wicker chair, his legs comfortably crossed with one ankle on the opposite knee. His head was bent over something, and he seemed to be deeply absorbed in whatever he was studying. Then she saw that he'd put down the magazine and was gazing at the picture of Grandma and Grandpa Fleming. She'd forgotten that she'd taken some of the photographs to the sitting room for further sorting. For reasons that were unclear to her, she felt pleased that Blair was staring at the picture with such obvious interest.

He looked up and smiled in her direction. "Are these your grandparents?" he asked, indicating the photo.

"Yes," she said. "That was taken on their wedding day."

A teasing light entered Blair's eyes. "So this is the man who taught you that toast about the space between us, huh?"

A current of sensual energy suddenly seemed to sizzle back and forth across the ten feet that separated the two of them. During her bath Justine's mind had conjured up the sharply etched fantasy of Blair bathing her with languid strokes on her naked, soapy skin. Because of those lingering images it was all she could do to keep her mind steady. Now, on top of her fantasy, he'd reminded her of the night before, when a similar erotic current had been kindled in the space between them.

Before Blair could see the blush that Justine felt creeping up her neck, she turned away and started to leave.

"Yes, he's the one who taught me the toast," she muttered.

"Wait," Blair called out. "Come back here a minute, will you?"

She hesitated, remembering how skimpily she was dressed. Beneath her robe were two little strips of silk and lace and nothing else. In spite of her misgivings, however, she turned and walked back to answer Blair's summons. She had the fleeting impression that her feet in their pink, high-heeled slippers had wills of their own and were compelling her to carry out their wishes.

She paused in the doorway. "What is it?"

Blair had picked up one of the photo albums. "Do you mind if I look at this?"

She shrugged. "Not at all. Although I can't imagine anyone being as interested in old family snapshots as I am."

He raised his head and gave her an odd look. A series of unreadable emotions passed through his eyes with such swiftness she wasn't sure she'd even seen them. Then he seemed to relax.

"I guess I've always enjoyed looking at other people's photographs because I don't have many myself."

"Oh?"

She wanted to ask him to expand on his vague comment, but before she could do so, he smoothly continued on another tack.

Gazing down at the open album, he chuckled. "What a cutie. This must be you. Come and look."

Ignoring an inner voice of caution, Justine walked in and glanced over Blair's shoulder. "Yes," she said, "that was taken on my sixth birthday. My grandmother made that dress for me. Just look at all those ruffles. It must've taken her forever."

"I suppose you and your sister were fussed over like little dolls."

"Yes, I guess we were."

She'd always taken her sheltered childhood for granted. Even after her parents had died, there'd been other adults to step in and take over. Of course she was aware that not all people had grown up under such protective, loving circumstances. Something in Blair's manner made her wonder about his interest in those old pictures. Perhaps his childhood hadn't been so fortunate. Perhaps he—

She jumped as Blair suddenly took her hand and pressed her wrist to his face. His breath felt warm against her skin.

"You smell wonderful, lady," he said. "Whatever it is, it must be expensive." He glanced up at her, a knowing look in his eyes. "I'll bet you didn't buy this powder around here."

Justine had the impression that he was making a point that went beyond a casual observation about her tastes. Before she could respond, however, he grazed her wrist with his lips. Although the touch was fleeting, it sent shivers through Justine. The air again seemed to crackle. Feeling the need to defuse the situation, she pulled her hand out of Blair's grasp.

"I . . . I'll be ready in a moment," she said as she left the room.

She firmly closed the bathroom door behind her and leaned against it to catch her breath. How on earth was she going to keep her resolve not to become involved with Blair if the merest brush of his lips so inflamed her imagination? She shook her head. This was going to be a tough assignment.

Chapter Five

By the time Justine and Blair were pulling up to Parker's Apple Inn, Justine's emotions had cooled, and she was feeling relaxed and composed. She wore a cotton sundress in a striking shade of fuchsia, a color that brought out the natural bloom in her cheeks. High-heeled sandals and a light shawl completed her outfit. Heads turned when she and Blair walked into Parker's, reminding Justine that she was with the most handsome man in the Shelby Valley.

Parker's was a small lakeside restaurant that catered to the summer tourist crowd and specialized in dishes made with eastern Washington beef and produce. Within the single room several dining levels descended to a wall of glass that looked out onto the water. The decor was low-key, the atmosphere restful. Justine counted a total of five plants in the whole place instead of the usual jungle that was in such vogue. The fine linen was in a soft shade of creamy pink, and the wood paneling was polished and gleaming. Soft music drifted from one corner where a young man sat playing a baby grand piano.

Blair and Justine were seated at a table near the windows. Several boats pulling water-skiers sped past, the roar of their motors a soft purr through the glass. The distant hills were golden mounds against a flawless blue sky.

"Nice place," said Blair, looking around with a smile of approval. "The tourists must love it."

"Yes," agreed Justine, "it's very popular."

They ordered the champagne brunch. A waiter poured them two glasses of the sparkling drink, then they visited the laden food tables.

Back in their seats, they ate in silence for a few minutes. Then Blair said, "Oh, this is fantastic, Justine. Did you get one of the apple crepes?"

"No, I guess I missed them."

"Here, try some of mine."

Justine assumed that he'd pass a portion of the crepe over to her plate. She was surprised when he instead held a forkful of the fragrant concoction near her mouth. Accepting food from another person had always been an act of great intimacy for her. Blair's offer to let her sample from his fork, and in such a public place, put her in a dither. Blair didn't seem to notice the effect that his little act of familiarity was having on her.

She took the food into her mouth and could hardly taste the warm, sweet-tart mixture because of her feelings of uneasiness. Glancing around quickly to see if anyone had witnessed the scene, she concluded that the other diners were preoccupied with their own food and conversation. She breathed a sigh of relief. It would be awkward if everyone in Shelby—for there were some locals in there, too—started wagging their tongues about her and Blair. After all, theirs was a business arrangement.

Funny, it didn't feel like a business arrangement, she mused and stole a glance at Blair. He raised his eyes and caught her looking at him; he smiled.

"How do you like the crepe?"

"It's wonderful," said Justine, trying to sound enthusiastic.

It was hard to keep her mind on the delicious brunch. She decided to give in to her curiosity about the man seated across from her. He'd learned quite a lot about her, but she knew almost nothing regarding his background.

"Tell me about yourself, Blair," she urged.

There was a pause. "Okay," he said slowly, "what do you want to know?"

"Oh, the usual stuff. Let's start with your parents. Are they still living?"

Blair darted a quick glance at her, then stared back down at his food. His tone was guarded when he answered her.

"No, they're both dead." He didn't seem inclined to elaborate as he speared a cherry tomato with his fork.

"Oh, I'm sorry."

He shrugged.

She decided not to delve any further into what appeared to be a sensitive area, the subject of his parents' deaths. Steering the conversation onto another track, she asked, "Did your folks own a retail business, too?"

He looked across at her. Something in his manner made her think that he was trying to appear at ease when he actually felt uncomfortable. Was the topic of his family a troubling one for him? She recalled his interest that morning in her photo albums. He'd sounded almost wistful when he'd asked about her childhood. And what about his comment regarding not having many family pictures of his own? There was something there that intrigued Justine.

"Uh, no," said Blair, "my parents were in agriculture."

His answer puzzled her. "They were farmers? But I thought that you'd grown up in San Francisco."

He tore a croissant in half, sending a shower of flaky crumbs onto the spotless tablecloth beside his plate. He brushed the crumbs to one side with impatient flicks of his hand. Some creases had appeared on his brow.

"Actually, I didn't live there until I was about twelve. Before that we lived in the country. We never had a farm. My dad traveled a lot...."

"Oh, you mean he worked for an extension service or something like that?"

He looked into her eyes, and there was an awkward pause. Justine suddenly realized that she was poking into territory that apparently held unhappy memories for Blair. She was instantly sorry.

"Blair, please excuse me. I didn't mean to pry. I'm just curious about you, I guess."

He shook his head, and some of the tension drained from his face. "That's okay." He paused and put down his fork. "No, my dad didn't work for an extension service. He—"

"Hello, Justine," a male voice exclaimed behind them. "It's good to see you."

Justine looked up and smiled. "Hi, Parker," she said. She turned toward Blair, who seemed thankful for the interruption. "Blair, this is the chef and owner, Parker Callahan. Parker, meet Blair Sutherland."

Blair stood, and the two men shook hands.

"Mind if I join you for a few minutes?" asked Parker.

"Not at all," said Justine and Blair.

Blair sat back down. Parker, a man in his sixties, pulled up a chair and lowered his somewhat portly frame onto it. He beamed at Justine, a look of affection creasing his tanned, leathery face. His white chef's jacket was immaculate, and his thinning gray hair was neatly combed back from his broad forehead. Parker's brown eyes twinkled with pleasure as he pressed Justine's hand between his two big ones.

"Little Justine," he said, "it's wonderful to get to see you so much lately since you've moved back to Shelby."

Justine turned to Blair to explain. "Parker was good friends with my grandfather," she said. "He's known me since I was born." She looked fondly at the chef. "I believe you still think of me as a little girl, Parker."

"Yes, I suppose I do." Parker grinned. "But I'd have to be blind not to notice that you've grown up into a lovely young woman. You're as beautiful as your mother was,

Justine." He paused and rested his hands on his thighs. "So
are you two nice people enjoying the brunch today?"

Both Justine and Blair responded with enthusiasm about
the food. Parker nodded toward the lake. "The great view
helps the digestion, doesn't it? Quite a place, Lake Shelby."

Justine sipped her champagne, enjoying the bubbly tang
on her tongue and lips. "I love your restaurant, Parker.
Let's see, when did you first open?"

"Three years ago," said Parker, smiling broadly. "Best
move I ever made." He laughed, his mirth a deep rumble.
"It sure beats that little hamburger joint I started out with
in the old days."

"I'm curious about something," said Blair, looking
around. "How do you fill this place during the winter?"

Parker wagged his head at Blair. "I just look stupid," he
said dryly. "The Apple Inn is strictly seasonal. When the
birds and the tourists leave in the fall, so do I."

"Why is that?" asked Justine. "I thought you loved
Shelby."

"I do, honey," said Parker, "but these days I love places
like Arizona and Nevada a lot more—at least for part of the
year."

"Arizona and Nevada?" echoed Justine.

"Sure," said Parker, "I've been spending my winters in
the sunny Southwest for the past several years. It sure is
better than staying here in the valley with the ice and snow."
He shook his head. "No, cold winters aren't for me any
more."

"But aren't you afraid that you'll lose your customers?"
asked Justine.

"Honey, Shelby closes up as tight as a tick during the off
season, so I'm not losing customers. I guess you don't know
much about that because you've only spent summers here
like the tourists. Believe me, this is one quiet town during the
winter." He chuckled. "Just call me snowbird. Besides, my
doctor told me that if I slowed down, I'd be healthier." He
grinned. "So I make my living during the spring and summer, then I move back into my motor home and go rock

hounding in Death Valley. I've met some of the darnedest characters down there."

For the next few minutes Parker regaled Justine and Blair with amusing stories about the "desert rats" whom he'd met in the Southwest. Justine only half listened as she mulled over his comments about Shelby going dormant during the winter. When the tourists left, most of the business apparently went with them. It was a theme that she'd heard before, and she was beginning to have some doubts about her plan to start a business there. Still, she was determined to give it a try.

"Say, that's enough about me and my crazy adventures on the road," said Parker. "What about you, Justine? Are you still planning to stay on here?" He regarded her with an expression of interest on his weathered face.

"Yes, I am," said Justine. "More than ever."

"One thing bothers me about that," said Parker, shooting a glance at Blair. "What are you going to do, if I may ask?"

Justine hesitated. She knew that her answer would probably unleash a grandfatherly lecture from Parker, who obviously had his life neatly organized. There was no way to dodge his question, however.

"I'm going to open up a bookstore here," she said.

Parker's mouth opened and stayed that way for a moment, then it snapped shut. The chef glanced at Blair again. Blair raised his eyebrows a fraction, as if to say that he was as perplexed by Justine's answer as Parker was. Parker again regarded Justine and frowned slightly. Finally, he spoke.

"You're kidding, right?"

Justine raised her chin a trifle, hoping that she looked more confident than she felt at the moment. "No, I'm not kidding," she said.

"Honey," he began, "haven't you been listening to your old friend Parker? Haven't I just explained to you that Shelby goes to sleep during the winter?"

"I understand that," said Justine, "but I'm willing to give my plan a try." She shrugged. "If it falls flat, then I'll go on to something else."

"But in the meantime, you'll have lost your capital," commented Blair dryly.

Justine glanced across at Blair, who shot back an I-told-you-so look that gave her no comfort at all.

"I've been talking to her about this, too," said Blair to the chef, "but she seems determined to cast her fate to the winds."

Justine laughed. "Oh, that's an exaggeration, Blair."

Parker leaned closer to her. "Look," he said, "I remember the things you told me last week when you were in here. You know, about being fed up with the city, crime and pollution and all of that. I can sympathize with you on those things. I'd just hate like the dickens to see you start a business here and go bust, that's all." He paused. "Have you got a particular property in mind for your store?"

"Not yet," she admitted, "but I have a real-estate agent looking for me. A couple of places did come up, but one was too small, and the other one was in a bad location." She paused. "And while we're on the subject, perhaps I should add that not everyone here thinks that my idea is off base. Several people have told me that they'd welcome having a bookstore in Shelby. After all, there's no library here, and the only place to buy books is in the grocery store—that is if all you want is Westerns."

"You forgot one other place," said Parker, his eyes twinkling.

"Oh? Where's that?"

"Baker's Feed Store. They've got a box of used paperbacks in the corner by the barn boots. They'll sell you any two books for a quarter."

Justine snorted softly. "You see what I mean? This town needs a bookstore."

Blair reached over and laid his hand on hers. "I think that Justine is a smart businesswoman, Parker. She may sur prise all of us and create the biggest success this valley has ever seen."

Warmth spread through Justine as Blair gave her hand a reassuring squeeze. She looked into his eyes and saw support there, as well as something else. She couldn't identify it, yet it pleased and intrigued her. Suddenly feeling flustered, she gently drew her hand away and again regarded Parker. She could tell by the interested gleam in his eyes that he'd noticed the emotion-laden current that had passed like lightning between her and Blair. The look on his face seemed to indicate that he approved of what he'd seen. Before he could voice his thoughts, however—in his typically candid way—Justine hastily changed the subject.

"Blair's here on a special project," she said.

"Oh?" asked Parker, looking at the younger man. "What kind of project?"

Blair explained to Parker about his future guidebook series. He also told him that Justine was helping him scout the area.

"Say," said the chef to Justine, "I hope you're going to show him the Colockum. You can't leave that place out of a recreation guide."

"You're right," exclaimed Justine. "I'd forgotten about that area." She turned toward Blair. "Of course, we must go there."

"What's the Colockum?" asked Blair. He took his notebook out of his pocket and flipped it open as she spoke.

"It's a mountainous region southwest of here, above the Columbia River," said Justine. "It's a beautiful wilderness, with trails and primitive roads and elk herds. Near Colockum Pass you get a wonderful view looking east across the Columbia and into the wheat fields. And in the south you can see Mount Saint Helens, the volcano. The Colockum is so big I'm sure no one's described it thoroughly."

"Sounds great," said Blair. "We can fly over it tomorrow or the next day." He scribbled something in his notebook.

"Fly over it?" asked Justine.

"Yeah, I've got my little two-seater in Shelby. That's how I got here from Seattle. The pickup truck is Noel's. It came with the houseboat." He paused. "Air travel sure saves time."

"Isn't it dangerous to fly through those mountain passes?" Justine asked.

Blair shrugged. "Not particularly at this time of year. But I certainly wouldn't want to try it in the winter," he added dryly.

"So," she continued, "you want to fly over the Colockum first, to get a feel for the region, before we go in on land. Is that your plan?"

Blair shook his head as he jotted some more notes on his little pad, then slipped it back into his pocket. "No, I don't think it'll be necessary to go in on land. By flying over the area I can get all of the information I'll need for now."

"I sure don't agree," said Justine. "How can you possibly find out what's really there by looking down at it from way up in the sky?"

Blair lowered his brows. Justine saw an impatient expression enter his eyes, exactly like the one she'd first seen at the fire lookout.

"I'm not going to be here very long, remember?" he said. "I have to squeeze in as much scouting around as I can. Now flying over the Colockum will save us some time and will just have to be good enough."

Justine turned in exasperation toward Parker. "Blair suffers from city jitters," she explained. "I thought that I'd gotten him to slow down, but I guess I was wrong. Help me out, will you? He—"

Blair broke in, holding up one hand. "Look, I know you're thinking that I live too much in the fast lane and that you're somehow going to change me while I'm here. But moving in slow motion isn't in my nature. I can coast for a while, and I did, but I've got to get rolling again." He snapped his fingers to emphasize his remarks.

Parker, who'd listened to this exchange in silence, now spoke up. "Justine's right," he said to Blair. "People do need to slow down now and then and smell the roses—or, in this case, the pine trees. To get a real feel for the Colockum, you'll have to spend at least three days up there. Flying over it simply won't do the job."

"Come on, Blair," urged Justine. "Give yourself permission to relax. Don't make work out of everything. Please."

It must have been her imploring tone that swayed him, for he paused, looked deeply into her eyes and finally sighed.

"Okay," he said, running one hand through his hair. "I surrender. With both of you ganging up on me to shift into slow gear, I don't stand a chance." He chuckled good-naturedly and turned to Parker. "How do we get to the Colockum?"

"There's only one way to do it right," said Parker, "and that's with Hattie June Harris."

"Isn't she that interesting woman who owns a ranch on the river beyond Reeve Orchards?" asked Justine.

Parker laughed. "Around these parts we call Hattie June eccentric, not interesting. She's a bit of a character," he added for Blair's benefit. "Besides running her ranch, she leads packhorse trips up into the mountains. The tourists eat it up. Hattie says she hates tourists but can tolerate them in small doses. The woman really knows what she's doing. Oh, and don't let her few odd habits bother you. She's a good soul. Why don't you give her a call right now? The phone's back there." He jerked a thumb toward the kitchen.

"Let's see, a three-day trip," said Blair, planning out loud. "We could leave on Wednesday." He looked over at Justine. "You know, this will give me a chance to try out some camping gear I brought along with me. It's a new line I've been meaning to test, but I simply haven't had the time."

"Haven't *taken* the time," corrected Justine. "Now, you see, there's another reason to do the Colockum the slow way—you'll be able to test your equipment."

"Okay, country mouse," drawled Blair, giving her a wry smile. "You've made your point. Now go and call Hattie, and let's get this plan rolling."

"Yes, sir," said Justine, smiling as she sketched a salute in the air. "I'll be right back."

A few minutes later she reseated herself at their table. By that time Parker had returned to his kitchen.

"It's all set," said Justine. "Hattie will provide whatever gear we'll need, plus the food and the horses. Her nephew Kurt will go along, too, to help out."

"I still don't know if I should take the time to do this." He was drumming his fingers lightly on the table.

"Hey, don't start that again. It's all arranged. Relax and go with it, Blair. You might even enjoy yourself."

"Yeah, I guess you're right."

Justine took a sip of her champagne. "I told Hattie about Aldora, and she helped me work out a plan for her."

"You told her about your falcon? Why?" He looked puzzled.

"Well, Aldora's permit will probably arrive soon—there's really no reason to keep her a secret any longer. Besides, I can't leave her alone. She'll have to come with us. I'm bringing my Jeep along. Hattie said that Kurt can drive the Jeep with Aldora perched in the back while the three of us ride horses. The roads through the Colockum are quite primitive, but a Jeep can make it just fine." She added brightly, "You see, it's all set."

"Thanks, I appreciate your help." Blair paused. "You know, you're turning out to be a terrific guide."

Justine felt her face grow warm under his compliment. "Thank you," she replied and fumbled with her purse. "Well, maybe we should think about leaving."

"In a minute. Justine, I've been mulling something over. Your plan to open a bookstore has me worried. I have an idea for you. Will you hear me out before you turn it down?"

Justine felt a knot of apprehension begin to tighten in her stomach as Blair's expression became sober. His gray eyes regarded her intently, and she flinched under their steady gaze.

"I . . . I guess so," she finally said. "What's your idea?"

Blair took a deep breath and leaned forward, his hands loosely folded together on the table. "I want you to visit Seattle with me."

"You want me to do what?" she asked. She must've heard wrong.

"I want you to visit Seattle," he repeated.

Justine gave a short, hollow-sounding burst of laughter and shook her head. "Is this a joke? Going to Seattle is not at all appealing to me. I think I've made it pretty clear that I—"

Blair held up his hand, halting her words. "Wait. You told me that you'd hear me out."

She sighed. "Okay, but you're wasting your time."

She leaned back in her chair and folded her arms across her chest. Trying to appear relaxed and nonchalant was a tall order when her heart was pounding and her stomach was aflutter. An objective corner of her brain noted with grim interest that the mere mention of going to a city sent her emotions into a tailspin.

"Now I'm not talking about living there," Blair continued, "just paying a visit. Seattle isn't all that big, you know."

"Oh, sure," scoffed Justine. "Seattle is the biggest city in the state, and it's growing. My parents took me there a long time ago when I was a child, and it was big even then. I don't remember a whole lot about it, except that the size was overwhelming."

"You were looking at it through child's eyes. Size is relative, Justine. Compared to, say, Los Angeles, Seattle is not huge. Besides, the people are friendly, the crowds aren't so bad and the prices haven't gone out of sight."

"Yet," she said with heavy emphasis. "Blair, you made this same pitch to me last night."

"I know, but I think it's worth repeating. Okay, I'll concede that Seattle has growing pains and that it will never be a small town again. But like I said last night, it offers the best of both worlds. I've only lived in Seattle for six months, but I already feel completely at home, as if I belong there."

"You do belong there, Blair. And I don't." She paused. "But go ahead—tell me why I should visit Seattle. Keeping in mind, of course, that I have absolutely no desire to do that."

Blair sat back in his chair and studied Justine across the table. "I think you're selling yourself short. Shelby's a wonderful place during the summer when there are tourists here and the service industries are operating. But I think that a Shelby winter would drive you crazy."

"Why do you say that? I crave peace and quiet, and I want a simpler life."

Blair again leaned forward, his expression earnest and intense. "You're a talented woman, a woman full of spirit and energy. You need to be where the action is, just like I do. I think you thrive on it and are unwilling to admit it."

His argument held a grain of truth, Justine had to admit to herself. She did miss some of the action and stimulation of city life. But the price for that stimulation had been too high.

She sighed. "It's nice of you to invite me to visit your adopted city, Blair, and I'll give it some thought. For now, though, the best thing for me to do is cut off my city ties altogether and make a go of it here. I'm putting down roots in Shelby just as fast as I can."

"I think you should test your reactions soon, before winter sets in," he urged. "Look, there's plenty of room in my apartment. It's right downtown in a handy location across the street from the Pike Place Market. Which is one of the most interesting outdoor markets on the West Coast, by the way. You'd love it. You could have your own key, and you could come and go whenever and wherever you like." He smiled engagingly. "Of course, I'd want to go with you."

Justine gazed across at him. She was trying to imagine what it would be like to be in Seattle with Blair. Share his apartment for several days? Hmm, that could be interesting. A little bit too interesting, a warning voice whispered inside her.

"That's very nice of you," she repeated, "but I believe I'll take a rain check on your offer for now. I still have Aldora to think about, you know. She's not ready to be set free yet, and—"

"After you release her, then?" he pressed.

"I'm not going to commit myself, Blair." She paused and mustered her courage. "Please don't ask me to."

A look of frustration flickered in his eyes, and his brows knit into a frown. Justine could see that her answer disappointed him.

"I suppose you're still thinking about what happened to your sister," he said, a muscle twitching at his jawline.

She nodded. "Yes, plus all of the other things that drove me out of L.A. I want to calm my life down, give this place a chance and see if I can adapt to the country." She smiled. "So far I seem to be doing nicely." She decided not to add anything about her irritation earlier that morning over expensive bath powder, fancy underwear and broken zippers. There was no sense in giving Blair fuel for his argument.

"Maybe you're using Aldora and your sister as excuses," he said. His tone was not accusatory but thoughtful, and Justine didn't take offense.

She shrugged. "That's possible, I guess, but I sure don't think so." Suddenly she felt restless and needed to change the subject. "Look, um, can we drop this for now?"

There was a tense pause as they continued to stare silently at each other. Justine could tell that neither of them would give in easily. She could buy time, but Blair would undoubtedly renew his campaign to change her mind at a later date. Her heart felt heavy as she realized that her first impression had been correct; their approaches to lifestyle were poles apart. Blair probably saw her as a challenge—altering her outlook would prove his point. She wondered if he always treated women as his pet project. Her doubts made her feel bleak and empty inside, and she sought to distract herself with action.

"Shall we leave?" she said.

They stood up.

"Where to now?" asked Blair. "Do you have any fascinating recreation areas to show me this afternoon?"

Was it her imagination, or did Justine detect a hint of sarcasm in his voice? Perhaps he was really annoyed with her and was fighting to hide his reaction. She tried to keep her demeanor light and upbeat to soften the effects of their obvious stalemate.

"Yes, I do," she answered, smiling up at him. "But first I need to give Aldora her workout. Would you like to join us?"

His frosty expression melted around the edges. "Sure."

Justine congratulated herself on having defused the tension with an invitation of her own. She'd thought that their disagreement would spoil the rest of the day; now she was sure that the afternoon could be saved.

They spent the next two hours up in the hills. Justine noted with pleasure how well Aldora performed her aerial maneuvers. She brought down her first live prey, an English sparrow. Justine and Blair laughed at how excitedly the falcon twittered over the tiny morsel. During that time they didn't mention their disagreement. It was as if they'd made an unspoken pact to keep the afternoon free of controversy, and for that Justine was thankful. It would've been a shame to ruin such a beautiful day. The sky was cloudless, the air full of bird song. The breeze was scented with sage and pine, and the lake gleamed below them like a puddle of azure watercolor.

As the falcon stooped and soared, Justine felt her heart fly with it. Only when she worked with Aldora could she forget her worries. She glanced at Blair a couple of times and caught him apparently deep in thought. He spoke very little, and his buoyant spirits seemed forced. She was grateful that, for whatever reason, he was striving to maintain his good humor.

Later that day, after they'd dropped Aldora back at Lilac House, they visited some camping areas near Shelby.

Blair took notes about the facilities that were available at each one. Then they hiked along the rim of Lupine Gorge, a dramatic canyon that attracted photographers.

Justine called Myra that evening. Her younger sister sounded much better than she had the night before. Justine explained to her about the trip into the Colockum and touched lightly on her arrangement with Blair. When they rang off, she heaved a sigh of relief. She'd been fretting about the coming trip, knowing that Myra wouldn't be able to reach her if she needed to. It reassured her to learn that Myra had recovered from the effects of her nightmare.

The next morning Justine called her real-estate agent. His rather glum report was that he still hadn't found property that would be suitable for her bookstore. "Things don't turn over very often in these parts," he told her for the tenth time. Justine felt frustrated and discouraged as she hung up the telephone.

The time sped by as she and Blair prepared for their trip into the Colockum. Although Hattie was providing almost everything, there were still many details to take care of. In the meantime, Ursula Pennington called to ask about the items that Justine had agreed to loan to the historical museum. Justine explained that she'd been extremely busy but had done a little sorting and had put aside a couple of boxes for the curator. Could Ursula pick them up that afternoon? The older woman agreed that that would be fine.

Whew, Justine thought to herself as she hung up the receiver. There was so much to do. When she'd first arrived in Shelby, she'd wondered how she'd keep herself busy in a small town. True to her nature, however, she'd quickly filled up her time with several projects as she put down some roots. Now, of course, showing Blair around took up even more of her time. It had dawned on her that most of her projects would eventually end. Then what would she do? Why, run her new bookstore, she reminded herself. *If* it ever gets off the ground, she thought grimly, recalling her agent's most recent and unpromising report.

Happier news arrived in the mail. Justine ripped open an official-looking envelope in which she found the permit for Aldora. Her relief was so great that tears of joy leaped to her eyes. The weeks of secrecy were over; she could now train the falcon without fear of breaking the law or angering her neighbors. She immediately called Blair with the good news.

"That's great," he said. "I knew my friend would come through for you." He paused. "Well, are you ready to go camping with me in the wild and woolly out-of-doors?"

"I sure am," she said. "Tomorrow's the day. Hattie wants us to meet her at seven sharp."

Blair gave an exaggerated groan. "That lady's an early riser." He continued in a joking tone, "You'd better get a lot of rest tonight, Justine. You'll be sleeping on the ground for the next three nights."

"Oh, I'll be fine," she lightly tossed back, a teasing note in her voice. "We country mice are used to roughing it, you know. I'm curious to find out if a city slicker like you can survive in the great outdoors."

"You were a city slicker yourself until a few short weeks ago," growled Blair, teasing her right back. "How soon we forget. We'll see who adjusts to the hardships of the trail better—you or me."

Chapter Six

The arrangements for the trip into the Colockum had been made over the telephone, and Justine had formed a mental picture of Hattie after she'd heard her voice a number of times. She was surprised to discover, then, that Hattie was not the tall, big-boned woman she'd come to expect. Instead, the horsewoman was short and wiry and looked to be about sixty. She had a tanned face as wrinkled as an apple that has lain out in the sun all summer, and her dark eyes glittered like polished river stones. When Justine and Blair arrived at the rendezvous spot, Hattie was already bustling about, making sure that everything was in order.

"Good morning, Justine," said Hattie in her low, gravelly voice.

"Hello," said the younger woman. "Hattie June Harris, this is Blair Sutherland." She nodded toward him.

"I'm happy to meet you, Hattie," said Blair, stepping forward.

They shook hands all around, and Hattie said, "How do, Blair."

Justine was amazed by the strength of the little woman's grip. The palm of her small hand was thickly callused. Her fingers were bony, and her skin felt dry and leathery. She'd obviously spent her life outdoors, working hard. And probably loved every minute of it, too, mused Justine.

"This here's my nephew Kurt," said Hattie, introducing the tall young man who was towering behind her left shoulder. "He's here for the summer, helping me out. Say hi, Kurt."

Kurt nodded in their direction and said, "How you doing?"

He had straight, dishwater-blond hair that hung to his shoulders. As he dipped his head toward them, Justine could see that his right ear was pierced but that he wore no earring. He appeared to be about seventeen and would be good-looking once he'd passed out of the spotty, adolescent stage. His blue eyes gazed directly into Justine's, and she got the impression that he was trying to look tough but was a softy inside. She felt a motherly twinge for the gangly youth.

Hattie wore old leather chaps over her jeans, a faded plaid shirt with metal buttons and a beaten-up straw hat on top of her steel-gray hair. She reminded Justine of a veteran rodeo rider.

After introducing them to Rawhide, her buckaroo, Hattie returned to her tasks. "Okay, you greenhorns," she said with a twinkle in her eye, "stand back while Rawhide unloads the horses."

Following the little woman's instructions, Blair and Justine stepped aside and watched. Rawhide led three horses out of the large truck that was parked nearby. Then Kurt and Blair started transferring gear from the truck to the Jeep. Because Aldora was perched in the back, most of the equipment had to go onto the rack on top.

"May I do anything?" asked Justine as Hattie scurried past her with a saddle blanket.

"Sure," said Hattie, "get to know your horse. Her name's Babe. Oh, and this here's Gypsy."

She nodded toward the black-and-white sheep dog that was frisking at her side, its plume of a tail held high. The dog pricked up her ears at the sound of her name.

Justine approached Babe, a gentle mare, and took the reins from Rawhide. The bay gazed into her eyes and whickered softly, and Justine knew that they'd be friends.

After some last-minute instructions to Rawhide, who was going to drive the truck back to Hattie's ranch, Hattie mounted a sleek black gelding named Chester. By that time Kurt was in the Jeep and had started the engine, and Blair was astride a gray-and-white Appaloosa mare named Sugar. Gypsy was making little forays into the sagebrush and back, eager to be off.

It was agreed that Kurt would drive ahead on the primitive road and meet the three horseback riders at a pre-arranged spot. By traveling cross-country Justine, Blair and Hattie would be better able to savor the wild country in quiet. The Jeep drove off in one direction and the truck in another, leaving a peaceful silence in their wakes.

Justine gazed around at the beautiful terrain as her horse fell in behind Hattie's. In the distance dry slopes rose to pine-encrusted hills and rocky cliffs. Here the land was flat and brushy. Meadowlarks caroled from the fence posts, and a hawk circled high above. Reddish-brown cattle browsed among the sage, and a raven flew in front of the horses. The pleasant smell of warm leather and the creak of the saddle played on Justine's senses. The sun warmed her back, making her feel that all was right with the world.

Hattie rode ahead, leaving Justine and Blair alone. He brought his horse up beside Justine's and leaned over toward her. He affected a cowboy twang.

"You look might pretty in the saddle, my little desert flower," he said in an admiring tone. "Yes, ma'am, I reckon you've got the cutest cheeks that ever sat a horse."

His frank compliment surprised her, and she caught her breath. "Blair, you're supposed to be admiring the view and doing research out here, not sweet-talking me."

One of his eyebrows shot up. "Oh, I'm admiring the view, all right," he said smoothly.

Then he fell back and let Justine ride ahead. She heard him chuckle softly, and she imagined that she could feel his eyes boring into her. The thought so unnerved her that she nudged Babe into a canter until she caught up with Hattie.

Later, when she looked back at Blair, he grinned wolfishly at her and made an elaborate show of tipping his hat. She turned away from his burlesque, feeling her pulse quicken. She was determined not to let his disturbing presence throw her off balance. The scenery was spectacular, and she meant to enjoy herself on this trip whether or not Blair flirted with her at the most unexpected moments.

Their route soon led the riders up into the hills, where the horses slowly wended their way between boulders and stands of pine trees. There was little talking on this first leg of the trip. All three seemed content to let the peace and quiet of the wilderness remain unbroken.

Although Justine tried to concentrate on the lovely surroundings, her mind kept straying back to Blair, who was again riding beside her. He was especially handsome in his jeans and open-collared blue shirt, she noted. As the temperature climbed, he'd rolled up his sleeves, revealing the bronzed skin of his strong forearms. In the sunlight the blond hairs on his arms looked soft and golden. She admired the way he rode his mount, his lean thighs flexing with the powerful movements of the horse....

"I see that you're admiring the view, too," Blair commented dryly.

She snapped her gaze up to his face. He'd caught her staring at him, and she knew that her facial expression must've been dreamy. She tried to cover up her embarrassment.

"I...I was just checking to see if..." Her voice trailed off. She was unable to invent a plausible reason for giving his thighs such close scrutiny.

He flashed her a knowing smile and chuckled deep in his throat. She could tell that he saw right through her feeble excuse. From then on she'd be more careful and not let him catch her stealing glances at him. Again she urged Babe forward, out of range of Blair's teasing laughter.

Around noon they met Kurt for lunch in a clearing near the road. The fried chicken, sourdough rolls and fresh peach pie went well with the hot coffee that Hattie brewed on a quick fire. Justine flew Aldora, who performed a magnificent power dive onto a blackbird, which became a meal for the falcon.

After lunch they rode for several more hours, then picked a camp spot for the night. Giant gray boulders partially surrounded a grassy meadow, where tall pines thrust skyward here and there like sentinels. Kurt unsaddled the horses while Hattie prepared dinner. Justine helped Blair set up the two tents that he'd brought along.

Later that evening Kurt disappeared into the darkness after helping clean up the dishes. The other three remained seated around the fire. Hattie explained that it was Kurt's habit to sleep outside on the ground instead of in a tent so that he could look at the sky and be near the horses.

"There's plenty of room in each tent for two or even three people," said Blair.

"Oh, that's just his way," replied Hattie, stirring the fire with a stick.

Sparks rose in the air, reminding Justine of a cloud of orange fireflies against the night sky. A light breeze sighed in the tall conifers.

"Kurt doesn't like to be hemmed in by a tent," added Hattie.

Justine stared into the flames, feeling a delicious drowsiness creep over her. "I suppose he's used to the wide open spaces," she said.

Hattie glanced over at her, the firelight reflected in her dark eyes. "No, but he's learning. Kurt's from Chicago. This is the first time he's been out of the city since he was a little tyke."

Justine sat up, her interest piqued. "You're kidding." She felt herself frown in puzzlement. "He does everything so well out here, I would've sworn that he'd been brought up on a ranch. He sure seems like an expert at handling horses and trail gear."

"That's because I've been training him," said Hattie, pride evident in her voice. She leaned forward a little and regarded them from under the brim of her straw hat. "Would you two believe that Kurt was almost a criminal before he came here?"

Blair and Justine exchanged surprised looks. Justine spoke. "Why, no, he seems like such a nice boy. What do you mean, Hattie?"

"Well," she began, "he's not headed toward crime anymore, that's for sure." She spat off to one side. "Kurt's mother is my younger sister. Several years ago Amanda's husband died. Up to that point Kurt had been a good boy, and his folks were proud of him. When his dad died, he gradually fell in with the wrong crowd. His grades went down, and he started hanging out on the street in some bad parts of the city. It wasn't long before he'd gotten himself into some trouble." She paused and stared across the fire at Blair and Justine. "Nothing too serious, mind you, but it would've led to much worse if his mom and I hadn't stepped in."

"What happened?" asked Blair as he added a couple of sticks to the blaze.

By now the wind had died down. The fire crackled softly, and mice rustled in the dry grass. Overhead the vast sky was sewn with star beads, glistening like glass, and a sickle-shaped moon was peeping over the horizon. Off in the dark a horse stamped its foot and snorted. Gypsy, who lay by Hattie's side, pricked up her ears at the noise, then put her head back down onto her paws.

"Amanda called me this spring," said Hattie. "I could tell that she was upset. Her voice was all shaky, like she'd been crying. She told me that she was at her rope's end with Kurt. Amanda's about my size, and you know how tall Kurt is. There was no way my sister could handle that wild boy all by herself." She took a pouch of tobacco out of her shirt pocket and began rolling a cigarette. "You two smoke?" she asked, holding out her pouch and papers. "Help yourselves."

Both Blair and Justine declined her offer. Hattie licked the paper and lit the lumpy cigarette with a burning twig from the fire. Then she exhaled the smoke, picked a strand of tobacco off her lip and continued her story.

"I told Amanda to put Kurt on the first bus out of Chicago and to send him to me. I knew what would straighten that boy out." Pride again gleamed in the dark eyes that gazed from beneath the weathered face. "And I was right, too. I wish you could've seen Kurt when he first got here." She paused and gave her next words special emphasis. "Why, he didn't even say please or thank you. Can you believe it?" Hattie grimaced as she recalled her nephew's lack of manners. "And his attitude was as ornery as a wet polecat's. He was surly and rude, and he had the worst mouth I've ever heard on a person." She shook her head, then frowned over at her listeners. "Not even my buckaroos talk the way Kurt used to."

"I never would've guessed that you're speaking about the same boy," said Justine. "Kurt's so polite and quiet. He goes about his chores without being asked, and he never talks back. You've done wonders with him, Hattie."

Hattie, who was obviously pleased at the compliment, stared down at the ground and pushed a few sticks around with her toe. "Oh, yeah, I helped," she said. "Lots of hard honest work was good for him, too." She looked up again. "But I'll tell you what really turned him around." She paused and dragged on her cigarette, seeming to relish the hold that she had on her audience.

"Well?" asked Justine, unable to stand the suspense.

Hattie exhaled, then tossed the stub into the flames. "The country life," she said simply. "Being on the ranch is what turned Kurt around and got him back onto the right path. Yep—" she nodded sagely "—the city almost ruined a good boy, but the country life has saved him."

Justine was intrigued by Hattie's analysis. She wanted to hear more from this mite of a woman whose alert eyes blazed as brightly as the dancing firelight. Before she could speak up, however, Blair voiced her thoughts for her.

"How do you figure that, Hattie?" he inquired.

Hattie shot him a glance. From the look on her face, she apparently wondered how he could ask a question whose answer was so obvious.

"Why, everyone knows that cities are terrible places," snorted the older woman, her eyes widening. "All of that crime! And those gangs of thugs wandering around, just looking for someone to bonk on the head! It's no wonder Kurt strayed. He was surrounded by hooligans, that's what happened."

"But not everyone who lives in the city is a hooligan," said Blair. "You don't really believe that, do you?"

Hattie chuckled, then gave a little cough and shook her head. "No, Blair, I don't believe that." She paused, then darted a glance at Justine, her eyes twinkling. "They're just crazy, that's all."

Justine turned to look at Blair. She was curious to see how he'd handle the city-versus-country issue with someone as feisty as Hattie.

Blair held up one hand. "Now wait a minute, Hattie. You're going to have to clarify that for me. Why are people crazy simply because they happen to live in the city?"

Justine sat back and watched the two of them. She suspected that Blair's keen interest in this friendly debate was not due to what Hattie believed but to his ongoing disagreement with Justine. She suppressed her urge to join in and satisfied herself with simply observing for the time being. Let Blair take on this tough horsewoman and her ironclad beliefs all by himself. This ought to be good!

Hattie ticked the items off on the fingers of her gnarled hand. "Crime is number one, of course. Who in her right mind would want to live where you can get mugged? Then there's stinky air, littered streets and honking, racing cars.

Push and shove, push and shove, everyone in a big hurry,
people being rude to each other—''

"Have you ever lived in a city?'' Blair broke in on her ti-
rade. His eyes shone with curiosity, and Justine could tell
that he was enjoying sparring with the older woman, even
though he probably knew that he'd lose this debate.

"Many years ago, before I wised up, I lived right in
Shelby,'' said Hattie.

Blair roared with laughter. "I said a city, Hattie, not a
wide spot in the road.''

The little woman drew herself up. "Well, now I reckon it's
according to your point of view, what you'd call a city. To
me Shelby is a city! Especially when those mobs of tourists
invade us like a plague of locusts.'' She shuddered. "I can
hardly stand to go into town during the summer. I have to
wait in line for this and wait in line for that. And the out-
siders whine about how Shelby doesn't have their favorite
brands of food or beer, same as they can get back home.
They bring their city troubles right along with them. Thank
goodness Kurt is willing to do the shopping for me.'' She
sighed deeply and stared at the flames. "No, sir, give me the
peace and quiet of my ranch any day. I would rather sleep
with rattlesnakes than live in a city.'' She poked at the fire
with such force that several large coals bounced out and had
to be corralled back into the circle of stones.

"What about during the winter?'' asked Blair, glancing
at Justine. Clearly he was trying to set Hattie up to score a
point for his side. "Don't things calm down then?''

"Calm down?'' said Hattie. "They plain die. Even my
apple trees go to sleep for the winter.''

"Isn't it rather dull?''

Hattie regarded him with a look of astonishment on her
wrinkled face. "Dull?'' she repeated. "I call it returning to
normal. The mobs go back to their... What's the word for
those things?'' She paused and seemed to search her memory. "Oh, yeah. They go back to their conderminerums—
beehives, I call 'em—and leave the country to us country
folks. I can actually breathe during the winter with all of

those people gone. Why, I can even go to the grocery store and get waited on without standing around for half an hour.'' She grunted. ''Winter's my favorite time of year these days.''

Blair sighed. It was plain that he'd accepted defeat at the hands of this peppery little woman. ''I can see that you're sold on the country life,'' he said.

''Young man, it's the only way to live,'' said Hattie with feeling. ''You can have your fancy restaurants and your fancy cars and clothes, but give me the simple life. Give me this.''

She gestured with her hand to indicate the pristine ebony sky with its array of glittering stars, the cool silver moon climbing into the velvet heavens and the dark outline of pines against the horizon. At that moment a chorus of coyotes began singing on a nearby ridge. Hattie grinned.

''Even got my own opry.'' She chuckled. ''Ain't it pretty?'' Then she yawned. ''Well, I think I'll turn in. We'll be up early tomorrow. Good night, you two nice people.''

''Good night, Hattie,'' said Justine and Blair.

The little woman levered herself to her feet and stumped off into the night. Justine couldn't hold in her mirth any longer. She laughed, pressing her mouth against her knees, which she'd drawn up and clasped with her arms.

''What's so damned funny?'' asked Blair. The look on his face told Justine that he suspected the cause of her laughter.

''That conversation,'' she said, gasping. ''Oh, it was great. Excuse me, but I got a kick out of watching you fence with Hattie.''

Blair regarded her with a sober expression. ''Surely you don't buy everything she said,'' he commented dryly.

Justine shook her head and wiped her eyes. ''No, of course not.'' Then her mood became serious. ''But I buy the gist of it: Kurt's been healed by the simpler life here, and Hattie knows that she'd never survive in a city. I identify with those ideas.''

Blair looked at her with an expression so intense and laced with meanings she couldn't interpret that she suddenly felt herself melting inside. Without a word he moved closer and brought his face to within inches of hers. Justine held her breath, waiting in nervous anticipation for his kiss. With some chagrin she realized she'd been hoping all day that he would hold her and kiss her. A trembling sensation erupted somewhere in her chest and rippled out to her arms and legs.

Instead of kissing her, however, Blair rose and pulled her up to stand beside him. "How about a stroll before we turn in?" he suggested.

Justine knew that accepting his invitation to leave the circle of firelight and enter the beckoning, sheltering shadows would be folly. But even as a red light of warning flashed in her brain, she found herself saying yes and allowing Blair to lead her out into the night.

It took Justine's eyes a few moments to get used to the darkness beneath the towering pines. Blair held her hand firmly in his, warming her fingers and palm, and guided her around the natural debris that littered the ground. Soon they broke out of the woods and stood bathed in starlight. Before them stretched a vast plain dotted with sagebrush and rocky outcroppings. A large shape skimmed near the ground, an owl hunting mice. With a few silent flaps of its wings, the owl disappeared over a rise. Coyotes again yipped in the distance. The sound had a poignant ring to it, and Justine shivered.

"Are you cold?" asked Blair, his head dipping low to talk to her. He must've felt her trembling.

"No," she said, "I was just thinking what a lonely sound that is—those coyotes singing in the dark."

"Come on. Let's sit over there and look at the sky. August is the best month to see shooting stars."

She followed him to the top of a little knoll that rose a few feet above the plain. They sat down on the soft, cool grass. Justine drew her knees up and hugged her legs to her as she gazed up at the spangled canopy.

"Why is this the best month?" she asked.

"Every August the earth passes through what's left of a comet that hasn't been seen for over a hundred years. Swift-Tuttle, I think it's called." He broke off to point at the sky. "There goes a shooting star. It might be debris from the comet's tail. Do you see it?"

Justine looked where he was indicating. "No," she said, "I missed that one."

"Keep watching, there'll be others. Have you ever seen a meteor shower?"

"I'm not sure," she admitted. "I don't think so."

She paused and turned to regard him. He sat so close to her their thighs brushed whenever one or the other of them shifted position. The intimate touch unnerved Justine, and she fought to keep her mind on the safe subject of comets and meteor showers.

"How, uh, how is it that you know so much about astronomy, Blair?"

It occurred to her that their easy conversation might eventually lead Blair into some revelations about his childhood. She recalled the scene at Parker's when they'd touched briefly—and painfully, it had seemed—on the subject of his past. She was sure that he'd been close to telling her something significant about his family when Parker had interrupted them. Perhaps Blair would welcome another opportunity to share personal details about himself. In any case, she'd let him take the lead this time.

Blair laughed. The warm, rich sound spread around Justine like honey. "I really don't know that much about astronomy. I'm a rank amateur. Astronomy's always interested me, but I've never had the time to really study it. Besides," he added, "it's a little hard to look at stars in the city."

"Why's that?"

"There's too much other light interfering."

"Aha!"

He leaned closer to her. "Aha?" he repeated.

"That's another reason to live out in the country. You can see the stars better."

"You just can't resist, can you?" he said.

"Resist what?" she asked in mock innocence.

"You can't resist trying to score points about your new lifestyle. I suppose what Hattie said tonight reinforced your decision to stay buried out in the sticks."

"Oh... not really," Justine responded slowly.

Blair looked at her. "But you told me that you identify with the gist of what she said."

"That's right, I do. But her point of view is pretty one-sided."

"Boy, you can say that again," he muttered with feeling.

Justine gazed up at the stars. "Something you mentioned to me recently, plus listening to Hattie talk tonight, has got me thinking." She laughed self-consciously. "You know, being out here where it's so peaceful sure clears the cobwebs out of your brain."

"What cobwebs, Justine? And what did I say that set you to thinking? Come on, you've got me curious."

"Well..." she began, uncertain how to proceed.

She wasn't sure that she could trust Blair with further revelations about her deepest feelings, but she knew that she owed him an explanation. After all, an insight of his had cracked open a door for her.

She cleared her throat and started over. "Do you remember saying to me at Parker's that I might be using Aldora and my sister as excuses?"

He nodded. "Yes, I remember saying that. It's only a hunch, kind of a gut feeling. Please don't take offense. I know that you and Myra are very close. But it seems to me that your total rejection of cities is a case of, well, over-reaction to what happened to your sister." He paused. "How about it? Do you think that's possible?"

Justine blinked away the tears that were suddenly stinging the corners of her eyes. This subject was still painful, but her perspective on it had definitely changed because of Blair's insights. The positive-sounding phone conversation she'd had with Myra the day before had helped, too. Her sister was obviously making progress.

"Yes," she admitted, "I probably did overreact." She paused. "Escaping to the country just seemed so much easier than staying to fight all those battles in the city. I was burned out from the hassles." Her voice became quieter. "I guess my outlook lately has been as one-sided as Hattie's."

"And now you feel a little differently about things?" he asked.

She brightened. "Yes, I do. What you said at Parker's made me stop and examine my motives." There was a long pause. "I guess I should thank you, shouldn't I?"

He laid a reassuring hand on her arm. "Thanks aren't necessary," he said. "Like I say, it was just a hunch on my part. I'm glad I could help." He paused. "So you're going to move to Seattle now, right?"

She laughed. "Hey, wait a minute, I've altered my perspective, not my entire plan. I still want to live in Shelby. That hasn't changed."

"But does this mean that you'll come and visit Seattle?" His tone was hopeful.

She took a deep breath. "Well, I've thought about your offer to share your apartment with me, and it sounds very interesting."

"Now you're talking." He looked at his watch and began pressing a little button on it. "Let's get this plan rolling."

Justine shook her head in amazement. "I can't believe you brought that thing along. Why on earth would you need a fancy wristwatch in the middle of a wilderness?"

He showed her the watch, where an October calendar had appeared on the luminous face. "Go ahead," he said, "look down your country nose at the symbol of my rat race lifestyle. But you have to admit it's a handy little gadget." He studied the calendar. "Okay, now where were we? Let's see, I've got a big sale coming up around the end of October." He seemed to be talking more to himself now than to her, Justine noted. "I'll be really busy getting ready for that." He suddenly snapped his fingers and looked at her. "I've got it. You could come over the last week in September." He was talking fast. "I'll be relatively free then and can show you around. We could—"

Justine held up her hands and leaned away from him. "Stop," she said. "Hold on, will you, Blair? I can't keep up with you."

"What's wrong?"

"I'm not going to go to Seattle during the last week in September."

"Oh, well, how about the first week in October, then? That's cutting it close to the sale, but I'm sure I'll be able to fit in some time for you." He grinned. "What am I saying? I'll just make time."

"Blair."

"Yeah, what is it?"

"You're not giving me a chance to explain. If I visit Seattle, it'll be next spring, not this fall. And I'll stay in a hotel, not at your apartment."

"Next spring?" His tone was incredulous. "Why wait that long? And why would you want to stay in a hotel? I told you there's plenty of room at my place."

"To answer your second question first, I'd feel better if I had my own place. That way, I wouldn't put you out, and, well, it would just be better."

He snorted. "Put me out? That's ridiculous. You know that—"

She again held up her hand. "No, really, I mean it." She paused. "To answer your other question, I want to settle in here before I take any extended trips. I think Sandra's close to finding a new partner. When she does, I'll have the capital to start my bookstore in Shelby."

"If you can find some property," Blair reminded her dryly.

"Oh, something will turn up eventually," she said. "So, you see, I'll probably be up to my eyebrows in my bookstore project just when you're planning your big sale."

There was a long, uncomfortable silence, then Blair spoke. "Spring." He made it sound as if it were a hundred years in the future. "You sure are an independent woman."

His resigned tone was tinged with admiration. "Maybe a little too independent?"

His remark surprised her. "I've had to be independent."

"Yeah," he said, "I guess so."

Justine leaned closer to him, feeling the need to shift the conversation away from further analysis of her personality. "Blair, would you do me a big favor?"

"Name it, lady," he drawled.

She drew her words out slowly, emphasizing each one. "Take off your watch."

He reared back, feigning shock. "What? But it's a part of me. Don't ask me to do that." Then he smiled, slipped the watch off his wrist and put it into his pocket. "There, are you happy now?"

"Yes."

He grasped her arm. "Is there anything else you'd like me to do, Justine? Come on, take advantage of me," he said as he pulled her down to lie beside him.

The grass was a soft, springy mat beneath her. The glittering heavens arced above, sheltering Justine and Blair as they lay secluded in the swirling universe. She could see a faint gleam of starlight reflected in his eyes as, propped up on one elbow, he leaned over her. One of his hands rested lightly on her waist. Justine felt her heart begin to race as Blair's head dipped closer to her. His breath was a warm whisper on her skin.

"You're terrible, do you know that?" she breathed, her voice sounding as soft and vulnerable as she felt. Her resolve to keep Blair at arm's length was fleeing, she realized, scattering into the balmy night like a handful of stardust.

At that moment a swiftly moving trail of silver caught her eye. "Oh, look," she exclaimed, "a shooting star."

Blair neither turned to gaze at the sky nor commented on the celestial show. Instead, he lowered his mouth to hers. His kiss began as soft pressure on her lips, then quickly evolved into a caress of such seductive intensity that Justine found herself being swept away. As she eagerly returned his kiss, she reached up her arms to clasp him around the neck. She felt warmth and strength there. She lingered over his firm skin, then laced her fingers into his soft hair. Blair's strong arms encircled her. He lifted her to him, pressing her body to his in an embrace that melded their two forms, making Justine ache for more. She longed to be held like that forever, protected by his warmth and power.

At last he dragged his mouth away from hers. "Oh, sweetheart," he whispered, his voice a ragged murmur on the night air. "You're such a responsive woman. I've been driving myself crazy all day, remembering how it feels to kiss you."

Justine tried to catch her breath and slow the fluttering in her stomach. She'd never felt that way before. Her fingers tightened on the rough wool of Blair's sleeve.

"This is crazy," she said. "We really shouldn't be..."

"Ah, shucks, ma'am," he drawled softly, again affecting a western twang. "A pretty little filly like you wouldn't turn down a lonesome cowboy, now, would you?"

"That's just the problem," she said. "It's so hard to resist you, Blair." She bit her bottom lip, afraid that she'd revealed too much.

He chuckled. The rich, deep sound thrummed pleasantly in her ears. "That's just the way I like it," he growled against her hair.

"Blair—"

Her feeble protest was cut short when he again possessed her mouth. For many long moments they clung together as he teased her with little nips and nuzzlings that left her feeling dizzy and hungry for more. Returning his intimate caresses, she reveled in the clean, silky feel of his lips and tongue on hers. He knew so many marvelous ways to explore those sensitive parts of her. She heard a low moan and realized that it had erupted from deep inside her own throat. Never had a man raised her to that level of excitement so quickly, so expertly, with but a few kisses.

Blair pulled his mouth away from hers and rained a trail of searing kisses along her jawline and neck. He explored the tender place behind her ear, the torrid imprint of his questing mouth teasing her inflamed senses. The spicy fragrance of his after-shave mingled with his faint masculine scent and filled her with yearning. She clung to his back, feeling the musculature there and the flexing of his body as he drew her ever closer to him.

He dipped his head lower and nuzzled the hollow at the base of her throat. Then he pressed fervent kisses on the skin that was exposed at the open collar of her shirt. Justine threw her head back, abandoning herself to the myriad emotions that were rocketing through her. She felt heat building between their two bodies and marveled at the delicious feel of Blair's lips and hands on her fevered skin. This was utter madness, she knew. But as another shooting star arced across the heavens, Justine felt as if she and Blair, straining against each other, were all that existed in the entire cosmos. Nothing else mattered. She twined her fingers in his hair and sighed again and again as he worked his magic on her.

Justine was faintly aware that coyotes were once again singing in the distance. Suddenly an answering howl, loud and eerie, pierced the night air about ten feet away from them. Justine cried out with surprise and struggled to sit up. Blair also seemed startled. He sat up with her, one arm still draped around her shoulders.

"What in the world was that?" exclaimed Justine.

Then she laughed, and Blair joined in as Hattie's dog, Gypsy, trotted over to them. She licked their outstretched hands and wriggled in greeting.

Blair rumpled the fur on the dog's neck. "So you're having a little duet with your wild cousins, is that it, Gyp?"

The dog wriggled even more and wormed her way between Blair and Justine, who chuckled in the darkness.

"Gosh," commented Blair in a dry tone, "I've been aced out before, but never by a dog."

He tried to gently push the animal away, but Gypsy stayed firmly planted between them. Justine could hear her panting, as if she were laughing about the clever joke she'd just put over on them.

Justine stood and brushed off her jeans, taking advantage of the distraction. "Let's call it a night, Blair."

Gypsy disappeared back into the shadows, snuffling close to the ground on matters that required her immediate attention.

Blair also stood, then stepped close to pull Justine to him. "Stay with me tonight," he whispered against her temple.

She pushed herself away, remaining within the circle of his arms but holding her body apart from his. She looked up into his eyes. "You know I'm sleeping in Hattie's tent."

He leaned forward to recapture her lips, but she stayed out of range. He groaned softly. "Hattie doesn't care where you sleep. Stay with me, sweetheart."

This time Justine firmly stepped out of his embrace. Gypsy's startling appearance had jarred her back to her senses, she realized. It was fortunate that the dog had wandered out and found them. If she hadn't, Justine might've become completely swept away by Blair's potent lovemaking. And that mustn't happen, she again reminded herself. She drew her jacket more closely around her. Then she thrust her hands into her pockets and started walking back toward their camp.

"Come on, Blair."

She heard him sigh deeply as he fell into step beside her. "Right," he muttered, disappointment evident in his tone.

Back in camp they found that the fire had burned down. The bed of hot coals pulsed with glowing patches of orange and red and yellow. Blair and Justine paused at the fire's edge and looked into each other's eyes. He reached for her hand and pressed it to his lips.

"Are you sure you won't change your mind?" he said.

The expression on his face was so full of longing that Justine felt herself waver. Then she mustered her resolve and drew her hand away.

"We mustn't let our attraction for each other carry us away," she said. "It just wouldn't work out—you and I getting involved with each other—don't you see that? You'll be leaving soon, and I'm building a new life for myself in Shelby. Oh, Blair, please don't make this so hard for me."

He raked one hand through his hair, and she could see a glint of anger shining in his eyes. His jaw hardened, and his brows lowered. She sensed the stiffening of his entire body as he regarded her.

"You're wrong," he said, his voice low and tight with tension. "You need to follow your instincts a little more closely, Justine. People who're as drawn to one another as we are should let their feelings out, not bottle them up. Our individual living arrangements don't have a damned thing to do with tonight and how much we want each other."

She rubbed her forehead, suddenly feeling exhausted. "Please, let it rest for now." She looked at him and tried to smile. "I'll see you in the morning." Then she walked away, leaving him in the fading light from the dying embers.

Chapter Seven

The next morning Justine awoke to find Hattie's sleeping bag already empty. She could hear the sounds of Hattie and Kurt making breakfast; the delectable fragrance of coffee brewing and bacon frying wafted to her through the open flap of the blue tent. She stretched, then lay still for a moment, mulling over last night's scene in the meadow with Blair. She bit her lip as she watched the shadows of the pine trees dance on the sun-washed nylon. That had been a close one, she thought. She hoped she wouldn't feel awkward and self-conscious when she saw Blair that morning. After all, part of her had wanted to follow him to his tent last night, and of course, he must know that. Never had she felt so torn. She wondered what kind of mood she'd find him in.

She felt uneasy about something else, as well, and searched her mind for the cause. It had to do with Blair's wristwatch.... Last night, when she'd asked him to take it off, he'd joked about its being a part of him. Behind his jest, however, was a kernel of truth. He'd already freely admitted that in his fast-paced life every minute counted. He

might be able to slip his watch off his wrist—temporarily—
but Justine doubted that he could shed his city ways entirely. Why, even out there amidst all of the peace and quiet
he'd shifted right into high gear when Justine had mentioned a visit to Seattle. He'd pounced on her comment like
the urban predator that he was and started pressuring her for
a commitment. He even picked out the week when her visit
would have the least impact on *his* schedule.

Justine stared up at the flickering patterns on the tent as
she realized that with the dawn came revelations. Blair was
so much like the men she'd dated in Los Angeles. His fast-
lane schedule and his goals in business would always have
priority over personal relationships. Any woman who became involved with him would have to adjust her life to accommodate his. And there would be many times, of course,
when the demands of his business would crowd her out
completely.

Justine sighed deeply. It was all so terribly familiar. And
the fact that Blair was unwilling to say much about his
family and childhood fit the pattern, too. Knowledge, after
all, was power. A high-rolling businessman like Blair obviously preferred to keep his competition—and everyone
else, apparently—in the dark about his roots. It disturbed
Justine to be with someone who was so unwilling to disclose personal details about himself. It made her feel as if
she weren't trusted.

Forcing these disturbing matters out of her mind, she
yawned and rubbed her eyes. She was determined to greet
the beautiful new day with optimism and good cheer, even
though her relationship with Blair might now be somewhat
strained. Dragging herself from the warm bag, she wriggled into her clothes.

After washing up at a nearby creek, she walked over to the
campfire. "Good morning," she said to Blair in as bright a
tone as she could muster. "How did you sleep?"

He was standing alone with his back to her, staring into
the fire, which had been rekindled with sticks and branches
to cook breakfast. He turned to regard her with an expres-

sion that seemed to hold many layers of meaning. Before answering, he took a sip of coffee from his tin cup.

"Not very well, I'm afraid."

"Oh? Didn't you use one of those pads you brought along? I was very comfortable on mine."

He raised one eyebrow. "I was comfortable, all right. I just didn't sleep well." He stared back into the flames. "I'll tell you about it sometime," he said with a bleak smile as Hattie approached.

After a hearty breakfast of bacon, blueberry pancakes and syrup, scrambled eggs and lots of rich, hot coffee, they continued their journey. For several hours Justine, Hattie and Blair rode through a series of valleys and along some high ridges that gave them spectacular views of the Cascades and Mount Saint Helens. As they'd done the day before, they met Kurt for lunch, and Justine flew Aldora. The falcon stooped on a quail, which she dined on with obvious enjoyment.

After lunch they again struck out, riding the horses up a dry gulch that climbed for about half a mile before leveling off in a narrow canyon where a stream flowed. Hattie suggested that they take a break and let the horses drink and crop the tender grass growing beside the water.

As they rested, Justine noted with relief that Blair's mood had lightened. Perhaps he'd catch up on his sleep tonight, she thought. But was it just lost sleep that had made him seem so edgy that morning? She didn't care to speculate about that.

At the next rendezvous site they were surprised not to find the Jeep already there. Kurt had had more than enough time to reach that spot. Hattie rode up the rutted track to check on him and was back within ten minutes.

"We've got trouble," she said as she reined Chester up beside Blair and Justine.

"What kind of trouble?" asked Blair.

"Something's wrong with the Jeep. Ride back with me and take a look."

Both Justine and Blair mounted their horses and followed Hattie. Soon they arrived at the Jeep. Kurt was sitting near a stump, where he'd tethered Aldora. The Jeep, its
back end stuck up in the air, rested at an angle on a rock that
was embedded in the road.

Blair dismounted and handed Sugar's reins to Justine. He
walked over to the Jeep and knelt in the dust to look under
it. Then he lay down and scooted beneath the vehicle,
emerging after about three minutes.

He got up and dusted his hands off. Clearing his throat,
he shot a grim look at Justine and Hattie.

Hattie spat into the dirt. "Well?" she asked, pushing
back the rim of her hat.

Blair took a deep breath. "The Jeep has a broken axle. It
looks like we're stuck here."

"Gosh, I'm really sorry," said Kurt. He'd walked over to
join the others as they surveyed the damage.

"Ah, it ain't your fault," said Hattie, laying a reassuring
hand on Kurt's forearm. "It's this dad-blamed road. You've
been dodging rocks the whole way, and one finally got you,
that's all."

"Are we really stuck here?" asked Justine.

"I'm afraid so," Blair replied. He nodded toward the
Jeep. "That thing's not going to turn a wheel until the rear
axle's been replaced." He leveled a wry look at her. "You
didn't happen to bring along a spare, did you?"

Hattie spat into the dust again. "Now wait just a minute. Let's think this thing through. We have three horses, so
we're not really and truly stuck here."

Justine said, "But how can all four of us ride on three
horses? Plus there's Aldora. What would I do with her?"
She shook her head. "I don't see how we're going to get out
of here unless . . ."

"Yes?" prompted Blair, hooking his thumbs into the
back pockets of his jeans.

"No," she said, "it's a crazy idea."

"Go ahead," he urged. "What's your plan?"

Justine looked at Hattie. "How far are we from the end of the trail?"

Hattie squinted her eyes and stared up at the sky. She appeared to be calculating the distance. Then she lowered her gaze. "At this point it's shorter to go on than to go back. If we stayed on the road, instead of taking the longer scenic route, I figure we could make it out by tomorrow morning sometime." She paused. "That is, if we started right now. There's still quite a lot of daylight left."

"I believe I see what you're driving at, Justine," said Blair. "One of us can ride out and bring back help."

"That's right," said Justine. "What do you think, Hattie?"

"It's a good plan," said Hattie. "We can't simply stay here and hope that someone will come along and save us."

"I'll go," Blair offered.

"No," said Justine. "I should be the one to go. After all, it's because of my falcon that we had to bring the Jeep in the first place."

Blair regarded her with a slight frown. "You plan to ride out all alone, Annie Oakley?" Although his tone was dry, Justine detected a hint of concern in his voice.

She shrugged. "I'm sure it'll be no problem, as long as I stay on the road."

Hattie was shaking her head. "No, no, Justine. Wait a minute. Blair's got a point. I think that both of you should ride out. Kurt, Gypsy and I can stay here to hold down the fort. We're old hands in this country, and if for some reason you can't get help to us right away, we'd be better off left in these woods than you two. Take my horse to pack the supplies you'll need overnight. By this time tomorrow you should be back here with help."

Justine opened her mouth to protest, but Blair silenced her with a wave of his hand. He grinned in her direction, and she got the distinct impression that he was stifling a whoop of pleasure at the prospect of spending a night alone with her on the trail. After last night's near seduction, how could she even consider going off with him under these circumstances?

Again she opened her mouth to voice her doubts, but this time Hattie stopped her. "Well," she said, "let's get you packed up so you can go."

The little woman had already begun bustling about and was telling Kurt which bundles of gear to pull down from the top of the Jeep. Clearly there would be no more debate about the plan, and Justine had only herself to blame for suggesting it. With a fluttery feeling in the pit of her stomach, she pitched in to help.

Soon Chester was loaded with camping gear and Blair and Justine were ready to go. Before they left, Justine gave instructions to Kurt about Aldora. She flew the falcon and Aldora captured another quail. Kurt seemed pleased to be put in charge of the regal bird. During the trip he'd become attached to her and was happy to stay behind and be responsible for her well-being.

The sun was still several hours from the horizon when Blair and Justine mounted their horses and started down the road, leading Chester. Justine glanced over her shoulder and saw Hattie unfolding one of the tents. Oh, no. She'd forgotten that their party had only two tents. That meant that she'd have to share the other one with Blair, for she knew that it was lashed onto Chester's back. Damn! How was she going to get out of this predicament?

But was it really a predicament? She glanced at Blair, who was riding ahead of her. Was she wrong to fret so much about her attraction to him? Maybe he was right—perhaps she should loosen up and let her emotions have freer expression. After all, she reasoned, our stay on this planet is short; why not grab pleasure whenever we find it? But that wasn't her style. She sighed, wishing she could make up her mind about such things once and for all. She'd had so much to think about since she'd left Los Angeles. Why did a devilishly attractive man—and precisely the wrong kind for her—have to drop into her lap at the worst possible time in her life?

Then an idea came to her. She knew how to solve the problem of their sleeping arrangements. Tonight she would bed down outside and let Blair have the tent to himself. She glanced up at the empty blue sky. It didn't look as if it were going to rain, and she'd be warm enough in her cozy sleeping bag. Plus it would be fun to watch for shooting stars. If Kurt could sleep without shelter, so could she. Now that her mind was made up about that knotty problem, she relaxed. She looked around at the slowly passing scenery with a deep feeling of contentment. Her decision to live in Shelby seemed so right at the moment. Gentle Babe stepped carefully along the dry roadbed, avoiding ruts and rocks. The sagebrush tinged the fresh mountain air with a pungency that mingled with the tangy fragrance of the pines. The swaying horse and the clop-clop-clop of its hooves lulled Justine as she contemplated the simpler life that she'd adopted. Memories of the pressures and fears of the city had receded in her mind, she realized, leaving her feeling rejuvenated and at peace.

The horses broke out of the trees and entered an open area. A patch of bright color on a distant slope caught Justine's eye. She looked more closely at it and was surprised to discover that it was a grove of vine maple whose leaves had already begun changing to fall colors. Fall... so soon? It still felt like summer, the air so warm and the sky so blue and free of clouds. Fall must arrive in the high country earlier than it did in the Shelby Valley, she mused. It wouldn't be long, however, before autumn colors also flamed on the hillsides overlooking the lake.

A chill wind suddenly whipped through Justine's soul. At that moment Blair turned around and called to her.

"How are you doing back there?"

"I...I'm fine," she hedged, trying to make her voice sound light, her mood upbeat.

"Just checking," he said with a smile.

He turned away from her again, and Justine picked up the threads of her thoughts. What had caused that cold pang of worry to pass through her? It had something to do with fall.... Then she realized that she felt a little anxious about the approach of autumn, followed closely by winter. Her mother had always said that winter was a time of drawing in, but Justine had never been comfortable with that notion. She didn't like drawing in. She preferred expanding, going out into the world, not closing herself off from it. This need of hers was the main thing that had driven her from her small hometown to the big city. Reardan simply hadn't been big enough to contain her dreams and her ambitions.

Justine then found herself comparing Hattie to Ursula. They held such different points of view: one woman embraced the country life, heart and soul, while the other one had never stopped missing the stimulation and fast pace of the city. Ursula had seemed to be looking into Justine's mind when she'd spoken her words of caution. Perhaps she had insights into the younger woman that even Justine herself didn't have.

Justine furrowed her brow. It was all very confusing, but one thing was certain: she was going to live in Shelby, and that was that.

Blair let Justine's horse catch up with his. "You seem so deep in thought," he commented. "What's on your mind?"

She looked over at him and found him watching her closely. Putting a smile on her face, she responded, "Oh, nothing much. I was just admiring the first fall leaves over there." She pointed toward the vine maple.

He looked where she was indicating, then returned his gaze to her. The expression on his face told her that his line of thinking might be following hers.

"You're worrying about what you're going to do with yourself during that long, cold winter, aren't you?" he said.

She lifted her chin. "Of course not. I'll be very busy in my new store," she said, feeling a twinge of pique. Couldn't he leave that topic alone? Why did he have to jump on every opportunity to remind her that he didn't think much of her plan?

"I hope you know how to knit," he tossed back, flashing her a wry smile that matched his tone.

"Why do you say that?" she asked. She hated herself for playing into his hands.

"Because you're going to need something to do between your few customers. That is," he added, dragging out his words, "*if* you even get your store going this year."

"I will, don't worry," she snapped, annoyed that she'd let his comments get under her skin. By a supreme effort of will, she changed her tone so that she sounded more flippant than defensive. She tossed her head. "It'll be a huge success, you'll see."

Even as she uttered those words, thorns of doubt pricked her, leaving her with that same cold feeling. In a way her move was an experiment, she admitted to herself, one that could either succeed or fail. Maybe Ursula was right: she might end up wishing she'd never relocated to a small town.

Firmly pushing those unsettling thoughts aside, Justine forced herself to concentrate on the beautiful surroundings. Her immediate goal was to get help for the broken-down Jeep. Other bigger problems would simply have to wait.

An hour later Justine heard the sound of running water coming from a grove of willow trees. Babe pricked up her ears and whinnied.

"Can we stop for water?" Justine asked Blair. "I think my horse is thirsty."

"Sure," he said, glancing at the sun. "We can spare the time."

They left the track and rode toward the willows. The dry ground suddenly opened up and sloped downward to form a narrow gulch. At one end of the cleft, a waterfall splashed over a twenty-foot ledge to a stream below. The stream flowed the length of the gulch, then emptied into a lakelet at the other end.

"How lovely," exclaimed Justine as she peered into the hidden canyon. "It's like an oasis."

Dry sagebrush grew to the edge of the cut, but all was lush and tender green down inside it. Willows crept up the slopes and were visible at the canyon's rim. The stream was clear and shallow and had a gravel bottom. Several fish swam along the edge, their tails undulating slowly in the lazy current.

The narrow trail down to the stream was steep and strewn with loose rocks. Justine and Blair dismounted and began to carefully lead the horses toward the water. About halfway down Babe's feet slipped, and the horse bumped into Justine. Crying out with surprise, Justine lurched forward and felt a stab of pain in her knee as she fell onto the rocky path. She immediately got up, but because of the twinge in her leg, she was unable to put her full weight on it. Trying not to show that she was in pain, she hobbled down the trail.

Blair called out to her from behind. "Justine, are you okay?"

"Yes, I'm fine," she fibbed, wincing at her discomfort.

At the bottom she gratefully sank down onto the warm grass beside the stream. She bit her lip and tried not to think about the pain.

Blair took charge of the three horses, leading them to a spot downstream. They lowered their heads to the water and drank, then they began grazing on the abundant grass.

Blair returned to Justine and knelt beside her. He put his hand on her leg. "I think you were hurt up there. Tell me about it." His face wore an expression of concern.

"I think I may have twisted my knee when Babe bumped into me," admitted Justine. "But I'm sure I'll be fine in a few minutes," she added. She didn't want anything to impede their trip out.

"Let's have a look," said Blair. He removed her dusty boot and sock, then rolled up the leg of her jeans. With gentle hands he examined her knee, cradling her leg in his lap. "Does this hurt?" he asked as he pressed here and there.

"A little." The pain wasn't as great as it had been at first. Maybe she didn't have a sprain, after all.

"I don't see any swelling or bruising," he said, giving further scrutiny to the vulnerable-looking joint that he held in his hands.

Justine found herself responding to his close attentions. His fingers were so gentle, so reassuring. Already she felt much better because of the warmth and caring of his touch, which seemed more like a tender caress than an inspection for injury.

He looked up and must've caught the dreamy expression on her face. "I think you lucked out this time, sweetheart," he said. "You pulled something, but I don't think you've got a full-blown sprain here." He smiled and added, "Perhaps a kiss will make you feel better."

He dipped his head and pressed his warm lips to her knee, then onto the sensitive skin of her calf, and Justine gasped with pleasure. How did Blair always know exactly what to do to make her feel good all over? It certainly seemed to be one of his special talents, she mused.

He looked up and regarded her. "I hope that helped," he said, a wolfish expression on his face. It was obvious that he was fully aware of the disturbing effect he was having on her. He continued, "I think you should soak your knee for a few minutes."

"That sounds wonderful."

Blair helped her edge closer to the stream. Justine shivered with pleasure at the massaging touch of his warm hands and firm fingers as he positioned her leg. Her skin felt starved for attention, and he seemed to sense her need as he lingered over the task.

She lowered her leg into the stream and sighed. Closing her eyes, she lay back on the soft grass. "Oh, that feels heavenly," she said as the water gently lapped against her skin.

By now the initial pain had subsided to a dull ache that was fading. Justine luxuriated in the silky feel of the water as it rippled around her knee and calf. What a soothing sensation, she thought. She savored the contrast of the cool water with the warmth of the sun on her face and arms. Swishing her foot from side to side, she grazed the pebbly bottom with her toes and the ball of her foot. Her hands lay motionless in the grass at her sides. A magpie chattered from the willows, its raucous scolding softened by the gurgling of the stream.

Blair spoke near her. "You look like you've drifted off somewhere." His voice was mellow, its rich timbre a caress on her senses.

She opened her eyes and found him leaning over her. She smiled up at his handsome face. "I guess I have. I didn't realize how much I needed a break. This has been a long day."

"Yes, it has," he agreed, then glanced at the sun. "Just relax. We still have enough daylight left to get in a few more miles." A look of concern crossed his face. "Are you going to be able to ride?"

"Oh, yes," she said. "You were right about my knee. I don't feel any pain now, and I'm sure I didn't sprain it." Then she quickly added, "Thank goodness. That's all we need—a broken-down Jeep *and* an injured woman." She laughed with relief.

Blair reached over with one hand and brushed her cheek with the backs of his fingers. His featherlight touch felt exquisitely gentle. The sun shone on his head from behind. Its rays cast a halo of light around his hair, lancing golden shafts through the honey-brown. His eyes regarded her with such glowing intensity, Justine felt herself being drawn into their mysterious depths. Her heart began to pound as he leaned closer. She knew that his kiss could transform this moment to one of sharpest clarity. Only Blair had the power to carry her to a world where all of her senses were supremely alive and fine-tuned. She parted her lips, and a ragged sigh escaped. She knew that she'd revealed her yearning when he acknowledged the little sound with a knowing smile.

"I'm glad we found this oasis," he murmured close to her, his breath a warm whisper on her skin. "It's so refreshing." He lowered his mouth to hers.

For several long, delectable moments the only physical contact between them was where their lips were fused in an ecstasy of hunger and sweet promise. As she had before,

Justine marveled at the potency of Blair's kiss. Expertly his mouth caressed hers, coaxing her lips apart for further intimacies. She felt a molten heat wave begin to course through her body and fan out to her fingertips. Clenching the grass with her hands, she willed herself not to throw her arms around Blair's neck. But she knew that her mouth was giving her away. Caress for caress, her lips and tongue returned his kiss until a groan rumbled deep in his throat.

Finally, Blair dragged his mouth from hers and caught her up in his arms. "Oh, Justine, what you do to me," he said, a ragged edge to his voice. "I've been thinking about you all day. I can't take my mind off how good you feel in my arms."

He buried his face in her hair and murmured words of such longing that a surge of sweetness welled up in Justine's breast. At last she clung to him, reveling in the strength that she felt rippling beneath the thin cotton of his shirt.

But this wouldn't do at all, she thought abruptly. Getting carried away now would surely prove troublesome later when they'd be faced with the realities of spending the night together. She gently pushed Blair away from her and looked up into his eyes. Before she could voice her reservations, however, he spoke.

"Do you remember my telling you this morning that I didn't sleep well last night?" he asked, gazing down at her upturned face.

"Yes." Her voice sounded shaky.

"You came to me during the night," he said, fire blazing in his eyes.

She was confused. "Came to you? But I...I didn't. I was in Hattie's tent the whole time."

His chuckle was a rich, throaty sound. "You came to me in my dreams, sweetheart. Not once but several times. After I turned in, I couldn't get you out of my mind. I lay there for what seemed like hours and thought about how wonderful you feel and how good you taste."

He gave an erotic growl and captured her earlobe between his teeth. Clearly the memory of his fantasies had a powerful effect on him. Justine could tell that he would probably love to ravish her on the spot. The mental image of them entwined in sweet abandon made her catch her breath.

Blair raised his head and continued, "You wouldn't leave me alone. When I finally dropped off to sleep, there you were again, tormenting me with your presence." He grinned. "I won't tell you about the wonderful things we did together. Just let me say that we did it all."

Justine grew warm as a blush began to creep up her neck. To cover up her flustered state she said the first thing that popped into her head.

"M-my," she stammered, "you certainly have a lively imagination." She moistened her lips nervously, and he watched the movement of her tongue with obvious pleasure.

"Yes," he said, "and it damn near ruined my sleep. Every time I woke up, my body felt like it was on fire." He lowered his voice. "Have you ever felt like you were on fire, Justine? Have you ever wanted someone so much you could feel it in every cell of your body, like an ache that wouldn't go away?"

She gazed up into his eyes, fully aware that he'd let her into a secret place of his heart. The desire to reveal secrets of her own was hammering in her chest. She opened her mouth to speak, but a sudden gust of wind seemed to snatch away her words.

"I want you to feel that way about me, Justine." An undercurrent of hidden messages flowed beneath Blair's words.

Her fingers tightened on his arms as her resistance began to crumble. "I . . . I . . . ," she began, fumbling for the right words to tell him what was in her heart. A kaleidoscope of mixed feelings whirled inside her.

Blair placed his fingers on her trembling lips. "That's okay," he said. "I don't want to put words into your mouth."

For a long moment they stared into each other's eyes. The only sounds were those of the grazing horses as they cropped grass, and the splash of the waterfall.

Then a surge of energy seemed to flow from Blair to Justine as he gathered her to him and kissed her with such intense passion she felt swept away. Suddenly they were tumbling together on the soft grass, straining against each other in a fever of desire. Blair rained a hot trail of kisses down her neck and onto her breasts. His hands moved over her body, caressing her narrow waist and hips and igniting the fires that lay dormant within her. She threw her head back in ecstasy, thrilled to her core at the exquisite sensations that were coursing through her.

Blair captured one of her nipples in his mouth. Through the thin fabric of her blouse, Justine could feel his heat. He bit her gently, sending molten shafts through every vein in her body, and she cried out with pleasure. Arching her back, she thrust her breast up to him, urging him to lavish more attention on it. He obliged her, cupping her wanton breast in his hand and raining kiss after kiss, nip after playful nip, on the eager mound that begged for his care. She clutched the firm flesh of his forearms, reveling in the flexing of his muscles. She was only half aware of her surroundings as his intimate caresses aroused her to a fever of desire.

"I want you so much, Justine," said Blair against her neck.

His urgent voice penetrated the sweet fog that clouded her mind. It was wonderful to lie there and lose herself in the sensations that were so fresh and new to her.

Then a shadow fell across her face. She opened her eyes. The sun had dropped below the rim of the gully, jarring her back to reality. She gently pushed Blair away and looked up at him. His face was flushed with erotic longing, his lips slightly parted from the pleasures that he'd been raining onto her taut breast.

"Blair," she said, her mood swiftly plummeting, "we can't stay here any longer. It'll be night soon. We should ride on and camp farther down the trail."

A chain of emotions crossed his handsome face as he regarded her. His hand rested on her waist, his fingers a soft, lingering pressure. She could see that his feelings were waging war within him. Given the choice, he would no doubt prefer to stay right there, to follow the mood of the moment and carry their passion to its natural conclusion. But she knew that he wouldn't do anything to keep Hattie and Kurt stranded any longer than necessary. Inwardly she sighed with relief, grateful that their trail partners had unknowingly snatched her out of a situation that had been sweeping her away in a flood of unchecked emotions.

With a groan of reluctance, Blair said, "Yeah, you're right, of course. I, uh, sort of forgot about the time." He chuckled at his understatement and glanced up at the sky. "We can still ride several miles before we have to stop for the night." He looked back down at her, and the expression in his eyes made Justine tremble. "It's too bad we can't stay here, this is such a Shangri-La." Kissing her lightly, he added, "Come on. We can continue this later."

Before Justine could respond, Blair rose and pulled her up to stand beside him.

"How's the knee?" he asked.

She placed her weight on her leg and took a couple of steps. There was no pain. "It feels fine," she said, "thanks to your expert help." She smiled up at him.

"Dr. Sutherland at your service, my dear." He sketched a salute in the air. Then he strode off to get the horses.

Before long they'd left the gully behind and returned to the dusty road. For the next hour they spoke very little. Blair seemed lost in thought, and Justine pondered the coming night. Purple shadows were already lengthening around them, and the air felt cooler as twilight approached. Her stomach fluttered as she wondered to herself how she was going to control her feelings for Blair. What would she do if he did try to continue what they'd begun at the oasis?

She brushed her hand across the breast where he'd recently rained a fever of kisses and erotic nibbles. A shaft of delight flashed through her as she recalled how wanton his caresses had made her feel. Blair's expert lovemaking carried her into realms of desire that she'd never before known existed. Would she be able to resist him tonight? With a firming of her jaw, she swore that she must. Living for the moment simply wasn't her style. Besides, Blair was definitely not her type of man, she reminded herself.

When they finally halted, the sun had dropped below the horizon, leaving deep shadows pooled beneath the pines surrounding their campsite. Blair set up the tent on a patch of soft grass while Justine took care of the horses. As she worked, she tried to keep her mind off the confrontation that she knew was coming. Fumbling with stirrups and horse blankets, she told herself that all would be well. Her stomach shouldn't be leaping wildly. She was in charge and would do what was best for herself, she kept repeating under her breath.

After dinner Justine found a concealed spot by the stream that gurgled nearby. Feeling especially dusty after their long ride, she stripped off her clothes and stepped into the water to bathe. Night creatures rustled in the grass. An owl hooted, its deep booming call mingling with the swish of the pine boughs overhead. Justine felt clean and tingly all over as she quickly rubbed herself dry and put on clean clothes. She brushed her teeth, then rejoined Blair, who was sitting by the fire.

"Well," she said, keeping her tone light, "I'm all ready for bed."

He looked up at her, his skin suffused with the reflected glow from the flames. She could tell that he'd also taken a dip in the stream. His face was smooth and clean, and his hair was damp.

"Good," he said, "I've put our sleeping bags in the tent. Shall we turn in?"

He stood and stretched. Judging from the hungry look in his eyes, however, he clearly wasn't ready for sleep. Justine took a deep breath and plunged ahead.

"Blair," she said, trying to sound brisk and confident, "I'm not sleeping in the tent."

A puzzled expression crossed his face. "What? I don't get it. Where do you plan to sleep then, out here in the open?"

She lifted her chin a fraction. "That's right." She headed for the tent.

She knelt on the ground and dragged her sleeping bag and pad outside, trying to ignore the sound of exasperation that erupted from Blair.

"This is absurd," he said as she breezed by him. She forced her step to look firm and full of purpose.

"Why do you say that?" she asked, lightly tossing the question over her shoulder.

She paused a moment, looking this way and that, then chose a spot between two trees. She arranged her pad and bag on the ground, then sat down and began pulling off her boots.

Blair stared at her, his hands on his hips. It was obvious that he couldn't believe she'd sleep outside. "It's absurd because you'll be uncomfortable," he answered. "It might rain and you'll get cold."

She looked across the fire at him. The ebbing flames cast dancing patterns on his jeans, which hugged his long frame in all the right places. . . .

"I'll be just fine," she said, banishing thoughts of Blair's sex appeal from her mind. "I'm going to sleep in my clothes, so I'm sure I'll be warm enough." She waved a hand at the blackened sky. "The stars are out. There aren't any clouds, and it isn't going to rain." She wriggled into the bag and zipped it up.

Blair walked over and squatted beside her. "You're avoiding me, aren't you?" he said quietly.

She pulled the sleeping bag up around her chin as a shiver passed through her body. "It's for the best, Blair, believe me."

"Is it something I said?" he asked dryly.

She laughed up at him. "No, you're just too potent to be around, that's all." She paused. "Good night. I'll see you in the morning."

He didn't speak for several moments. Justine could hear the soft sound of his breathing, an occasional pop from the dying embers and the soughing of a breeze in the branches overhead.

Finally, Blair stood. "All right, have it your way. But you're wrong about this, Justine. We need to be together; I wish you could see that." He walked a few steps away from her, then stopped and looked back. She could tell from his tone that his sense of humor had emerged to reclaim the moment. "Well, I guess it'll be another restless night for me. I'll see you in my dreams, Justine," he said wryly.

Then he strode to the tent and disappeared between its flaps. Justine heard him rustling inside, then there was silence as the night closed in on them.

Sighing deeply, Justine shifted her body inside the narrow bag. Even though the pad beneath her was soft and cushiony, she could feel the unyielding hardness of the ground. She tried to empty her mind, but her thoughts kept returning to Blair. Behind closed lids she imagined his lean frame towering over her. She could still hear the longing note in his voice as he'd bid her good-night. Her mind was a jumble of confused thoughts as she wondered if she were doing the right thing. Why did life have to be so complicated?

It occurred to her that she was to blame for that night's awkwardness. Maybe she should be resigned and philosophical about her relationship with Blair. Instead of trying to avoid a casual summer fling, she should relax and enjoy herself for as long as he was around.

No, that wouldn't work, and she knew it. Resolutely she squeezed her eyes shut and willed herself to fall asleep.

Justine didn't know how much time had passed when she awoke. Her heart was pounding. A noise had startled her out of an uneasy sleep. She sat up and looked around,

straining to see in the blackness that enveloped the campsite. The fire had burned low, leaving a few orange coals that
glowed like eyes. Then she heard hooting in the distance.

She lay back down and expelled her held breath. It had
only been an owl that had awakened her. She mustn't allow
herself to get a case of the jitters out there. If she gave her
fertile imagination free rein, she'd start seeing shapes lurk-
ing among the trees and hear menacing noises in the brush.
Idly she wondered about bears and cougars. Hattie had said
that they were found in the Colockum, but would they prowl
close to a campsite? She shivered and stared into the inky
darkness. Was that a branch snapping? And what was that
squeaky sound and that swishing noise over there?

She closed her eyes and forced herself to breathe normally. She'd read too many spooky stories as a child, she
chided herself, and was now paying the price for all of that
lurid stimulation.

She'd just begun to drift off again when some raindrops
fell onto her sleeping bag, making soft pattering sounds on
the nylon. She opened her eyes and looked up. The stars
were no longer visible. Oh, no. Clouds had rolled in while
she'd slept and were now about to pour rain on her. She'd
be soaked.

Or would she? Maybe there would only be a sprinkle or
two. She thought about Blair, all snug and cozy in the tent.
Even if it rained hard, he'd remain dry and comfortable
within the little shelter. For a moment she regretted her decision to sleep outside. Impatiently she swept that reaction
aside and burrowed deeper into her nylon cocoon.

It began to rain harder, the heavy drops plopping loudly
onto her sleeping bag. Cursing the storm, Justine finally
wriggled out of the bag and picked it up, along with the pad.
Blair or no Blair, she was going to claim her half of that
tent. She ran in her stockinged feet toward the shelter, trip-
ping over her sleeping bag and stubbing her toes on rocks.
Swearing under her breath, she parted the tent flaps and
pushed her bedding in ahead of her.

Chapter Eight

Hmm?" inquired a sleepy voice. "Wha-what is it?"

"It's only me," said Justine, trying to sound brisk and businesslike. "I'm sorry I woke you up," she added as she struggled with her bag, "but it's raining. I'll get soaked if I stay out there."

Justine fancied that she could feel Blair grinning in the darkness of the small, warm tent. "Is that a fact?" he said, the sleepiness now entirely gone from his voice.

There was a rustling sound as he propped himself up on one elbow. As Justine's eyes became accustomed to the darkness, she could barely see Blair's frame silhouetted against the wall of the tent. He reached over and helped her arrange her bag so that it lay next to his.

"Thank you," she murmured as she slipped down into the warm folds.

Blair chuckled. "I'm glad you decided to join me, Justine." His deep voice throbbed with hidden meanings.

"Now don't get any ideas about this."

"I knew you couldn't resist spending the night with me," he teased.

She searched her mind for a suitable retort to his banter. Her heart hammered in her chest, and her voice shook maddeningly. "As you can hear," she said, "it's raining. That's the only reason I've moved into the tent."

"Just the same, I'm glad."

"Yes, well, good night, Blair."

She turned her face away, suppressing the sudden impulse to snuggle close to him. His bulk, mere inches away, radiated such an inviting warmth. At that moment a clap of thunder crashed nearby, and lightning lit up the tent's interior. Justine leaped in her sleeping bag, her nerves on edge. She snapped her head around and saw Blair still leaning on one elbow. He was staring across at her, a provocative smile on his handsome face. As if operating with a will of its own, her hand flew out and clutched for him.

She was immediately sorry that her body had betrayed her, for Blair lifted her hand to his lips and kissed her fingers.

"Wait," she said, "I didn't mean to do that. The thunder startled me, that's all."

"Don't worry," he murmured against her palm, where he was pressing kisses that scorched her skin. "I'm right here."

"Blair," she said, her voice weak and whispery, "don't do that. It makes me feel so..."

"Yes?" he asked, raining kisses along her wrist. His warm lips on her sensitive skin told of the erotic power that he was barely holding in check.

"It makes me feel dizzy." She paused, her breath coming in short gasps, her nerves tingling from the exquisite sensation of his mouth on her wrist and palm. Her resistance was quickly fading. "Oh, this is crazy."

"Crazy wonderful," he murmured as he drew her to him. "Am I dreaming again, Justine? Or have you really come to my bed this time? Ah, sweetheart."

His hand tugged at the zipper of her sleeping bag, and Justine felt her good intentions floating away like dandelion fluff on the wind. Perhaps it was the velvet darkness that sheltered them, or maybe it was the fact that the two of them were alone together in a vast wilderness. Whatever the reason, Justine suddenly realized that nothing in the whole world mattered except giving herself up completely to the emotions that were pulsing through her body. She'd found that resisting Blair's sensual demands only left her feeling sad and empty. Suspecting that this could be the most delightful night of her life, Justine decided to follow Blair's lead. She firmly silenced the little voice in her head that was telling her giving in was folly. *I'll deal with that tomorrow,* she told herself. *Tonight is mine.*

"Let me make love to you, Justine," Blair whispered against her neck. His breath was a hot wind on her already fevered skin. "I want you so much. And I think that you want me, too."

"Yes," she said, her voice ragged with desire. "I do want you, Blair. Very much."

He moaned deep in his throat and began unbuttoning her shirt. She reached out in the darkness. Her hands touched his naked chest, and she cried out with delight. He probably slept with no clothes on, she thought. The mental image of his powerful nude form was strongly arousing to her. She splayed her fingers in the soft, springy hair that covered his chest. Beneath his firm skin she could feel his heart beating in a tempo that matched her own racing pulse.

Dipping his head low, Blair pressed his mouth to the sensitive skin above one breast. Justine shuddered and felt her nipple instantly grow taut in sweet anticipation of the wonderful things she recalled he could do to her. He undid the front clasp of her bra, and her breasts broke free. Eagerly, they thrust themselves up to his seeking mouth. He caught one of her nipples between his teeth and teased it to a throbbing bud, swirling the tip around and around in his mouth. Justine felt as if she might swoon from the sensations that were coursing through her body. The stimulation of his warm, silky mouth drove her to clasp his bare skin tightly and call out his name.

Her body writhed with uninhibited, shameless desire, the waves of lust rocketing through her until her five senses felt drugged. At the same time she was aware of the sharp-edged clarity of everything around her. She could smell the faint spicy fragrance that she'd come to associate with Blair. It mingled pleasantly with his rugged male tang, teasing her nostrils and causing her to breathe deeply to savor his scent. She could hear the rain pattering on the tent. Or was that the pounding of her racing heart? From far off came the low rumble of thunder. The worst of the storm had moved on. Left behind was a deep silence, punctuated only by the drip-drop of rain and the cries of two lovers being swept away on a tidal wave of delight.

Blair dragged his mouth from her throbbing breast, leaned back and said, "Let's get out of these bags." His voice was husky, his tone laced with an unmistakable urgency that thrilled Justine.

"Won't we be cold?" Even as she uttered these words, Justine knew that her fevered skin might never feel cold again.

Blair chuckled. "I'm on fire." Then he added, his voice rich with meaning, "I'll keep you warm, sweetheart."

He helped her out of her sleeping bag, then joined her outside his. As Justine had suspected, he was wearing no clothes. Together they smoothed the bags out, forming a soft bed that filled the tent. Then Blair knelt beside Justine and helped her remove the rest of her clothes. In the duskiness surrounding them, she could make out the vague outlines of their bodies as they came together in a passionate embrace that exploded against her senses.

Blair kissed her deeply, penetrating her mouth with his questing tongue. She returned his kiss, clasping her hands around his neck. He pulled her closer to him, rubbing his broad chest intimately against the twin mounds of her breasts. He leaned down and captured first one, then the other of her breasts, suckling and biting until the nipples were pebble hard and pulsating. Shafts of molten pleasure ripped through Justine as she savored Blair's expertise. Although she was far from inexperienced, never in her wildest dreams had she imagined that lovemaking could be this exciting, this tantalizing. She felt as if she'd never get her fill. Each embrace, each touch, stroked her to higher peaks and promised even more.

As they kissed again, Blair fondled her breasts, then his hands drifted down to her waist. He touched the sensitive skin there with slow strokes that aroused her nerves to a higher pitch. Placing her on her back, Blair pressed down upon her, molding together the peaks and valleys of their bodies. Justine cried out with delight as she felt his flaring manhood straining against her thigh. She worked her hand between them and captured him in her eager grasp, caressing him until he groaned against her open mouth.

"Justine, Justine," he repeated again and again. "I can't tell you how much I've wanted you. I've never wanted a woman this much before. You're driving me crazy." He bit her neck with an erotic nip, sending tremors of desire shuddering through her.

Lying beside her, Blair swept his hand down her length, lingering often to savor particular aspects of her form. He stroked her flat belly, then cupped the rich tangle of silk that hid the center of her womanhood. Justine gasped with pleasure as he possessively parted her thighs, and his caress became more intimate. He kissed her deeply as his hand worked its magic on the trigger of her senses, stoking the fires that leaped from her center and pulsed to the tips of her fingers and toes. She arched her back, marveling at the wanton impulses that Blair was coaxing from her. His potent kiss and the knowing pressure of his hand were fanning flames that burned beneath her skin.

He lowered his head and, with a groan, pulled at one of her nipples with demanding lips. She twined her fingers in his hair and pressed him down upon her breast with eager hands. Breathless murmurs were torn from her throat. All the while his hand continued its sweet persuasion, exploring her silky folds and carrying her toward far-flung peaks of pleasure. Her trembling knees fell further apart of their own volition, and she cried out into the darkness that embraced their straining bodies.

"Please, Blair, please," she begged, "I want you."

She hugged him to her and nipped his chest with her teeth. Nothing existed for her now except the wildfire that was racing unabated through her tensed body.

He knew what she wanted. Levering himself above her, he eased his body into the welcoming embrace of her outspread limbs. The little tent shook with the power of their desire as they cried out to each other in voices that were ragged with passion. Never before had Justine experienced such sweet, unbearable anticipation as she felt at that moment with Blair's bulk looming over her. Time stood still as she waited for him to bring them together in the ultimate act of love.

Then with a muffled sob Blair lowered himself to her and claimed her with one clean, powerful stroke that took her breath away. The sheer wonder of that moment astonished Justine. She felt as if her body were opening up like an exotic flower, yielding its honeyed sweetness freely in celebration of the proud manhood that was stroking the deepest part of her.

"Oh, Justine," Blair gasped against her temple.

He hugged her closer to him as he moved above her. Together they found a rhythm that pleased them as they rocked in each other's arms. Sparks exploded in Justine's brain as she responded, stroke for stroke, to the fierce-tender loving that flamed in the night.

A more intense heat was being kindled somewhere deep inside her. As the sensation coursed through Justine, she clung ever more tightly to Blair. He and she, and this feeling that was growing and growing, were all that mattered. Suddenly a series of cries ripped from her throat. A tidal wave of pleasure swept over her, claiming her in a release that sent ripples pulsating from her center to her extremities. Again and again the waves washed over her, battering sweetly at her senses. Stars seemed to explode inside the tent, scattering little bits of fire all around their two bodies. She arched herself toward Blair, thrusting against his sturdy length and thrilling to the firmness that filled her and was there for her. Blair rocked her in his arms, murmuring into her hair and cradling her in his giving embrace.

Still marveling at the intensity of her release, Justine became aware of a growing tension in Blair's body. Sweeping the length of him, her hands paused at his waist, at the small of his back and then moved down to his upper thighs. His strokes became quicker, more lancelike. Then he paused, and Justine felt a quickening of his pulse and a trembling in his legs and belly. Sighing against her neck, Blair lunged forward one more time. Powerful shudders claimed him as his body reached the peak of its passion. Justine held him to her, coaxing from him the last few tremors that shook his frame.

Many minutes later Blair moved to lie beside Justine, tucking her body against his, spoon-fashion. She stroked his arm and lay still and quiet as the powerful sensations slowly ebbed from her spent body. Cradling her in the darkness, Blair kissed the nape of her neck and whispered his appreciation into her ear.

"You've made me so happy," he said.

"I'm happy, too. You're a wonderful lover."

He laughed softly. "Allow me to return the compliment. You are a wild woman." He kissed her again, his lips warm against her cooling skin. "You're shivering, sweetheart. Come on, let's get these bags zipped together."

They quickly arranged their bedding and slipped between its cozy folds. Holding Justine to him, Blair was soon breathing deeply.

Before she also dropped off to sleep, Justine pondered where her impulses would lead her. One thing was certain, she vowed to herself—she absolutely refused to have any regrets in the morning. If all that ever came of this relationship were a few brief days of pleasure and happiness, she would accept that. She had never before felt such joy as she had that night in Blair's arms. She would savor the joy that came her way and let the future take care of itself. This was not what she would've planned for herself. Indeed, she'd tried to resist this kind of thinking, especially where Blair was concerned. But it was clear that she could hope for no more, so she would try to be thankful for what she had.

Not altogether convinced that she could maintain that attitude, she sighed deeply and finally fell asleep.

"Good morning, Sleeping Beauty," said Blair.

Warm sunshine was pouring through the open flaps of the tent. Justine sat up and looked at Blair, who'd poked his head inside and was grinning at her. She rubbed her eyes. Was it morning already? She'd slept so soundly the hours of darkness had sped by.

"Good morning." She smiled back at him. "Is that coffee I smell?"

"Yes, breakfast is almost ready. Come on out and join me at the fire." He reached over and held her ankle for a moment, squeezing it through her sleeping bag. Speaking less briskly, he regarded her with eyes that shone with concern. "How do you feel?"

"Just fine."

"Great. I'll see you at the fire." Then he backed out of the tent and left her to dress.

As Justine pulled on her clothes, she recalled in vivid detail their lovemaking during the night. A blush crept up her neck and into her cheeks as she remembered specific details of the fierce passion that had rocked the little tent. She touched her skin and felt the warmth there. What had she promised herself? To feel no regrets. Deciding to try to keep that promise, she crawled from the tent and headed for the stream to wash up and comb her hair. By the time she joined Blair at the fire, she'd assumed a philosophical outlook. While they ate, her demeanor remained as determinedly sunny as the bright new morning.

Her nagging doubts returned, however, after she and Blair had broken camp and started riding down the road. As the sun climbed into the sky, it seemed to illuminate the corners of her mind. The realities of her situation were exposed, gripping her with anxiety. Why had she thought that he could carry off a relationship that was doomed to be short-lived, with a man who was so wrong for her? How could she ever imagine that such a relationship would satisfy her? It irked her that Blair seemed so happy and carefree that morning. Obviously their brief encounter during his stay in Shelby was quite the thing to amuse and entertain him. It pained her to think that he might be that shallow, that uncaring. But then she'd suspected as much.

Her emotions were in a turmoil by the time they reached Malaga, a little community on the Columbia River near the end of the road into the Colockum. Blair seemed puzzled by her withdrawn manner but, thankfully, didn't press her for details. Leaving her to watch the horses, he entered a telephone booth to call for help.

Arrangements were soon made to have a service station send a mechanic up to the Jeep and repair it. By late afternoon the Jeep and Aldora were safely back at Lilac House, and Hattie and Kurt had returned to Hattie's ranch.

Justine emerged from Aldora's pen after settling the falcon on her block. She avoided looking at Blair, who stood nearby.

"Will you have dinner with me tonight?" he asked.

Justine felt herself stiffen. She knew that the evening would surely evolve into more than dinner. Her body ached for the touch of Blair's hands and mouth caressing her into another sweet frenzy. Yet she dreaded miring herself deeper and deeper in a relationship that was going nowhere.

She shook her head. "Not tonight, Blair. I . . . I'm really very tired from our trip."

"It wasn't last night that wore you out, I hope," he chuckled.

The intimacy of his implied meaning hit her like a thump to the midsection. She fought down the blush that always seemed to be right there at the edge of her awareness, threatening to reveal how much this man affected her.

She looked straight up into his eyes and feigned a courageous front. "No," she insisted, "I just need time to rest and think, that's all."

His brows knit together into a frown. "Oh, I get it. You're tormenting yourself about us, aren't you?"

"No, Blair, really," she hedged, fumbling for words. "I..."

His mouth hardened into a line. He grasped her shoulders and gently shook her. "You're such a worrier," he murmured. "Why do you do it to yourself? Can't you take life one day at a time? It's really all you can count on, you know." He paused. "I had the impression that you'd decided to relax and enjoy what we find in each other."

"I had decided that," she admitted, "but I don't seem to be able to maintain that approach."

Sparks of irritation ignited in his eyes as he dropped his hands from her. His steely expression made her flinch.

"I suppose now you're going to tell me that you don't want to see me again, is that it?" It was clear that he found her attitude insufferable.

"Blair, please," she began, making imploring motions with her hands. "Let's not quarrel. I—"

"Well," he interrupted, his tone laced with irony, "now that you have your permit for Aldora, you can dump me. That isn't hanging over your head anymore. You've got what you want, and there's no reason to continue with our original agreement, I suppose."

He loomed over her, hands on hips, lips pale with anger. She'd never seen him like that before and wasn't sure how to deal with such intensity. The moments stretched into an eternity as they stared at each other. Justine watched a wide range of emotions pass through Blair's eyes. She was unable to name what she saw there and was left feeling confused and shaken.

Then her own anger flared. "I wouldn't dream of backing out now," she tossed up at his accusing face. "We made a deal, and I intend to honor my part of it. I agreed to show you around, and that's exactly what I'll continue to do."

She hesitated and felt her stomach lurch as she thought of something else. "Besides, you won't be here that much longer, anyway. Surely you and I, as reasonable adults, can maintain a businesslike attitude." She paused. "What bothers me is that we've become involved in more than a business arrangement. Don't you see that it can only lead to problems?"

"No," he said, his tone softening, "I don't see it that way at all." He gazed deeply into her eyes. "I want to spend time with you while I'm here, and I was hoping that you felt the same about me."

It suddenly occurred to Justine that she'd somehow hurt him, and the realization pained her. As brash and matter-of-fact as Blair could be, he definitely had his soft spots. Or was his seeming vulnerability just wishful thinking on her part? Mentally she shrugged. She supposed that she'd probably never know for sure. One thing was clear, however—he was as committed to his lifestyle as Hattie was to hers. Justine knew there was no way she would ever change that fact, and this knowledge lay at the very heart of their conflict.

Suddenly she wanted to smooth things over. "Look, I really am tired. Why don't you come to my house for dinner tomorrow night? I could use some time to catch up on things around here, but I'd love to see you in the evening." She smiled. "Besides, it's my turn to feed you. Could you possibly do without my guide service until then?"

He returned her smile, and she felt the tension ease between them. "Sure, I think so. I've been meaning to talk to some of the locals, anyway. I can take care of that, then come here for dinner."

"You know, I miss the dinner parties I used to put on for my friends in Los Angeles. Would you mind if I tried out a new menu on you?"

"Not at all." Then he added, "Do you want me to bring anything?"

"Just your appetite."

He gazed at her warmly. "Oh, I'll bring that," he said, the implied meaning of his words revealed in his eyes.

In spite of the balmy air surrounding them, Justine shivered. She knew that the hunger he felt had nothing to do with food. She wondered for a moment if inviting him to dinner was such a good idea. Oh, well, she did miss the elaborate meals she used to prepare for her friends. She hadn't had the chance to do that since she'd moved to Shelby. Blair would certainly appreciate her special efforts. And, as he'd once said to her, they had to eat anyway—it might as well be together.

They agreed on a time for Blair to arrive the next evening, then he left. Justine watched his truck disappear around a curve in her driveway and was surprised to note how empty she suddenly felt. The hours before she'd see him again seemed to stretch into infinity, and she found herself wishing that she could hasten them along.

"Nonsense," she muttered under her breath. There was plenty to do, and she needed time to herself.

Turning around, she went inside to call Myra. She wanted to check on how her sister was doing. Plus she knew that positive action would erase the let-down feeling that had been caused by Blair's departure.

Myra answered on the third ring. "Hello?"

"Hello, Myra."

"Justine," said her sister, her tone light and happy. "I was thinking about you a little while ago. How was your adventure in the wilderness?"

For the next few minutes Justine described the trip into the Colockum, carefully omitting the part about her night in the tent with Blair.

Her voice must've given her away, however, because after a pause Myra asked, "Is everything okay, Justine?"

Justine's laughter sounded forced and a little too bright. "Of course. Why do you ask?"

"Well, you seem sort of..." Myra hesitated. "I don't know, it's just a feeling. You sound as if you have something on your mind. Is it your store? Hasn't Sandra sold your share yet?''

Justine was relieved that Myra had opened up a different topic, one that Justine could blame for her present mood. She hastened to expand on the subject, talking about the store as if that were the only thing that was pressing on her mind.

After the sisters hung up, Justine sat and stared out the window at the lake. The two women were so close it was impossible to hide things from each other. Justine could tell from Myra's voice that her younger sister was growing stronger each day, and for this improvement she felt thankful. By the same token, Myra had obviously picked up on Justine's mood. She'd read between the lines, sensing Justine's anxiety and confusion. Although Myra knew about Blair, she wasn't aware that Justine's involvement with him had deepened and that this was the cause of her sister's worry. Justine needed someone to talk to about her mixed feelings, but she didn't want to burden Myra. Her younger sister had troubles of her own. Maybe later, when Myra visited her... She'd wait and see. In the meantime, she had to get Aldora back onto her training schedule and check with Leonard about the grounds cleanup. There were a hundred things to do.

Determined to keep herself busy, Justine stood up. She'd spend some time at her computer, then she'd eat and go to bed early. Tomorrow was a new day, and she'd fill the hours with projects to keep herself distracted.

Justine flew Aldora in the morning. Then she cleaned out another room at Lilac House and took a box of antique hats and dresses to the museum. Ursula invited her home for tea. Justine accepted, and the two women spent a pleasant hour or so in Ursula's elegant rose garden overlooking Pennington Orchards. Justine kept her conversation light and general and was careful not to mention Blair or her worries.

Back at Lilac House she called her real-estate agent, who informed her that no suitable properties had turned up in town. Would she be interested perhaps in a little farm outside of town? he asked her. Maybe she could convert the old barn into a bookstore.... Justine politely rejected his idea, shaking her head as she rang off.

Late in the afternoon she checked her dinner menu, then drove to the store for groceries. This was her first chance to entertain in Shelby, and she wanted everything to be perfect.

Shortly before Blair was due to arrive that evening, Justine took one last look in the mirror to check her hair and makeup. She was wearing a summery dress in a vibrant shade of heliotrope, with matching sandals and silver earrings. Noting the time, she went outside to talk to Leonard, who was working near the lake's edge. His teenage assistant Ellen and Ellen's best friend, Caroline, were there, too, talking to each other with great animation.

As she walked across the manicured lawn, Justine again felt thankful that she'd found Leonard. He was a widower in his early seventies and an expert gardener. Together he and Justine had worked out a plan to clear the grounds of weeds and brambles. Restoring the park to its former state of loveliness would take a long time, but Justine knew that the results would be well worth the effort.

Ellen was a small, bubbly minx with a mop of curly brown hair and eyes that were bright and lively. In spite of her youth and size, she was a capable helper and worked as hard as Leonard. During the past several weeks Leonard and Ellen had cleaned out the flower beds, pruned the trees and trimmed the hedge. A sense of order had slowly emerged, but there was still lots to do.

Leonard was raking around an elegant old snowball bush when Justine walked up. "Isn't it time for you to quit for the day, Leonard? I can see that Ellen already has."

Ellen, who was standing off to one side with Caroline, grinned at her. "Hi, Justine," the girls sang out.

Caroline was tall and freckled with sun-bleached hair. Like Ellen, she'd graduated from high school at the beginning of the summer. Both girls were wearing shorts and T-shirts bearing the 4-H logo.

"Hi, girls," responded Justine, then she turned back toward Leonard.

The gardener leaned on his rake and smiled at her, his lined face full of friendliness and good nature. "Hello, Justine," he said. He pulled a red handkerchief from the back pocket of his bibbed overalls and wiped his forehead. "Yeah, I suppose it is about time to knock off. I've been taking advantage of these long days. There's so much to do before winter sets in." He paused. "Say, what do you think of this old bush?" he asked her. "Isn't it a beauty?"

Justine regarded the snowball bush, its thick trunk surrounded by newly turned earth. "It looks great, Leonard." Then she pointed to some nearby flower borders that were models of weed-free neatness. "Did you and Ellen do all of this while I was gone?"

"Oh, that and a lot more," he said. "Wait until you see your grandparents' tree collection."

Ellen and Caroline suddenly giggled. Justine noticed that they were looking at a pamphlet with rapt attention. Before she could ask about it, however, she heard Blair's truck pull up at the house. She turned and motioned for him to join them.

As she watched him walk across the lawn, Justine felt her heart do flip-flops. He looked wonderful. He was wearing tan slacks, an open-necked shirt and a summer-weight sports jacket. As he got closer, she noticed that Ellen and Caroline had stopped reading the pamphlet and were staring at Blair instead. Suddenly she felt foolishly proud that he was her date.

Justine introduced Blair to Leonard and the girls.

"I'm pleased to meet you, Leonard," said Blair, shaking the old gardener's hand. "Justine told me about the great job you're doing here." Leonard nodded and smiled, ob-

viously pleased by Blair's compliment. "Hi, girls," Blair
said in their direction.

Ellen and Caroline laughed lightly as they chimed their
hellos. Justine saw them exchange self-conscious glances, as
if they hardly knew what to do or say in the presence of such
an attractive, worldly man as Blair. She silently chuckled
with amusement.

"We were just admiring this old snowball bush," she told
Blair.

The three adults chatted about the restoration project for
several minutes. Behind them Ellen and Caroline again giggled. Justine turned toward them and smiled with curiosity.

"Girls," she said, "what on earth are you looking at?"

Ellen handed her the pamphlet. It described the campus
of the University of Washington in Seattle.

"Is this where you two will be attending classes in the
fall?" asked Justine, sharing the pamphlet with Blair and
Leonard.

"That's right," Ellen replied, her eyes sparkling. "We're
driving to Seattle first thing in the morning to register and
get our dorm room."

"We can't wait!" exclaimed Caroline.

"We'll be in Seattle for two days," added Ellen, whose
bubbly tone matched her excited hand gestures. "First we'll
go to the university and get all of that stuff taken care of.
Then we'll sightsee."

"Where do you think you'll go?" asked Justine.

"Lots of places," said Ellen with enthusiasm. "We've
heard about the Pike Place Market, so we'll go there, of
course. Then we'll visit Pioneer Square, where there're lots
of interesting little shops. Oh, and we'll probably walk
through the lobby of the Four Seasons Olympic Hotel, just
for fun. I hear it's so posh." She rolled her eyes, and Caroline giggled at her. "There's a Laura Ashley shop by the
hotel," added Ellen. "I'm going to buy a dress there."

"Don't forget the Space Needle and the Science Center,"
Caroline chimed in.

Justine laughed at their high spirits. "You're going to do all of that in two days?"

"Sure," said Ellen with a shrug and a smile.

"We haven't even told you the best part," said Caroline.

"What's the best part?" asked Justine.

Leonard shook his head. "Now don't get them started on that. I've heard about nothing except this trip of theirs for the past two weeks." He wagged his finger in mock rebuke at the girls.

"The best part is the men," exclaimed Caroline.

Ellen let out a little squeal.

"We can't wait to see them," continued Caroline, nudging Ellen in the ribs. "Imagine all of those gorgeous hunks at the university."

Justine glanced at Blair, who'd been listening in silence. He had an expression of amused indulgence on his handsome face.

She again regarded the girls. "But there're men right here in Shelby," she said. "What about the fellows you dated in high school?"

"Oh, those," said Ellen in a tone of aloof disdain. "Those are just plain old country boys. We're ready for city men."

Justine squelched the broad smile that was threatening to spread across her face. Ellen and Caroline were so wide-eyed and unsophisticated; what could they possibly know about men? She was reminded of herself at that age, so eager to break away from the small-town existence that had held her prisoner. She'd been as determined as they were to escape to the big city, hungry for excitement, bright lights and worldly men. Silently she wished them luck and hoped that they wouldn't become as disenchanted with urban life as she had.

Leonard snorted. "Is that all your girls think about—men and romance?"

"What else is there?" Ellen giggled and looked at Caroline, who rolled her eyes and sighed dramatically.

"Well, there's your education, for one thing," said Leonard. "I hope you two will knuckle down and study your books while you're at the university, in spite of all those—" he goggled his eyes skyward, then raised his voice in a falsetto that mimicked the girls "—handsome city hunks."

The girls laughed. "Oh, don't worry," said Caroline, "we'll study. But we'll save time for fun, too." She paused. "And speaking of romance, isn't that Bluebell over there, Leonard? Hmm?"

"Huh? What's that you say? Where?" said the gardener, suddenly acting a little flustered. He turned to look where Caroline was pointing.

A fawn-colored Siamese cat, its tail held high and proud, had just strutted through an opening in the lilac hedge. Behind Bluebell appeared another cat. It was orange and fluffy, with white boots and perky ears. The cats bounded straight over to Leonard, where they meowed and started twining around his legs. He put down his rake, then picked up Bluebell and held her against his chest.

"Hi, there, Blue," he crooned. "How's my pretty puss?"

Blair picked up the orange cat, which immediately started to purr loudly. "What's this one's name?" he asked.

"That's Caramel," said Ellen. "Well, Leonard," she teased, "any romantic notes today?"

Leonard spluttered, his face turning red. "Shush, shush, Ellen," he said. "I don't know what you're talking about."

As he spoke Justine noticed that he was feeling along Bluebell's leather collar. The cat kneaded on his chest, her eyes closed to contented slits. Leonard peeled a little strip of paper from her collar and quickly tucked it into his pocket, as if he didn't want the others to notice it.

"Aha!" exclaimed Ellen. "I saw that, Leonard. What does it say this time?"

Justine was puzzled. "What's this all about, anyway?" She stared at the two girls, who had knowing expressions on their schoolgirl faces.

"Leonard has a sweetheart!" piped Caroline.

"Oh, now, now," said the gardener, but he was obviously enjoying all the attention.

Ellen turned toward Justine and Blair to explain. "Bluebell and Caramel belong to Mrs. Berwick. You know, the widow lady next door? They come over every day to play in the park. Caramel likes to ride in the wheelbarrow, and Bluebell follows Leonard around like a little dog." She rolled her eyes owlishly at the gardener. "About two weeks ago Leonard found a note taped to Bluebell's collar."

"A note?" asked Justine.

"That's right. It was from Mrs. Berwick, inviting Leonard to drop by after work for some of her homemade dandelion wine." She grinned. "You get one of those notes almost every day now, don't you, Leonard?"

The old gardener shifted his weight from one foot to the other and nodded his head. "Yeah, I guess I do," he admitted, looking pleased with himself. He took the slip of paper out of his pocket and read it silently, then tucked it away again. "Abigail—" he coughed self-consciously "—that is, Mrs. Berwick wants me to come to dinner tonight. She's making crullers for dessert." He smiled, a dreamy expression in his eyes. "That woman sure knows how to make crullers. Ahh." He hugged Bluebell closer and scratched her under the chin.

"So Bluebell plays Cupid, huh?" remarked Blair, his tone revealing that he found the notion delightful. He shot Justine a glance that made her cheeks grow warm.

Justine suddenly wanted to change the subject. Leonard's after-work liaisons with the Widow Berwick made a charming story, but the topic of love and romance was a rather touchy one for her right then. Seizing upon an idea that had occurred to her earlier, she addressed Ellen and Caroline.

"Girls," she said, "would you mind picking up a few things for me in Seattle?"

They smiled. "No, not at all," said Ellen. "What do you want?"

Justine began listing things, ticking the items off on her fingers as she spoke. Blair broke in.

"Whoa," he said, laughing, "they'll never remember all of that stuff. You'd better write it down for them."

He shifted Caramel in his arms and reached inside his pocket, pulling out his small notebook and pen, which he handed to Justine.

"Thanks," she said, accepting his offer. "I guess my list is longer than I thought." She began writing. "Now where was I? Let's see…a pound of proscuitto, a package of dried figs, a jar of pickled grape leaves and the best walnut oil you can find." She scribbled in the notebook. "Oh, and some wild rice."

"Can't you get that stuff around here?" asked Blair.

"Are you kidding?" she responded.

Then she glanced over at him and caught the look of mock innocence on his face. He knew very well that she couldn't buy such specialty foods in a small town like Shelby and was just baiting her to get a reaction. Well, she could play that game, too.

"Actually," she said, keeping her tone light, "the store had just run out of all these things when I went shopping today." Then she laughed wryly. "To tell you the truth, my grocery list was much less exotic than this, but even it was impossible to fill. I finally had to change my menu for tonight. We're having pot roast and potatoes. And instead of Gâteau Dauphine for dessert, we're having plain old angel food cake." She quirked an eyebrow at Blair. "It's not exactly the gourmet meal I'd planned. I hope you don't mind."

He shrugged. "It sounds fine."

In spite of his reassurance, Justine felt that he was watching her closely to see how she dealt with the inconvenience of small-town shopping. She tried not to think about that as she continued writing.

"Let's see, get me some fresh cilantro, a couple cans of chestnut puree and a small package of candied violets."

Blair whistled. "Wow, we are getting fancy."

"I make a special cheesecake that's decorated with candied violets," explained Justine. She frowned slightly. "The girls can get these things at the Pike Place Market, can't they, Blair?"

"Absolutely," he said. "It's a fantastic place. I'll bet they can fill that order in five minutes at the Italian grocery there."

Justine ripped the list from the notebook and handed it to the girls. "Are you sure you don't mind picking these things up for me?" she asked them.

"No problem," replied Ellen. "Would you like to go with us, Justine? You could shop while we're at the university. Then we could meet for lunch at the Four Seasons."

"Yes, come with us," urged Caroline. "We're going to have so much fun."

Justine felt herself wavering. It was exciting to listen to the girls talk about their upcoming trip. She could imagine herself browsing in Seattle's best lingerie department, then strolling over to the perfume bar to buy her favorite fragrance and bath powder. She was sorely tempted.

Blair must've sensed her indecision, for he moved closer to her and said, "Why don't you go, Justine? It would do you good."

She bit her bottom lip and looked up at him. She could see in his eyes that he knew she wanted to go, and somehow that nettled her. He'd probably like to see her get swept up in the fast pace of Seattle, for it would prove his point—she belonged in the city, not out there in a small town.

Finally, she shook her head. "Thank you both," she said to the girls, "but I really should stay here. I have so much to do. Maybe some other time." She began walking toward the house. "Come on, I'll give you some money." Ellen and Caroline fell in beside her. "Oh, and buy me a *Seattle Times*, will you?" said Justine. "And a *Wall Street Journal*." She paused. "Are you sure I'm not asking too much of you?"

"We're sure," chimed Ellen. "But we'd still like you to come with us. Think of the fun you'll be missing."

"Go with them," called Blair.

"No," Justine tossed back over her shoulder, the issue closed. "I'll see you tomorrow, Leonard. Enjoy the crullers tonight. Dinner in ten minutes, Blair."

Chapter Nine

Justine was pensive during dinner and wondered if Blair sensed her mood. She glanced across the candle-lit table and found him studying her. She forced herself to smile, then stared back down at her plate, searching her mind for the cause of her worry. It had something to do with the girls and their trip.... She thought about the list she'd given them. It was true that she'd acquired big-city tastes in Los Angeles and that she'd grown used to being able to find exactly what she wanted there. Sighing, she picked at the food on her plate.

Blair broke the silence. "What's on your mind, Justine?"

She looked over at him. "Oh, I was thinking about Ellen and Caroline and their trip to Seattle. And about how frustrated I became today when I shopped for our dinner and had to change my entire menu. It was pretty irritating."

Blair sipped his wine, a thoughtful expression on his face. "Small towns can't cater to gourmet tastes," he said. He raised his eyebrows and continued in a tone that bordered on "I told you so." "You're giving up a lot to live here and not just candied violets, either."

"I know that," she said, an edge creeping into her voice, "but I see it as a trade-off. And I obviously believe it's worth it, or I wouldn't be here, would I?"

Blair remained silent for several moments as he continued to regard her across the table. Slowly he swirled the wine in his glass. "I sometimes wonder if you do believe it's worth it." Then he shrugged. "But I suppose you'll have to find that out for yourself."

"That's right, I will," she snapped.

They ate in silence for several minutes. It distressed Justine to note that the air in the dimly lit room seemed to crackle with a current of combativeness. It certainly wasn't how she'd planned the evening to unfold. She again searched her mind, trying to pinpoint the cause of her anxiety. Something had put her on edge so that she was snapping at Blair and taking offense at everything he said.

The trip the girls were taking to Seattle had stirred some uncomfortable feelings in her. But there was something else, something even more worrisome than the ambivalence she felt lately about her move to Shelby. What was it?

She glanced over at Blair when she thought he wasn't looking in her direction. He was buttering a piece of roll. The candlelight suffused his face with a golden glow, emphasizing the firm set of his mouth, his strong jawline and the faint scar that ran through his eyebrow.

The scar. She remembered the day they'd met, high up in the hills. She'd wondered then how he'd gotten the scar. In fact, she mused, she'd wondered a great deal about him since then. There was a cloud of mystery that hung about him. It was as if he had no past at all, the way he skillfully parried her questions about his family and childhood. His reluctance to reveal personal details about himself bothered her a great deal. And now that she'd slept with him, this fact troubled Justine even more.

She recalled the men she'd dated in Los Angeles. They'd been like Blair, caught up in the brisk business of making

money, always planning their next big killing in the
marketplace. They'd lived strictly on the slick surface of life
and had fended off Justine's attempts to delve deeper into
their personalities. Those men had disappointed her, for she
craved intimacy, a sharing of heartfelt thoughts and emotions. That was the kind of relationship she'd always
dreamed about, and she knew that anything less could never
satisfy her.

As she again glanced covertly across the table at Blair, she
knew what was really bothering her: Blair was hiding himself from her. Perhaps he was emotionally crippled and
could never disclose his inner self to another person. Maybe
he would always relate to others—even to his lover—only on
the surface, where life was impersonal. Where life was safe.
Why was he so secretive? Justine was determined to find
out. There'd been enough of this charade.

"Blair?" Her voice sounded too loud in the quiet room.

He looked up. "Yes?"

"I hope you won't mind my asking, but how did you get
that scar?"

He touched his eyebrow. "This?" He chuckled. "I got it
from being a greedy little boy. When I was about five, I
found out that my mother had hidden some chocolate up on
a high shelf in the kitchen. She'd put it out of reach because she was saving it for something special. One day, when
she was doing some chores outside, I climbed onto a chair
and tried to get the chocolate." He smiled ruefully. "Instead, I lost my balance and my head bumped into something with a sharp edge. It hurt like hell. I screamed, of
course, and my mother came running in and found me with
blood all over myself. She was scared to death, poor thing.
I got about ten stitches and then this scar to show for my
greediness."

"But every child does things like that," commented Justine.

"Yeah, I suppose," Blair agreed. "But we so seldom had
anything like chocolate around—too expensive, you know—
that I always went a little crazy when I knew there was a

special treat in the house.'' He sipped his wine thoughtfully.

A little bit of chocolate was too expensive? Justine remembered Blair's comment on the road from the lookout that an aversion to poverty was what drove him so hard in his work. She suddenly felt that she might now be on the right track in finding out more about him. He was being so open with her at the moment she decided to press on.

"Blair," she began, licking her lips nervously, "why are you so reluctant to talk about your past with me?"

He shrugged, but she could see a guarded look enter his eyes. "Reluctant? But I just told you a story about my childhood, didn't I?"

"Yes, I know, but before, when I've asked you about your parents, you've seemed so unwilling to talk about them." She hesitated. "It's as if..."

"As if what?" His eyes never left hers.

"Well, as if you're hiding something. It makes me feel very uncomfortable. Especially now after we've..." Her voice trailed off.

"Now that we've slept together?" he finished for her.

Her voice was barely a whisper. "Yes." She gathered her courage. "We've been physically intimate with each other, but I really don't know much about you except that your parents are dead, you used to live in San Francisco and you're in the recreational equipment business. Why won't you tell me more about yourself? Why won't you trust me?"

There was an awkward silence as Blair stared down into his wineglass. Then he looked over at Justine and spoke in a quiet voice.

"I don't think it's all that important to dig into our past. I much prefer to live right now, in the present."

"Live in the present, yes, I agree," she said. "But we're products of our past to a large extent, and we can't simply ignore what came before us. Recording my family history here in this house has taught me that. When I moved to Los Angeles, I was kind of running away from my roots, denying who I was. Now that I'm back, I'm starting to appreci-

ate where I came from and who I am. My family was
working-class for the most part—loggers, bakers, farmers.
No one rich or famous, just sons and daughters of immi-
grants and pioneers, who earned their living the old-
fashioned way with lots of hard work. I'm proud of that.''

"No, I don't suppose there's anything to be ashamed of
in your family," said Blair, an odd look crossing his face.

"Ashamed of?" His remark puzzled her. "Why, no. But
even if I did have a criminal or a black sheep in my family—and I suppose I'll find one eventually—it wouldn't be
a reflection on me. We can't help who we're related to."

Blair's hand formed a fist on the tablecloth. "No, we sure
can't." There was another long pause. "I started to tell you
about my parents at Parker's," he added softly.

"I remember that. And then we were interrupted."

He raked his fingers through his hair. "Look, it's a long
story. . . ."

"We have all evening," she said gently. "I'm a pretty
good listener."

He smiled, but she could see the uncertainty in his eyes.
"Yeah, you are." He glanced restlessly around the room, as
if he were suddenly looking for the exit. "It's not a pretty
story, Justine."

"I don't care," she insisted.

"Tell you what," he said, his voice assuming a tone of
false bravado, "I'll give you the whole grisly tale in the
morning. Let's not put a pall on the evening, shall we?"

"You're sidestepping the issue again," she said quietly,
feeling him draw away from her.

"No, honestly, we can talk all about it tomorrow. I want
to tell you but in my own way. Okay?"

She could see that pressing him further would do no
good. He'd decided not to talk about himself that night, and
that was that. She wondered if he'd really follow through the
next day. In the bright light of morning, would he be willing to expose the shadows that lurked in his past? Or would
he find another excuse to put her off? Perhaps he believed
that he had nothing to gain by telling her about himself.

After all, their relationship was temporary; why stick his neck out? Yes, the book on Blair Sutherland would probably remain closed. The realization saddened Justine, but she knew there was nothing she could do about it.

"All right, Blair," she said, feeling resigned and defeated. Suddenly wishing that she hadn't brought up the subject, she arose from her chair. "We can have our dessert and coffee in the living room," she said briskly and began clearing the table.

"Here," said Blair as he also stood, "let me give you a hand."

They worked for several minutes, gathering the silverware and plates, then Blair carried a stack of dishes into the kitchen. As the swinging door closed behind him, Justine walked around to his side of the table to push in his chair. Then she noticed his wallet lying on the floor. It must've fallen out of his pocket when he'd stood.

She bent over and picked up the wallet. The expensive leather felt cool and rich in her fingers. As she placed it on the table, a small black-and-white photograph fell out of it and landed on the carpet. The photo was old and creased and had deckle edges. Justine reached down to pick it up and tuck it back into the wallet. Then she caught a glimpse of the picture and her interest quickened. She knew that she shouldn't give in to her curiosity, and yet...

She glanced over her shoulder. She could hear Blair stacking dishes in the kitchen. Feeling guilty for looking at the picture without his permission, Justine nervously moistened her lips and held the photo nearer the candlelight.

She studied the picture closely. It was of a woman who appeared to be in her mid-forties. Justine suspected, however, that she was probably much younger. Her careworn face had simply aged before its time. The woman wore a shapeless old cotton dress and broken-down shoes. Her hair hung in lank strands around her wrinkled face, and in spite of her smile, Justine could detect no trace of humor or joy in the woman's eyes.

In the background was an old house, whose sagging front porch was propped up on one side with bricks. A battered galvanized washtub rested among the weeds, and a shabby quilt hung from a clothesline.

Then Justine noticed the child. Peering from behind the woman was a little boy who was about ten. He stared shyly at the camera, his expression unsmiling. The small hand clutching the woman's dress made Justine think of a fist balled up against a harsh world.

As she stared at the photograph, Justine's brow knit into a puzzled frown. Why would Blair carry this kind of picture around with him? He was such a worldly man and was so used to getting exactly what he wanted. Surely he didn't have any direct connection to these people, did he? But in light of their conversation at dinner tonight, maybe he did, she mused. It seemed hard to believe, but perhaps this woman and her little son were somehow related to Blair. Could this be an aunt and a cousin? They seemed to be living out in the country, and he'd said that his parents had worked in agriculture. Or maybe these people had been neighbors down on their luck, people whom Blair's parents had helped out. But why would he carry their picture around with him? Then another explanation for the photograph occurred to her, but she quickly rejected it as unlikely, impossible, even outlandish.

It was all very confusing, and her mind was whirling with a hundred questions. She longed to ask Blair about the picture but knew that she didn't have the nerve. Just as she was about to tuck the photo back into his wallet, Blair spoke from behind her.

"What are you doing, Justine?"

Startled, she spun around, her heart suddenly pounding. She'd been so intent on trying to interpret the picture she hadn't heard Blair reenter the dining room. Still holding the photo, she felt the heat of shame creep into her neck and cheeks.

He took in the scene at a glance, and his expression hardened. A muscle twitched at his jawline.

"I said, what are you doing?"

His voice was low and accusing. It carried a rebuke laced with something else. Fear? No, that's not possible, Justine thought. This powerful man had nothing to fear.

"I . . . I . . ." she stammered and licked her lips. "Your wallet must've fallen out of your pocket, and I . . . I was just . . ." Because of her embarrassment she was babbling. Silently she cursed her tongue.

In three quick strides he was beside her. He snatched the picture from her hand. "And this just happened to fall out, right?" he said.

He tucked the picture into the wallet, then jammed the wallet into his pocket. He towered over Justine, his anger rippling toward her in scalding waves. She suddenly felt small and defenseless.

"Yes," she managed to say, "that's exactly what happened. I was pushing in your chair, and I found your wallet on the floor. When I picked it up, that picture fell out."

"And you simply couldn't resist looking at it, is that it?"

His lips were compressed into a tight line of anger, and his eyes lanced warnings at her. Why was he so upset? she wondered. Surely he was overreacting. Maybe their dinner conversation had disturbed him more than he'd let on and he was now blowing off steam. She drew herself up and stared directly into his eyes, trying not to let her glance waver.

"I was wrong to look at it, Blair," she confessed. "I shouldn't have been so impulsive and I'm very sorry." She paused. "But I don't see why you're so angry about it."

His face darkened. "I think you'd be pretty angry, too, if you caught me looking through your purse while your back was turned. First you grill me about my past, then you snoop in my wallet. I said that I'd tell you what you're so keen on knowing tomorrow. That should've satisfied you. Apparently it didn't."

"I said I was sorry. And I wasn't snooping. It was just an accident. Besides, I don't see why an old picture of a woman and a little boy should make you blow up like this. It's as if you—"

"Never mind about it!" he lashed out at her.

Justine thought she saw an arrow of pain dart through his eyes. The impression was so fleeting, however, that perhaps she'd only imagined it. Still, there was something there that deeply disturbed Blair. Maybe she should ask him about the photograph and try to draw him out.

She reached toward him and touched his arm. "Blair, do you want to talk about that picture? I've never seen you act this way before. Do you know those people? Are they—"

"That's none of your business," he said abruptly and stepped back. Her hand fell to her side.

Suddenly Justine had had enough. The temper that she'd been struggling to hold in check flared at his brusque rejection of her offer to talk. She leveled her gaze at him and bit off her words.

"Fine," she said, "have it your way. I told you I was sorry, and I meant it. It was wrong of me to look at that picture, but now that I've seen it, you can forget it. It means nothing to me, but I can tell that it means a lot to you. If you don't want to discuss it, that's okay with me. Keep your secrets!"

Her chest heaved with the anger that she was expending on him, and she realized that some of her emotion was misplaced. She was discouraged that Sandra hadn't yet sold her share of the L.A. store. And she was disappointed with the poor showing of the real-estate agent here, who'd come up with nothing more promising than a couple of tiny storefronts and an old barn. To top everything off, Blair was now exploding at her, overreacting to a blunder for which she was genuinely sorry. Well, to hell with all of it!

She turned on her heel, grabbed her purse and sweater and headed for the front door.

"Justine, where are you going?" Blair called out behind her.

"None of your business," she cried. Then she whirled around and looked back at him. Her face felt flushed with emotion, and tears were stinging her eyes. "Excuse me, that's your line," she said. "I'll tell you where I'm going, Blair—as far away from you as I can get." Then she turned and grasped the doorknob. "Oh, and there's no need to lock the door when you leave."

"Come back here!" she heard just before she slammed the heavy door behind her and ran out into the night.

Tears coursed down Justine's cheeks as she started the engine of her Jeep. The vehicle roared into life. She floored the throttle pedal and heard a cascade of gravel spitting out behind the rear wheels. She sobbed as the headlight beams bounced in front of her on the driveway.

Turning right at the road, she took a deep breath and forced herself to slow down. She wiped the back of her hand across her cheeks, brushing away her tears. How ironic, she thought. Just when she'd simplified her life, the biggest complication of all had appeared on the scene. If only Blair had stayed in Seattle where he belonged.... She cursed the day she'd met him.

A few miles down the road she parked in an isolated spot beside the lake. Whispering pines towered over a small sandy beach that was concealed from the road. This was one of her favorite places to be alone and think things over; no one would bother her there.

She got out of the Jeep and kicked off her sandals. It was a beautiful night, still and star-spangled. The full moon cast a limpid, silver sheen across the silent lake. Justine walked to the water's edge, her bare feet caressed by the soft, warm sand. She sat down on a drift of fragrant pine needles, wiped away the last traces of her tears and calmly assessed what had happened at dinner. She was sorry that she and Blair had quarreled. His angry reaction to her seeing the photograph had seemed so out of proportion, but there was obviously something about the picture that greatly disturbed him. Her heart went out to him as she swore to herself that she wouldn't ask him about it in the future. If it caused him that much discomfort, she'd never put him on the spot again.

She felt hurt that he'd spoken so harshly to her. It wasn't like him to lose his temper that way, and it distressed her that he was so unwilling to trust her. She shrugged. Oh, well, she thought as she stood, there was no point in mulling it over and over. The night was so lovely, the air so warm and balmy; a moonlight swim would soothe her emotions and help her forget.

She slipped out of her clothes, dropping her dress and bra and panties onto the pine needles. Then she waded into the lake, her nude form a carved column of moonlit ivory. She dove beneath the water and swam for several yards. Then she broke the surface and tossed her head back, flinging droplets from her thick hair. The water caressed the tension from her body and cooled her heated skin. She breathed the calm night air and looked up at the sky. What a spectacular sight. The few lights that shone from town were insignificant when compared with the light show wheeling overhead.

Justine slowly swam farther out until the bottom dropped away and she was alone in the black water. She eased over onto her back, reveling in the flow of the silky liquid over her naked limbs, belly and breasts. How peaceful it was to lie there, suspended between heaven and earth. She felt the last shreds of her anger drift off like water grasses being drawn away by a gentle current. She could float like this forever, she thought.

A noise abruptly intruded upon her peaceful reverie. She broke out of her floating position and began treading water. She peered through the darkness toward shore. A pair of headlights shone across the lake for a moment, then went out.

Damn! Someone else had pulled into the little space beside her Jeep. Maybe he or she was also planning a moonlight swim. She continued to tread water and was wondering what to do when she heard a familiar voice call from shore.

"Justine? Are you out there?"

It was Blair. He must've cruised around the lake, checking her favorite haunts until he'd found her. He'd probably figured that she'd seek solace in the healing waters of Lake Shelby.

"Yes," she called back, "I'm here."

The words almost stuck in her throat as her emotions welled up again. The sound of Blair's voice brought back the tension of their quarrel in awful clarity, and she fought to keep from spilling fresh tears. Perhaps Blair's anger was spent, and he'd searched for her to smooth things over. The thought was painful and moving at the same time.

"I'll be right out."

There was a pause. Justine watched his dark figure on the beach. She imagined his powerful male strength reaching across the glassy surface toward her. She shivered and knew that her sudden trembling was not because of the temperature of the water. Then she heard a splash. With a few strong strokes Blair was beside her, water streaming down his face, his hair wet and gleaming in the moonlight.

"Justine," he began, "I'm sorry I yelled at you. I really am. Please forgive me."

He reached for her hand, then stroked the water and drew her along until they were standing on the bottom. Their shoulders and heads rose like water nymphs from the rippling, mirrorlike surface. Blair's arms went around Justine, holding her close as the stinging tears spilled from her eyes. She pressed her face into the hollow of his neck, sobbing out her misery as she clung to him. All the while Blair caressed her back and murmured comforting sounds into her hair.

Finally, Justine stopped crying. She licked her lips; the salt of her tears had mingled with the flat taste of the lake water. As she took a deep breath, she became aware that her naked breasts were pressed against the solid warmth of Blair's chest. His silky hairs tickled her skin in subtle stimulation. Her nipples hardened, and her thighs tensed as she noticed that the entire length of Blair's body was melded to hers. Belly to belly, thigh to thigh, they clung together in the blackened velvety water. Somewhere across the lake a night bird called.

"Thank you, Blair," said Justine, her voice soft but steady. "I'm sorry, too. I didn't mean to make you feel uncomfortable."

He squeezed her shoulders, his grip strong and reassuring. "Hey, that's okay. I overreacted. Come on." He started moving toward shore. "Let's get out and dry off. I'll explain everything."

They waded toward the sandy beach. When they emerged from the lake, water streamed down their slick bodies and formed little trails of wetness as they walked, hand in hand, toward the trees. Before they entered the deep shadows beneath the pines, Blair stopped and turned to look at Justine. His hungry eyes swept the length of her, then he squeezed her hand and lifted it to his mouth. He kissed her fingers and palm.

"You're the most beautiful woman I've ever seen," he said, his voice thick with emotion. "I'm so lucky I met you."

Justine felt a wave of pure delight ripple through her. His tone was so adoring, his touch so pleasurable, that she felt her heart would burst with joy.

"Wait here," he said. "I'll be right back."

He walked briskly to his truck and opened the door. Soon he was back with her, carrying a couple of blankets and something small and metallic that reflected the moon's glint. He spread one of the blankets on the soft pine needles. They sat down on it and draped the other blanket around their shoulders.

Justine had begun to shiver from the coolness of the night air on her wet, naked skin and welcomed Blair's idea. The comforting warmth from his body reached out to envelop her, and as they huddled together, skin touching skin, she sighed with contentment.

"Are you starting to warm up?" he asked.

"Yes, it feels wonderful."

"This'll help, too."

He picked up the shiny object; it was a metal flask. He opened it and poured liquid into the large cap. Justine accepted the cap from him and took a deep swallow. The fine old brandy filled her senses with its rich, woody flavor. She closed her eyes and sipped again, savoring the brandy's mellow fire as it slid down her throat. Its heat spread a warm glow up to her face and neck and out to her fingertips. She finished drinking, then handed the cap back to Blair. He refilled it and drank, then replaced the cap on the flask. He set the flask down and put his arm around Justine, hugging her close.

"I owe you an explanation," he began. He brushed her lips with a kiss that was gentle and featherlight. "You deserve to know why I got so upset when I saw you looking at that old photograph."

"You don't have to tell me if you don't want to."

"I want to."

"All right," she said quietly.

His voice was husky when he spoke again. "That's a picture of my mother."

There was a long pause as Justine tried to digest this startling bit of news. His mother? That woman with the worn dress standing in front of one of the poorest shacks she'd ever seen, that woman with the haunted, sad look in her eyes—that was Blair's mother? Justine was confused.

"I don't understand."

Blair took a deep breath and stared out at the black-and-silver lake. On the far shore the lights of a farmhouse flickered warmly. Justine hugged the soft wool blanket to her and gazed at Blair's profile, at the finely chiseled nose and strong chin and at the planes of his cheeks and broad forehead. She sensed his inner turmoil; telling her these things wasn't easy.

"Have you ever been poor, Justine?" he finally asked.

She thought about it. "No, we never had a lot of money, but we always had enough food and clothes and a roof over our heads. We weren't rich, by any means, but we weren't poor, either."

"Then what I'm about to tell you might be hard for you to understand."

She placed her hand on his forearm, wanting to reassure him with her touch. "I'll try, Blair."

"My family was very poor. The way we lived was quite different from the way you lived when you were growing up." He chuckled ruefully. "The old house in that picture was one of our better arrangements. For years, on and off, we lived in an old station wagon that my dad had fixed up with a bed in back."

Justine suddenly realized something and squeezed his arm. "The little boy behind the woman—that was you, wasn't it?"

"That's right," he said.

It was almost more than Justine could take in at one time, yet she encouraged him to continue, sensing that he needed to get this story off his chest.

"Go on," she murmured.

He tossed a stone toward the lake. It skittered on the water, then sank, sending ripples out in widening circles that captured the moon's glow and scattered it like shards of glass.

"My folks were uneducated," he said. "They made it through the eighth grade, I think. All they knew how to do was perform stoop labor on other people's farms." His tone was ironic but contained not a trace of self-pity, Justine noticed. "When I told you that they were in agriculture, what I meant was that they followed the harvesting of the seasonal crops. We must've driven around the state of California a hundred times so that my parents could pick grapes, lettuce, oranges—you name it, my folks helped get it to market." He paused. "Your family might've eaten produce that my family picked."

"What about you? Were you able to go to school?"

"Oh, yeah, I went to school wherever we went, but it was rough. Just when I got to know the teacher and my classmates, off we'd go again, headed for the next crop." He shook his head. "It's a wonder I learned anything at all during those years. I was always behind.

"My folks finally scraped enough money together to buy that house. It was way out in the country and was so old and rotten probably no one else wanted it. I'm sure that my folks got it for very little, although to them the price must've seemed like a fortune." His voice thickened, and Justine pressed closer. "They wanted to settle down so that I could go to school with the same teacher and the same children. They were afraid that I'd end up like them, so they tried to make my life better than theirs."

He tossed another rock into the lake. Flung with greater force than the first one, it landed much farther out. Justine could tell that these powerful memories were difficult to share.

"What about their work?" she asked. "Wasn't it hard to follow the harvests and still keep you in one school?"

"My mother stayed at home with me and took in sewing while Dad traveled with the crops. They made less money at first, so Dad worked even harder and sent home every dime he earned." He paused. "My folks really loved each other. But they gave up being together most of the year so that I could have an education. I'll always be grateful for that."

"You said that your folks are no longer living, I remember."

He stared at the ground and cleared his throat. "Dad died a couple of years after we moved into that house, when I was twelve. My mom died shortly after that. I think they just worked themselves to death. I have no living relatives that I know of, so I was put into a children's home in San Francisco. That's where I lived until I was eighteen." He suddenly laughed; the hollow sound contained no trace of humor. "Now don't think I feel sorry for myself, Justine. I don't. But I do feel sorry for my folks because they really didn't have a chance in life."

He turned to regard her, and Justine could see the fierce look that had entered his eyes. His forceful tone matched his expression, and she suspected that he was about to tell her the most important thing of all. She shivered a little.

"You wonder why I'm a driven man, don't you, Justine? You asked me once why I spend so much time and energy figuring out how to improve my business and make more money. I'll tell you why. I swore to myself, when I was in that children's home, that I would never be poor again. I decided that I would do whatever it took to rise above that kind of life. I made that promise when I was thirteen. In school I worked as hard as I could, and I took advantage of every opportunity that came my way.

"When I graduated from high school, I was third in my class. And because I had no money but good grades, I received a full scholarship to attend college. Even though my tuition and room and board were paid for, I always had a couple of part-time jobs on the side. I washed dishes in the student union cafeteria, I pumped gas, I worked as a short-order cook, that sort of thing. By the time I had my degree, I'd saved enough money to start my own business." He stared into the distance. "And the rest, as they say, is history. My business kept growing and expanding, and I added one store after another." He turned to look at her. "I love it, Justine," he said with passion. "I love my work, I love making money. If you're going to understand anything about me at all, it's that I love what I'm doing."

Justine felt overwhelmed by his disclosures. She was amazed that this wealthy, powerful man had sprung from such humble beginnings. It was clear that what motivated him—indeed, what perhaps drove him like a demon on his back—was the ingrained fear that he would one day wake up and find himself poor again. As she studied his handsome profile, she felt a wave of compassion for him sweep over her. It was an impressive accomplishment to have worked his way to the top in spite of an impoverished beginning. The term "self-made man" surely fit Blair more than anyone else she could think of. Admiration for his determined struggle to succeed filled her breast, and she squeezed his arm again.

"Blair," she said, "this is an incredible story. Thank you for sharing it with me. I feel like I know you so much better now."

"I've never told anyone else about my family, Justine," he said with feeling. "I hate to admit it, but I think I've always been ashamed of how I grew up. It's been easier to keep those details to myself instead of dragging them out for other people to look at." He paused. "To be perfectly honest, I'm not sure I would've told you the whole story if you hadn't accidentally seen that photograph. Not now, at least. By the way, that's the only picture I have of my mom. I used to have one of my dad, too. I don't know what happened to it."

Justine recalled the day when Blair had asked to look through her photo albums. "Is that why you're so interested in other people's family pictures? Because you only have one of your own?"

He nodded. "That's right. It's always fascinated me that everyone else seems to have such a lot of physical evidence about their past. The few family roots I have don't exist anywhere but in my head. There's no Lilac House for me to go back to." Again there wasn't any self-pity in his voice; he was merely stating facts. "I keep that picture with me all the time to remind me of the kind of life I will never live again." He emphasized those words by hitting the ground with his fist. "Things have worked out well for me," he continued after a pause. "I do have one regret, though."

"What's that?" she asked gently.

"I never got to help my parents," he said, his voice catching. "Both of them died before I made it. If only they'd lived, there'd be so much I could do for them now, so many things I could give them to make their lives more pleasant and comfortable. I'll never be able to do that."

He cleared his throat, and Justine saw something small and glittering slide down his cheek. Without a word she reached up and tenderly wiped away the single tear. He immediately responded to her touch by taking her hand in his and kissing her palm.

"So you see," he said, his voice strong and sure again, "that's why I'm such a confirmed city dweller, I guess. When I was a kid, we always lived way out in the country where the farms are. I know this will sound crazy, but I can't seem to shake off the idea that country and small towns mean being poor." He laughed. "I know that isn't always the case, but that's what I feel in my guts. My education, my business—my salvation, Justine—all came from the city. That's where I found opportunity, action, the way out."

"Is that why you keep pressuring me to go back to the city? It's not the answer for all of us, you know."

He looked deeply into her eyes. "I have my own selfish reasons for wanting you to come to Seattle. I'd love to be able to see you whenever I wanted, but there's more to it than that. I honestly believe that you'll regret it if you bury yourself out here. Look at me. My apparent talent for business would've been wasted if I'd adopted my parents' lifestyle." He shook his head. "It's ironic—I came so close to being a farm laborer. Think about it, Justine. I'd be picking oranges today instead of running my own little empire."

It was a chilling thought. Justine pondered for a moment how many other potentially talented lives were being wasted because of a lack of education and opportunity. Suddenly she felt very fortunate and also curiously envious of Blair. He had something that she would never have: a tough resilience for meeting every challenge that came his way. She shivered and clung closer to him as she wondered at his strength. Her own inner resources seemed puny by comparison.

"What's on your mind, sweetheart?" he asked.

"I'm thinking about how much I admire you, Blair," she responded. "And I'm also thinking that because I didn't grow up the way you did, I don't have your drive to make money and conquer the business world. It isn't in me anymore to live the crazy lifestyle of the city. I'm perfectly happy in this quiet little corner of the world."

"I believe you'll change your mind after one winter here," he said softly. "Maybe I'm wrong. I hope so, for your sake." He paused and cupped her cheek in his warm, rough palm. "I admire you, too. You're very determined." He chuckled. "We're cast from the same mold. We both go our own ways and accept the risks and the responsibilities. You're some kind of woman."

Suddenly Justine felt overwhelmed by all that had passed between them that night. A warm cocoon of trust, created by Blair's disclosures, embraced her. She was more drawn to him at this moment than she'd been to any other man in her life. A sweet yearning blossomed in her breast and reached out toward him in the darkness. She longed to be held by him, to nestle in his embrace and cling to the strength that loomed beside her.

She lifted her arms and twined them around his neck. Pressing close, she rubbed her smooth cheek against his and felt a light skimming of whiskers. They clung together wordlessly, then Blair sought her mouth and kissed her with infinite gentleness. His lips were warm and firm. Then the intensity of their emotions seemed to sweep over both of them, for suddenly they were throwing off their blanket and rolling on the soft wool. The crushed pine needles released a pungent fragrance as their straining bodies pressed down on them. Justine felt as if Blair were kissing her in a dozen places at once. His hungry lips and hands roved over her body, nuzzling here, tasting there, imprinting a string of hot kisses from her collarbone to her breasts. She felt drugged by the potent sensations that were rushing through her tingling body. They raged within her like a hot wind blowing in a savage land, a land where exotic flowers bloom and birds dip low to taste their strong, wild honey.

A wanton cry erupted from her throat as Justine surrendered herself completely to her lover and to the emotions that were rocketing through her. With hands that moved with confidence and took what they wanted, Blair stroked her lean waist, her warm thighs and the flat plain of her belly. She heard his ragged sigh against her hair. He kissed her temple, then claimed her mouth again, dragging muffled cries from deep in her throat. His tongue and lips explored the sweet interior of her mouth, arousing her to a near frenzy. Her fingers dug into the lean hardness of his shoulders, where she felt the muscles flex as he clasped her to him. Her breasts rubbed erotically against his firm chest with its feathering of silky hair, and she felt her nipples harden at this intimate friction.

With a boldness that surprised her, Justine pressed Blair's head toward her upthrusting breasts, which were eagerly awaiting his special attentions. He made her wait, softly sliding his tongue around her nipple, teasing it into turgid anticipation.

"Blair," she gasped, her head thrown back, "I can't stand it."

His laughter thrummed against her heated skin. "What do you want, Justine? Name it—it's yours."

In answer she pulled his head down onto her breast. He took the nipple into his mouth, drawing on it until it ached with sweet sensations. Expertly he taunted the hard little bud, swirling around it with his tongue and nipping gently with his teeth until Justine cried out with unbearable pleasure.

Covering her breast with his hand, Blair turned his attention to its twin and worked the same sorcery there. Justine forgot where she was as she wandered lost in the sweet haze of Blair's expert lovemaking. Then he was lifting her hips as he nuzzled her belly and tasted her satiny skin. His hands clasped her bottom, arching her body toward his questing mouth, his breath a hot wind that inflamed her nerve endings.

Justine gasped as Blair's caress became more intimate, his head dipping low to kiss the silky patch that curled below her belly. Her hands clutched his shoulders as he possessively parted her thighs and drew her closer to his exploring lips and tongue. For a moment she thought she would faint from the sweet agony of his mouth on the very center of her throbbing womanhood. Never before had any man stoked the fires of her passion into such uninhibited ecstasy. Her awareness of time stopped. She knew nothing beyond the sensations created by Blair loving her. A fire raged out of control, building in her loins and rippling out to her fingertips and toes. With hands and mouth that stroked her in a rhythm as ancient as the mountains, Blair urged her body on to ever higher plateaus of arousal.

Justine reveled in the waves of heat that fanned throughout her entire body. Her mind whirled with a varicolored pattern of lights as her excitement peaked, exploding in a series of shudders that shook her like a willow in a windstorm. Through a honeyed fog she heard the breathless cries that ripped from her throat. Like velvet moths, her gasps floated on the night air and vanished into the sheltering pine branches above. And still Blair caressed her, coaxing from her every last pulse of pleasure that rocked her body.

Then he raised himself above her and plunged between her thighs. His stunning manhood stroked the inner chamber of her being with such molten intensity Justine felt lightheaded. Flinging her legs around Blair's waist, she clung to him, pressing up to meet him thrust for thrust. She felt a faint sheen of perspiration break out on his back as she listened with the keenest of pleasure to the endearments that spilled from his lips.

"Oh, Justine," he gasped against her throat, "I love being all tangled up with you like this." He growled erotically. "Ahh . . . I can't get enough of you."

Justine urged him on, grasping him with encouraging hands that revealed the depth of her emotions. And then she held him close as his tempo quickened. Clutching Justine to him, as surge after surge claimed him, Blair again called out her name. Powerful shudders shook his body, like an earthquake along a mighty fault line.

Spent and breathless, they clung to each other for many long moments. Justine savored the dreamy languor that had spread throughout her body like a potent balm. She breathed the perfume of their lovemaking; the faint musky smell mingled so delightfully with the tang of crushed pine needles. A cool breeze from the lake blew against her skin, and she shivered. Blair pulled the blanket over them, enclosing them once more in a cozy woolen cave.

Lying entwined with her lover, Justine realized that she felt completely whole, as if she'd found with Blair a part of herself that had always been missing. Was this what poets meant when they rhapsodized about two people becoming as one? She wasn't sure, but she was certain of something else—she'd never been this happy in her life. At the edge of her awareness nagged the same doubts about where all of this involvement was leading her. Resolutely she pushed those demons out of her mind and sent them skittering into the shadows. Her time with Blair was the most valuable thing she had now. She would waste not one precious moment on her fears.

Chapter Ten

In the morning Blair and Justine took Aldora up into the hills for her workout. The splendid peregrine flew magnificently. Her shiny brown feathers reflected the sun's fire, and her power dives displayed a breathtaking mastery of the air. It wouldn't be long, Justine reminded herself, before she'd cast Aldora into the sky for the last time and wish her well. The fall migration would begin soon; that would be a perfect time to release the falcon. Those thoughts put a lump in Justine's throat, and her eyes misted over as she watched Aldora arrow through the air.

Blair seemed to sense her inner turmoil and put his arm around her shoulders. She forced herself to smile up at him, for she didn't want to put a damper on the beautiful morning.

They spent the afternoon exploring some ski resorts and visited a little town in the mountains that had been remodeled as a frontier village. As the hours passed, Justine struggled to maintain her cheerful facade. Yet the thought kept nagging at her that, like Aldora, Blair would soon be gone, as well. He'd already hinted at his approaching departure, referring again to the big sale that was coming up at his Seattle store. During lunch in a café she overheard him on a pay phone, talking to his manager about the Norwegian skiing star who was going to appear at the opening of the sale. As he discussed this part of the promotion scheme, Justine noticed that his body was tense and alert and that his facial expression showed full concentration. She realized that she was glimpsing Blair in his favorite role of the shrewd businessman. When he hung up the phone, he scribbled some quick notes, slipped the little pad back into his pocket and smiled at her. She knew from the contented look on his face that he was in his element. Even over the phone, taking care of business gave him joy.

Any faint hope that she'd entertained about him easing out of the fast lane faded as she looked into his lit-up eyes. Asking him to gear down would be like...like expecting Aldora to remain forever on the ground. Like the falcon, Blair needed to chase the wind, to find out how far his drive and creativity would take him. She was especially aware of this requirement in light of his heartfelt disclosures of the night before. At last she knew what made Blair tick.

Suspecting what his response would be, she nevertheless looked across the café table and posed her idea, anyway. There was no harm in asking, she told herself. Had he ever thought about opening a small version of his Seattle store in the Shelby area? she asked him. Like Parker's Apple Inn, it could operate during the summer only, just to accommodate the tourists.

He smiled indulgently and laid his hand on hers. The topic of positive cash flow dominated their conversation for the next few minutes, but what Blair's words boiled down to was no, he didn't think that a recreational equipment store would do well in Shelby, not even on a part-time basis. Justine busied herself with her hamburger, trying to hide her disappointment. Hers had been a tentative feeler, and she could see that Blair thought it was a crazy idea. She was embarrassed to have suggested it.

One afternoon a couple of days later, Blair and Justine were sipping iced tea in the shade of the maples at Lilac House when Ellen and Caroline drove up. The girls joined them under the trees for a brief, enthusiastic chat. Their trip to Seattle had been a huge success. Both wore new T-shirts: Ellen's, which was from the University of Washington, read Go, Huskies! and Caroline's proclaimed that she'd visited Seattle, The Emerald City.

After the girls left, Justine dug into the sacks they'd left behind and inspected the food and other items they'd bought for her in Seattle. As she and Blair savored some Turkish delight from the Pike Place Market, Justine scanned the entertainment section from a copy of the *Seattle Times*. Suddenly she sat forward in her lawn chair and exclaimed under her breath.

Blair looked up from the business section he'd been studying. "What is it, Justine? Did you find something interesting?"

"*Throw Her a Kiss* is in Seattle." She showed him the full-page ad. "It's a New York musical that's touring the country. I bought a ticket to see it in Los Angeles, but I had to sell it when I moved up here." She bit her bottom lip. "I really wanted to go, too. Oh, well."

Blair put down the newspaper and fixed her with a thoughtful look. "You can go," he said. "Be my guest. I can get on the phone and order tickets, then you could fly over with me, and we could—"

Justine shook her head. "Blair, you know I can't leave now. Aldora's very close to being released, and I can't make any plans until after that." She smiled at his slightly frowning face. "Besides, I already told you that I really want to stay put until spring." She shrugged. "Thanks, anyway."

Blair refolded the paper as he spoke. "Spring's a long way off. As soon as Aldora's released, you're free to come and go anywhere you like. Why wait?" He reached over and took her hand, his eyes twinkling. "Think about it, Justine—a New York musical, a candle-lit dinner, the two of us out for a night on the town."

She felt sorely tempted. "Well," she said slowly, "it does sound inviting...." She abruptly tossed down the paper and stood up. "Sorry, there's the phone. I'll be right back."

When she returned some time later, Justine was bubbling with excitement. "That was Sandra," she exclaimed as she sat back down on her lawn chair. "She sold my share of the bookstore this morning. That means I'll soon have enough capital for my new store here."

"Well, there goes *Throw Her a Kiss*," Blair muttered.

Some of Justine's ebullience faded. She wanted Blair to be happy for her. Instead, he'd chosen that moment to point out that she'd once again miss seeing the musical. Of course, Sandra's news meant that Justine's waiting was behind her. She could forge ahead with her plan at last and would no doubt be very busy over the next few months. There would be no time for trips anywhere until the spring. It amazed her that Blair seemed so unwilling to let that tentative plan of theirs ride. How like his type to pressure her to cram more activities and commitments into a schedule that she'd purposely scaled down.

She had to admit to herself, though, that it excited her to think about the busy time ahead. Lately she'd felt as if she'd been living in a kind of limbo. She'd been able to fill her time with projects, but deep down she knew that only by plunging into her business again could she adequately occupy her mind and energy. Looking at Blair's frown, she decided not to let him detract from her happiness over Sandra's good news. She shrugged one shoulder and kept her tone light.

"So I'll miss the musical," she said. "It's just another trade-off for living here." She smiled hopefully. "Come on," she said, "be happy for me, Blair."

He squeezed her hand. "Of course I'm happy for you." Then his facial expression became rueful. "I was just thinking, though, that this means you'll dig yourself in even deeper here."

"But I want to dig in. This is my home."

"Yeah," he said softly after a long pause, "I guess it is."

An emotion that Justine couldn't identify passed through
Blair's eyes. Perhaps she was imagining it, but he seemed
vulnerable all of a sudden, just as he'd been on the night
when he'd confided in her. She felt a twinge of guilt, as if
she'd hurt him or let him down in some way. Could it be that
she felt sorry for him because of his rough start in life? Did
she feel guilty because she'd had a sheltered childhood and
now lived in a house full of memories that comforted her
and reminded her that she had a secure place in a family?

She almost expressed these thoughts to Blair but stopped
herself in time. He wouldn't want her sympathy or pity.
How she longed suddenly to include him in the warm circle
of her family. But he was so independent. Would he ever let
anyone do that for him? Before she could further ponder
these unexpected ideas, Blair stood up and pulled her to her
feet.

"Hey," he said, "I'm starving. When's dinner, Chef
Fleming?"

Justine was relieved that Blair had shifted into a lighter
mood. She smiled up at him. "I'm sure I can whip up
something from these goodies the girls brought back. Come
on," she said, banishing the last of her negative feelings,
"have a glass of wine in the kitchen while I cook."

"You're on." He smiled and grazed her forehead with his
lips.

After a candle-lit dinner they climbed the stairs to Justine's bedroom. As a soft lake breeze wafted through the
open doors to the balcony, Justine and Blair made love in
her big antique bed, roiling the covers and finally kicking
them to the floor. The mellow night air throbbed with the
sounds of the two lovers crying out their passion and later
laughing softly as they snuggled into each other's arms for
sleep.

The next morning Justine awoke and discovered that Blair
had already left. She lay there with a sinking feeling in the
pit of her stomach and stared at the ceiling. Last night at
dinner Blair had told her that he'd be leaving early in the

morning. He was going to fly through the mountain passes and spend a few days at his Seattle store. Although she knew he'd be back, having him gone now made Justine feel lost and sad. The next time he left would be his last, and it was her nervous anticipation of that day that made her feel so dispirited.

Then she caught her breath and shut her eyes, recalling last night's lovemaking in vivid detail. It had been in turn so tender she'd been moved to tears and then so fierce she'd thought that the old house might shudder on its foundation. Never in her life had she imagined lovemaking could be that way, and she dreaded giving up this newfound passion.

Impatiently she got out of bed. She'd made up her mind to enjoy the time that she and Blair had together, and she wasn't going to waste one minute regretting her decision. There was no sense in wishing for the moon, but that didn't mean she couldn't appreciate what they had together right now. In another week or so he'd return to Seattle for good, and she'd be left with her memories. She'd deal with that when the time came.

She wondered if she would actually visit Blair in Seattle next spring. He was right—spring was a long way off. A lot could happen between now and then. Blair could meet someone else in the city, for example. Then Justine's trip to see him would only embarrass everyone. Perhaps she could visit Seattle to sightsee and shop and not tell him that she was in town. She smiled ruefully, knowing that it would be impossible not to call Blair if she were anywhere near him. Tabling these distressing thoughts for the time being, Justine went into the bathroom to wash and get dressed.

Later she took Aldora up into the hills and watched her chase the wind. At one point the falcon called to a red-tailed hawk that was soaring overhead. Aldora seemed to fixate on the hawk as it disappeared over the southern horizon, and she stirred restlessly on Justine's fist. Did the falcon feel the urge to join its wild raptor cousins in the fall migration? As

Justine hooded Aldora and walked back to her Jeep, she felt sadness welling up in her; she would miss the peregrine.

Justine spent the rest of the day working at her computer. There was much family information to be gleaned from some bundles of letters and papers she'd found under the eaves in the attic. By this time, she'd cleaned out almost every room in the big old house. She'd given a few more items to the museum, burned several barrels of trash and donated some old clothes to a local church. Most of Lilac House was now neat and orderly, with furniture dusted and mirrors polished. As she stared at the computer screen, Justine realized that her project of cleaning out the house and recording the family history would soon end. This thought gave her a feeling of accomplishment, but she was also thankful that she'd soon have her own bookstore to fill the void.

Later, as Justine sat alone at the kitchen table and picked at her dinner, she had a lot to think about. An hour earlier she'd received a phone call from Paul Bradburn, Myra's former editor at the *Los Angeles Globe*. Paul wanted Justine to persuade Myra to return to his newspaper staff. Myra was arriving the next day for a visit, Justine had told Paul. She'd broach the subject to her sister then, although she doubted that Myra would want to return to L.A. Paul had thanked her, then offhandedly remarked that he'd recently run into one of Justine's old flames, Jason Emery.

Now, as Justine poured herself a glass of wine, she pictured Jason Emery. The handsome, well-groomed man's main goal in life was to accumulate as many material objects as he could. She stared out the window and sipped her Burgundy. Paul's casual mention of Jason had brought back painful memories. At one time Justine had thought that she was falling in love with Jason. She'd finally realized that as his wife she'd be treated as just another of his acquisitions, a useful adornment in his tireless quest for the good life.

Justine's thoughts turned to Blair, and she found herself comparing him with Jason. Both men were ambitious and thrived on competition, but there the similarity seemed to end. Beneath Jason's glamorous veneer of suavity and charm lay a void, an emptiness that would always be there. Blair's personality, on the other hand, was richly complex. He'd shared a vulnerable facet of himself with her, which had humanized him in her eyes unlike no other man she had ever known.

Lately she'd wondered if he might compromise his views with hers. Perhaps there was some way they could arrange to be together, to somehow mesh their disparate lifestyles so that both could pursue their individual plans and dreams. Her tentative suggestion that he open a branch of his store in the Shelby area had been an attempt to broach this subject. Then she recalled how swiftly he'd rejected her idea as unfeasible.

She poked at her food, which was getting cold on her plate. It was pointless to think about compromise, anyway, when she was on the verge of starting her new business in Shelby and Blair was planning his biggest sale of the year. Both of them were digging deeper and deeper into their own areas of interest, and a compromise seemed out of the question.

Then the bleak thought occurred to her that maybe Blair wouldn't even be interested in a compromise. After all, why should she believe that she had any special place in his heart? He hadn't spoken of any such feelings for her and seemed content to remain single. They'd shared some passionate moments, and there was a profound tenderness between them at times, but what commitment had they made to each other? None. It saddened her to think that Blair might not be capable of commitment. Because his teen years had been devoid of a nurturing home and family, he'd perhaps learned the lessons of self-sufficiency too well.

She sighed and took a bite of food. Normally she loved her homemade lasagna, but that night for some reason the savory sauce and tender noodles tasted flat. She put down her fork and sipped some wine. The Burgundy was sud-

denly sharp and acidic on her tongue. Pushing her plate and
glass aside, Justine stood. She wasn't hungry anymore.

"Justine!"
"Myra, it's so good to see you!"
Justine threw her arms around her petite sister the next
day as Myra got out of her vintage VW Beetle in front of
Lilac House. The two young women hugged and laughed.
Then they stepped back to look at each other, Justine still
holding on to her sister's shoulders.
"You look great," she said, gazing down into Myra's
eyes, which were the same color as blue forget-me-nots.
Myra was wearing slacks and a cream-colored polo shirt.
Her fine blond hair, cut close to her well-shaped head,
feathered around her face pixie-style. Her delicate coloring
and porcelain skin had always made Justine think of a fragile doll. As she studied Myra, Justine noted with pleasure
that her sister's eyes held a merry glint and that her smile
seemed neither forced nor strained. Her impression on the
phone lately had been correct: Myra was recovering from
her ordeal.
Justine hugged her sister again. "Come on in," she said.
"I've got some homemade peach pie, and I'll make us a pot
of tea. I'm so glad you could come."
Linking arms, the two sisters climbed the wide steps and
entered the house. Both were talking at once. Soon they
were seated in lawn chairs under the maple trees, eating pie
and sipping mugs of tea. The park rang with their laughter
as they shared stories and got each other caught up on the
news since their last phone call.
Finally, their empty plates set aside, Justine broached the
subject that was uppermost in her mind. She gazed over at
her sister's face. A pattern of filtered sunlight danced across
its delicate contours.
"Myra," she began, "you look and act so much better.
How do you really feel?"

Her sister's demeanor became sober as she stared up into the maple, on whose wide branches she and Justine had climbed as children. Then she looked Justine in the eye.

"I think I'm over it," she said quietly.

"How about the nightmares?"

"Oh, I still have one now and then," admitted Myra. "But it's pretty hard to keep bad memories alive when you have someone like Uncle Bob to talk you out of it." She laughed. "Honestly, he and Aunt Dora have been great. I'll never be able to repay them for their kindness."

"I'm sure that seeing you get better is payment enough," said Justine. She hesitated before continuing. "How about your writing? Have you done any more of that lately?"

Myra's eyes glowed warmly. "Yes, I have. You know, it felt like going home when I started writing again. I hadn't realized how much I'd missed it. I wrote that profile I told you about, then I did some other pieces for the local paper. And I discovered something kind of scary."

Justine's stomach fluttered with apprehension. "What?"

Myra laughed, her voice as soft as the breeze that was blowing off the lake. "I discovered that I'm hooked for life. There's no way I could ever give up writing for good, not even if an entire gang of thugs held me captive for a year."

Justine reached over and squeezed Myra's hand. "Oh, Sis, I'm so happy to hear that. You're such a good writer. It worried me when you stopped."

"It had me worried, too," said Myra. "But I understand all of that now, thanks to my counseling sessions with Uncle Bob. I believe I've come out of this a stronger person, Justine. I really do." She returned her sister's squeeze.

Justine reached for the teapot and refilled their mugs. Steam rose into the air, which had begun to cool with the approach of dusk.

Myra continued. "I want to thank you, too, Justine. Poor thing. I'm sure you got sick and tired of hearing about my—" she paused and rolled her eyes "—problem."

"Not at all," Justine hastened to reassure her. "You'd do it for me." She laughed. "Come to think of it, you have done it for me. Remember all those times in Los Angeles when I called you up to complain about the break-ins at my apartment? And remember how you helped me when my car was stolen? You've been there for me, Myra. Don't ever worry that you've bored or burdened me.''

"Well, I appreciate everything you've done," said Myra, her voice tinged with emotion. Then she sat up and took a deep breath. "I've been doing a lot of thinking the past few weeks. It finally dawned on me that one of the reasons I caved in after the bank incident was that I was still too much of a country kid when I moved to L.A. I had no idea what I was getting myself into."

"Lamb to the wolves?" suggested Justine.

"Yes, you could put it that way." Myra chuckled. "Anyway, that's all behind me now." Sipping her tea, she gazed out at the lake for a moment. Then she again regarded Justine. "I'm thinking about moving back to L.A. My editor called me the other day and told me that I could have my old job back."

"Paul called me, too, just yesterday."

Myra's eyebrows rose. "He did? Why?"

"He wants me to talk you into going back," said Justine. "But it sounds like you've already made up your mind."

"Yes, I'm about ninety percent certain," said Myra.

She set down her mug and leaned forward. Justine could tell that the prospect of returning to the city excited her sister.

"Paul told me about a journalism competition that's coming up," continued Myra. "He wants me to visit the bank where I was held hostage, then write up my experience there for the competition. He says that my timing would be great and that I might have a good shot at the prize."

"Go back to the bank? I don't know, Myra...." Justine bit her bottom lip. "Do you think that's a very good idea?"

"I asked Uncle Bob what he thought," said Myra, "and he said that it might be exactly what I need to do. Maybe it would help me shake off the rest of the bad feelings that I still carry around with me."

"Don't do anything that you're not truly comfortable with," cautioned Justine. "Frankly, I'm surprised that you'd even consider going back to L.A."

Myra laughed. "I'm a little surprised, too. But when I stop to think about it, except for the bank incident, I was happy there. I didn't have all the bad luck that finally drove you out of the city."

"That's true," admitted Justine.

"Besides," continued Myra, "I've been in hiding long enough. It's time to jump back into the mainstream and start taking a few risks again. I'll never have the kind of career I want if I stay up here."

"Yes, I see what you mean," said Justine thoughtfully.

What her sister said made a lot of sense. Justine was very happy for her, and yet Myra's decision to return to city life gave Justine a vague feeling of uneasiness. She searched her mind for the cause. It had something to do with Blair....

Myra broke into her thoughts. "Justine, what are you thinking about? You look so pale and distant all of a sudden. Are you all right?"

Justine looked at her sister and forced herself to smile. "Yes, of course. I was thinking about how happy I am for you. I'm sure that everything's going to turn out okay."

Myra was staring at her. A slight frown cast a shadow over her delicate features. "There's something else on your mind, isn't there? I can tell."

Justine tried to appear nonchalant. "You mean, besides your move back to L.A.?" She shrugged one shoulder. "No, not really," she hedged. But her lower lip began to tremble, and she could feel her hands start to shake. She laced her fingers together in her lap, hoping that Myra wouldn't notice.

But of course she did. Justine couldn't hide anything from her perceptive sister, any more than Myra could conceal the truth from her.

"Come on, Justine," said Myra softly. "What's up?"

Justine raised her hands in a gesture of resignation, then dropped them onto the arms of her chair. She sighed as she leaned her head back. The deep green of twilight was beginning to pool among the branches above.

"It's a man," she said.

She realized as she uttered these words that a heavy weight seemed to lift from her shoulders. She'd been keeping her feelings bottled up much too long and desperately needed someone to talk to. She hadn't said a lot about Blair to Myra before this time because she hadn't wanted to burden her sister. Now that Myra was coping so well with her own emotions, however, it seemed all right to share her mixed feelings with her.

"A man," exclaimed Myra. "I knew it." She paused. "Is it Blair, the guy you've been showing around?"

"That's right."

"When do I get to meet him?"

Justine looked at her. "He's in Seattle right now, so introductions will have to wait."

The thought of Blair being so far away, on the other side of the Cascade Mountains—the formidable natural barrier between eastern and western Washington—filled her with sadness. She dreaded his return, knowing that it would force her emotions to the surface, leaving her ill fit to cope with their final parting. Her stomach twisted into a knot.

Myra settled back in her chair and fixed her sister with a thoughtful look. "Tell me about it," she urged.

Then, as shadows lengthened on the lawn, Justine told Myra the whole story, beginning with a description of the startling way that she and Blair had met. It seemed to Justine that the scene in the upland field had occurred a hundred years ago. So much had happened since then, she mused, so many things had been said. And not been said, she added silently.

"So," she concluded, "he'll be leaving here soon after he comes back from this trip to Seattle, and I may never see him again." She almost choked on the last words.

Myra was silent for several long moments. "Blair sounds wonderful. You want to see him again, don't you?"

A sudden wind from the lake rattled the leaves overhead. Justine shivered. "No," she said. "Yes... Oh, I don't know."

A tightness had crept into Justine's throat, making her muscles ache and her mouth feel dry. The pain of her emotions threatened to overwhelm her. She put her head back, fighting to keep from crying.

"You're in love with Blair, aren't you?" said Myra softly.

Justine snapped her head up and frowned at her sister. "Absolutely not!" she declared.

Even as she denied it, Justine knew in her heart that Myra, with her usual keen insight, had zeroed in on the truth. Sometimes her sister seemed to know her better than Justine did herself.

"I am not in love with Blair Sutherland," she repeated, but even to her own ears this second denial sounded feeble.

Myra's eyebrows rose a fraction. She laced her fingers together under her chin and fixed her sister with a steady gaze.

"I don't believe you," said Myra. "I think you're trying to convince yourself that you don't love him because that's easier than admitting how much you'll miss him when he leaves."

Suddenly the tears were streaming down Justine's face. "No," she said. "No, I don't love him. I don't. I don't." Then she sobbed, "Yes, I do. I do love him. Oh, Myra, I love him so much it hurts me. It hurts, Myra. What am I going to do?"

Justine covered her face with her hands and cried for several long moments. As the scalding tears wet her palms, she realized again how much emotion she'd been holding inside. Ever since she and Blair had become lovers, she'd tried to convince herself that she could handle a summer romance, then let go of it in the fall without regrets. How wrong she'd been to ask that of herself. She wasn't capable of loving just on the surface, then casting that love aside. It felt good to admit that she loved Blair, but there were serious problems connected to that.

Myra asked, "Does Blair love you?" She pressed a handkerchief into her sister's hand.

Her question brought renewed weeping from Justine, who regarded her sister with eyes brimming over with tears. "I don't know," she said, choking on her words. "There've been times—" she recalled their lovemaking, which was both tender and passionate, and their moments of easy companionability "—times when I've thought that he might love me. But he's never said so. And, Myra, he's so dedicated to his business. I'm afraid that I'd always be in the background because of that." She dabbed at her eyes. "What he and I have is probably nothing more to him than a summer affair."

"And yet he's coming back here again."

Justine waved her hand impatiently. "Oh, that doesn't mean anything." She crumpled the handkerchief in her lap. "We haven't gotten around to all of the recreational areas I'd told him about. He's probably coming back to check those out, that's all. He just has business on his mind."

"Has it occurred to you," said Myra, "that he might be holding back from letting you know how he feels? Maybe he's waiting for a sign from you that you're willing to love him on his own terms."

"What do you mean?" Justine was confused.

"Well, look at it this way," said Myra. "Here's a man who's very powerful and successful. He loves running his business and making money. He meets a very independent woman, who has also been successful in business. He's attracted to her, of course, because she's probably more woman than he's ever met before."

"Oh, I don't know about that," scoffed Justine.

Myra held up her hand. "Wait a minute—hear me out." She continued. "This very independent woman has decided to drop out of the rat race and scale down her lifestyle. The place where she starts her life over is miles and miles away from where he has his base of operations.

Something is going to have to give, and he knows that. Long-distance romances don't usually work out. Blair may be wondering if he can pry you loose from here. And can he hope for a commitment from you since you obviously feel so strongly about living here?'' Myra leaned forward. ''He might be waiting for you to make the first move, Justine. Do you think that's a possibility?''

''Well, he does seem like a man that a woman would have to meet halfway....''

Was it possible that Blair loved her? She'd wondered about it lately but had always pushed the idea to one side. Believing what wasn't true would only fill her with regrets when he left Shelby. Then her thoughts turned even blacker. If he loved her, surely she'd know it by now, wouldn't she?

On the other hand, he'd asked her more than once to visit him in Seattle. What was his game, anyway? Or was it a game? She gave a weary sigh. It was all very confusing, and suddenly she felt a headache coming on.

''I think you need to hang on to Blair,'' said Myra. ''I've never seen you so worked up about a man. There's something powerful going on here. Don't let it slip away.''

Her words rang in Justine's ears. Their message was elusive; if only she knew what to do! If she knew how Blair felt about her, things might be different. She'd thought that she'd gotten her life neatly planned—like the newly organized rooms in Lilac House—then Blair had entered the scene, throwing her life and her emotions into chaos. A cool breeze rushed across her bare arms, and she shivered.

''Brr,'' she said as she stood, ''there's a touch of fall in the air. Let's go in, shall we?'' She began stacking the dishes, then stopped and looked at her sister, who was helping her. ''Thanks, Myra. I appreciate your listening to me.''

''It's been a rough year for both of us. I think my problem's behind me.'' Myra paused. ''I want you to be happy, too.''

''I know,'' murmured Justine, ''and I will be.'' But deep inside she wondered about that. She wondered about a lot of things.

Chapter Eleven

A couple of days later Justine stood in the morning sunshine and waved goodbye to Myra. As her sister's car rounded the curve in the driveway, Justine felt sorry that Myra's visit had come to an end. She'd wanted her to stay longer, but Myra had become restless; there were things she needed to do in Reardan before she moved back to Los Angeles.

Justine went inside and sat down at her computer, but her concentration simply wasn't there. At last she gave up and drove Aldora into the hills for a workout. Being high above the lake always cleared her mind and calmed her nerves, and it was the same that day. The sight of the bullet-fast falcon in flight, with the Indian summer sun glinting off her smooth feathers, lifted Justine's heart. Her spirits seemed to fly with the bird, and she temporarily forgot her worries.

Later, back at Lilac House, the telephone rang. Justine ran to answer it, her heart pounding. Blair had called her last night, just to chat. She knew that he was returning to

Shelby that day. Maybe he was calling now to let her know that he was back.

"Hello?" she said, clutching the receiver. Her pulse leaped with nervous anticipation.

"Hello," said an unfamiliar male voice. "Is this Justine Fleming?"

She sank down onto the nearest chair and stifled her disappointment. It wasn't Blair, after all.

"Yes," she said.

"This is Noel Houston in Seattle," said the man. "I'm a friend of Blair's."

"Oh, sure," she said. "He's mentioned your name to me. It's your houseboat he's been staying in over here."

"That's right," said Noel. "I had lunch with him yesterday, and he mentioned your name, too. I called information to get your number because I've been unable to reach him today." He paused. "Look, I hope you don't mind, but could you give Blair an important message for me? I have to catch a plane to Phoenix, or I'd keep trying myself."

"No, I don't mind at all. I expect him back later on." She reached for a pencil and paper. "What's the message?"

"Tell him that the property he was asking about is available and that he can get it at the price he offered. A mutual friend of ours has been working on the deal, and he just gave me a call," he added.

Justine's eyes widened with interest. What property was Noel talking about? Blair hadn't mentioned any property to her. She shrugged. He was probably expanding his Seattle business. Then she caught her breath as another possibility occurred to her. Dare she hope that Blair was buying land in eastern Washington, after all? But why? Her head suddenly swam with exciting thoughts, and her hopes soared.

Noel's voice interrupted her happy conjecturing and brought her back down to earth. "Have you got that?" he asked.

"Um, yes," she said, trying to sound casual.

She was dying to ask where the property was located but didn't want to pry. Besides, she was probably wrong, anyway, about its being on this side of the mountains. Blair had been pretty firm in rejecting her idea about his opening a store over there. Even so, her little flame of hope refused to go out.

"Thanks, Justine," said Noel. "I appreciate your help." He chuckled. "You know, when I loaned Blair my house-boat, I had no idea that he'd become so attached to Lake Shelby."

"How do you mean?"

"Well, he sure acted different at lunch yesterday. Oh, he's the same old Blair, all right, but there's something changed about him. I think that being out in the country has done him a world of good."

"Oh?" Justine's interest quickened.

"Yeah," Noel continued, "he was more relaxed than I've ever seen him. He's not wearing a watch anymore, for one thing. When I asked him about it, he just shrugged and said that he didn't want to be too preoccupied with time. And he seemed really eager to return to Shelby. I've never seen Blair like this before, and I've known him for years." He paused. "I can't help wondering if you might be one of the reasons why he wants to get back across those mountains."

Justine's heart flip-flopped, and she felt a warm flush creep into her cheeks. "What makes you think that?" she asked in a tone of uncertainty.

"Oh, your name kept coming up," said Noel. "And when he talks about you, he gets a certain look in his eyes." Again he paused. "I think you've really made an impact on my old buddy."

Justine nervously picked at the arm of her chair. Noel's words pleased her, of course, yet she hesitated to put too much store in them.

"He and I've spent a lot time together lately. It's natural for him to mention me. After all, I've been his guide over here."

"Yeah, he told me about that," said Noel, "but you may not realize that Blair has spent much more time in Shelby than he'd originally planned."

"Oh?"

"That's right. And I can think of only one reason why workaholic Blair Sutherland would stay away from his business for so long: he's on to something very interesting. And I'm not talking about his guidebook project, either."

As the implied meaning of Noel's words sank in, Justine felt a bit light-headed. Suddenly the topic of their conversation was too personal for comfort. She hastened to end the phone call, hoping that she wouldn't seem abrupt.

"Well," she said, "it's been nice talking with you, and I'll give Blair your message as soon as I see him."

Their goodbyes exchanged, Justine replaced the receiver with an unsteady hand. So Blair was eager to get back to Shelby. But what was the real reason for that? He had more than enough material to launch his guidebook project. She frowned slightly. Could she dare to believe Noel's assessment that she was the main reason why Blair was taking extra time away from his business?

Feeling restless, she stood up and went out onto the back porch. Down near the water's edge Leonard was burning some cuttings from the park. The gentle breeze carried the rich smell of woodsmoke to her, reminding her that autumn was just around the corner. Soon the frosty air would be filled with the pungent aroma of many fires as the valley's residents raked and burned fallen leaves. She glanced at the lilac hedge and was startled to notice that it looked a little brown and shriveled around the edges. Bluebell and Caramel were chasing each other around on the lawn. Before long the cats would be rustling in piles of dry leaves.

Justine waved at Leonard, then went back into the house. She didn't want to think about the seasons changing or about the passage of time. Time... She glanced at the clock. She wondered when Blair would land in Shelby. Even though she was eager for his return and longed to feel his strong arms around her, she somehow dreaded seeing him. He was probably coming back for a day or two at the most to wrap things up, then he'd go back to Seattle for good. Her mood turned edgy and apprehensive.

What she needed right then was action, any kind of action, to take her mind off Blair. She hadn't heard lately from Mr. Gordon, the real-estate agent; she'd give him a call. Now that her L.A. capital was available, she wanted to push forward her bookstore plan.

"Hello, Mr. Gordon," she said when the agent came on the line. "This is Justine Fleming. I was wondering if you'd found any property for me yet."

"As a matter of fact," he said, "I think I have. I'd like you to take a look at it. Are you free this afternoon?"

"It isn't another old barn, is it?"

He chuckled. "No, this is a bona fide commercial property, Ms. Fleming, and it's right on the main street of town."

"That sounds interesting," said Justine. "Yes, I could look at it today. Shall we say around three?"

"That'll be fine, Ms. Fleming."

When Justine viewed the property that afternoon, she discovered that it had less floor space than she'd wanted but that it had real possibilities. She would simply scale down her original plan. After all, the Shelby economy wouldn't support a large bookstore, like the one she'd shared in L.A. The property currently housed an arts and crafts center. The owner had recently suffered a mild stroke and wanted to sell out and retire.

"This place could be yours for a very reasonable price," Mr. Gordon told Justine.

They were standing on the sidewalk after their tour of the premises. Mr. Gordon was tall and lean. He wore gold-rimmed glasses, and his gray hair was cut into an old-fashioned flattop.

"The owner's in a big hurry to pack it in and move to California," he went on. Then he nodded toward the building. "Are you interested in making an offer, Ms. Fleming? I think this would be perfect for your business."

Justine peered through the window and imagined book-shelves lining the walls. "It certainly is the best thing you've found for me," she said. "And I know it would work out with a little bit of remodeling...." Her voice trailed off.

"Fine, let's go on back to my office, and we'll start filling out the paperwork—"

"Um, wait a minute," interjected Justine.

How ironic, she mused. Selling her share of the L.A. store and locating property here had seemed to take forever. Now that things were finally beginning to roll, she felt that she was being swept along too fast. She shivered as a cold wind suddenly blew around her ankles.

"Mr. Gordon," she said, feeling foolish, "do you mind if I give it some thought?"

He shrugged. "Not at all," he said, "but I wouldn't wait too long. This place is going to be snapped up, especially now that we've got a little economic boom on the way."

Justine's interest was piqued. "What do you mean?"

"Oh, maybe you haven't heard the news. Someone's buying that piece of land over by the grange hall. No one knows yet what's going to be built there, but it's bound to give our economy a boost." He smiled at her. "Your timing might be perfect for starting up a new retail business in Shelby."

Justine barely registered his last words because her mind was in a whirl. "Who... who's buying that land? Do you know?"

The real-estate agent shook his head. "No, I didn't handle the deal. Sorry, I don't have a clue." Then his face brightened. "Wait a minute, yes, I do. When I got my hair cut this morning, the barber mentioned that he'd heard it was some big shot from the coast." He grinned. "It could be interesting, Ms. Fleming."

It could indeed.

Justine cleared her throat. She felt a bit light-headed. "Well, thanks for showing me this place. I'll get back to you on it as soon as I've made up my mind."

"Right. Just give me a jingle."

Justine hummed to herself as she drove back to Lilac House. Mr. Gordon had said that the buyer of the Shelby property was "a big shot from the coast." The coast—that could be Seattle. Perhaps Blair had given additional thought to her idea about opening a branch store in Shelby, that expanding on this side of the mountains would be worth the risk, after all. Could she dare to hope that Blair was buying the property or even that his decision was based on his desire to be closer to her? If it were true, did that mean that he loved her? Was this his way of reaching for a compromise to mesh their two lives? Oh, life was wonderful!

She skipped up the steps at Lilac House and headed straight for the telephone. She dialed Mr. Gordon's number.

"Hello, Mr. Gordon?" she said when he came on the line. "This is Justine Fleming. I'm calling about that storefront you showed me a little while ago."

He chuckled. "My, you didn't waste any time. I just this minute stepped back into my office. Have you decided what you want to do?"

"Yes, I have," she responded a bit breathlessly. "I'd like to make an offer on that place. When would it be convenient for me to drop by your office and start the paperwork?"

"We can get going on the earnest money agreement right now, if you'd like to drive over—" He stopped. "Say, can you hang on a minute, Ms. Fleming? My secretary has something she wants to tell me."

"Go ahead. I'll hang on."

Justine could hear a muffled conversation, then Mr. Gordon came back on the line. "My wife called while I was out of the office," he explained. "Some of our calves got loose and are wandering through our neighbor's orchard. I'm going to have to get on home and help round them up. Dang it, I'm sorry, Ms. Fleming. Could you stop by tomorrow instead?"

She hated to wait now that she'd made up her mind. Be patient, she told herself. "Um, sure, that'll be fine."

They agreed on a time to meet in Mr. Gordon's office the following day, then they rang off.

The hours crawled by. For the first time since she'd left L.A., Justine caught herself watching the clock. She fidgeted at a window, staring at the driveway as if she could will Blair's truck to appear. Where was he, anyway?

When the phone rang later that afternoon, Justine's heart skipped a beat. Maybe that was Blair calling. She jumped up from her computer, where she'd been trying unsuccessfully to concentrate on some birth records from an old family Bible. Running into her bedroom to grab the receiver, she tripped over a throw rug in her haste. She broke her fall by sprawling across the bed on her stomach. She snatched up the receiver.

"Hello," she breathed, her heart pounding.

"Hi, Justine," said a wonderfully familiar male voice. "It's Blair." The rich sound of his chuckle charmed Justine through the phone line. "You answered on the second ring. Does that mean you're anxious to see me?"

"Oh, I happened to be near the phone, that's all."

She felt guilty for fibbing, but she didn't have the nerve to reveal that she'd practically slipped a disk rushing to answer the call.

"I just landed in Shelby," said Blair. "In fact, I'm calling from the airstrip." There was a pause. "I've missed you. Are you free tonight? I'd like to take you out to dinner."

I've missed you. The words played in Justine's mind like a beautiful symphony. Her grip on the receiver tightened as she pictured Blair in the outdoor phone booth, the late-afternoon sun burnishing his hair with gold. The plane had hardly touched down before he'd gone to the nearest phone to call her. The realization made her stomach flutter.

"Justine?" said Blair. "Are you still there?"

"Yes," she responded self-consciously. "Yes, I'm here."

"You . . . already have plans for tonight, is that it?"

"Oh, no, I'm free," she said quickly. "I'd love to have dinner with you."

She heard a sound from him that might've been a sigh of relief. "Good," he said, "then it's settled. I'll pick you up around seven."

"Terrific," she responded with feeling.

There was a long pause. Then Blair spoke. "There's something I need to tell you."

Justine almost blurted out her guess that he was buying land in eastern Washington. But she restrained herself. She could be wrong; and even if she were right, she'd learned that he liked to tell things in his own way when the moment seemed right for him. So she confined herself to a one-word response.

"Oh?"

"Yes, you see I . . ." He hesitated.

Justine got the impression that he was about to share his news then and there but something was holding him back. He cleared his throat.

"Look," he continued, "I'll tell you tonight, okay?"

He probably wanted to share his news in person so that he could watch her eyes light up. Justine bit her tongue to keep from chuckling with delight.

"Sure, that's fine," she managed to say. "I'll be ready."

"Oh, I almost forgot. Do you have any fancy dresses here with you?"

"Well, yes, but—"

"Good," he said. "Wear one tonight. Really dress up, Justine."

She was puzzled. "Are you sure we're going out here, in Shelby?"

"That's right. Just leave everything to me."

"Okay, but now you've really got me going."

"Trust me, sweetheart," he said with a chuckle. "I've got some fragile cargo to unload, so I'll see you later."

There was a soft click as he hung up the phone. Justine replaced the receiver and pondered what he could have in mind. He was taking her out to dinner, and she was supposed to wear her best dress. Hmm, what on earth was he planning? It wasn't as if Shelby had an abundance of supper clubs and glittery night spots. The one nice restaurant, Parker's, had already closed for the season, and Parker was no doubt motoring south at that very moment. So where was Blair taking her? Her brow puckered with curiosity.

She stood and walked over to her closet to search through her clothes. Because she hadn't worn them in so long, her fancy dresses had gradually been pushed to the back of the closet, and she had to move her casual summer clothes to get at them. She took out the half-dozen dresses and laid them on her bed, finally settling on the floor-length electric blue chiffon with the drop-dead plunge in the back. The vibrant color was perfect to set off her skin and midnight-black hair. Worn with strappy silver sandals on tiny heels and silver jewelry, the dress had never failed to turn heads in the past. Yes, definitely the blue chiffon, she told herself. He wants the dressiest clothes, he'll get them, she thought as she put her less dramatic gowns back into the closet. She glanced at the clock. No time to lose. She began peeling off her clothes, dropping them on the floor as she headed toward the bathroom. She'd take a leisurely bubble bath and make careful preparations for what promised to be an interesting evening out.

Later, when Justine opened the door to Blair's knock, she stepped back at the sight of him. She'd never before seen him this dressed up. Magically, the man who usually wore casual shirts and faded jeans or sports jackets had transformed his appearance into that of a polished man of the world. The vision nearly took her breath away.

Blair lowered his gaze, sweeping her chiffon-draped curves with appreciative eyes. "Mmm," he murmured, "you look fantastic."

Justine laughed lightly. "Thanks," she said, "I was thinking the same about you."

Blair waved a casual hand at his richly tailored dark suit, crisp shirt and understated silk tie. "Well, I could hardly show up in my country clothes after I'd told you to dress to the teeth, now could I?"

Justine returned his easy smile. Then she said, "I'll get my wrap."

She turned around to fetch the evening jacket that she'd tossed onto a chair in the hall. Before she reached it, however, she was surprised to hear Blair catch up with her. He grasped her shoulders from behind and held her still.

"Will you look at the back of this dress," he commented, giving a long, slow wolf whistle. "Or maybe I should say where the back used to be. I'm not sure you ought to leave the house in this little number, sweetheart. I mean, is Shelby ready for stunning, half-naked women to be sauntering in its midst?"

Justine laughed, warmed by his praise. "Don't be silly. This is a resort town, remember? During the summer the tourists run around in bikinis, and no one thinks twice about it."

"Ah, but those women don't have backs as gorgeous as yours." Justine felt Blair's warm breath on her sensitive skin as he dipped his head closer to her. "And they sure don't have this provocative little dip right here...."

He placed his hand on the small of her back and gently fondled her bare skin. Then his hand dropped even lower, this time coming to rest possessively on the fabric that was molded to her bottom. He kissed her shoulder, and Justine felt a thrill of desire zing through her veins. He continued.

"And I'll bet that none of them has such a cute little—"

Unable to stand any more, Justine turned in Blair's arms and pressed herself against him. She felt him flex with pleasure as he wrapped his arms around her, bending her soft curves into his hard contours.

"Much more of this," she murmured, "and our date's off."

He leaned away from her a bit, his brow puckered into a small frown. "Was it something I said?"

She twined her arms around his neck and kissed his jawline. "Oh, something you said, something you did—just everything, that's all." She gazed up into his handsome face.

"If you keep touching me that way, we'll stay right here, where I may have to ravish you on the hall carpet."

He chuckled low in his throat, and it sounded more like an expression of hunger than mirth. "Now you're talking."

He sought her mouth, muffling her small outcry of pleasure with a kiss that told her volumes about how much he'd missed her. They clung together for several long moments, and Justine felt the familiar light-headedness that often accompanied Blair's caress. It felt unbelievably delicious to be held in his arms and to feel the strength of his body against hers. She experienced a drunken giddiness caused by his kisses, as if she'd been sipping a heady wine all afternoon, a honeyed essence made from flower nectar, sweet hidden springs, the mist from a rainbow....

When at last their mouths broke apart, both of them were breathing more quickly. A fine dew shone on Blair's top lip, and his eyes smoldered from wanting her. It took all of Justine's self-control to keep from pulling him down to lie with her, then and there.

Blair spoke, his voice ragged with barely suppressed desire. "Much as I love your bawdy suggestion, we really should be getting along, or we'll miss the sunset. Maybe later you can demonstrate for me how to ravish someone on a hall carpet."

Justine reached for her handbag. "Honestly, Blair, you have me so curious about tonight."

"Good," he said. "That's how I want you to be."

"But where are we go—"

He held up his hand. "No hints." He wrapped her jacket around her shoulders, then held the door open and gestured toward his pickup. With a slight Cary Grant accent, which he managed to make sound both posh and playful at the same time, he said, "Your coach awaits you, madame."

A few minutes later they pulled up to a dock that jutted out into the lake. Blair helped Justine alight from the truck, then he grabbed a large picnic hamper from out of the back.

The skirt of Justine's chiffon dress billowed around her as
a soft breeze blew off the lake. Twilight was descending on
the land. The Cascades were already streaked with bands of
deep purple, their upper peaks gold-tinged by the setting
sun. A hush had fallen with approaching night. The only
sounds were those of the lake waters lapping against the
pilings and the gentle wind whispering in the tall pines.

Justine breathed in the sweet evening air, which was still
warm from the Indian summer day, and took Blair's prof-
fered arm. They began walking down the dock. The sound
of Justine's high heels on the timbers punctuated the dusk
with staccato beats that matched the excited pounding of her
heart.

A white rowboat was tied up at the end of the dock. On
its prow was painted the name *Water Nymph*. Justine cried
out with delight when she saw what was inside the little
craft. Soft cushions lay plumped invitingly at either end of
a low platform. The platform was set as a table, with a
creamy linen cloth and an unlit candle inside an amber
globe.

"Do you like it?" asked Blair close beside her.

There was a touching note of tentativeness in his voice,
which made Justine realize how much he wanted her to be
pleased with his efforts. She looked up at him.

"It's..." She gazed back at the boat. "It's simply wonderful."

"I figured that since I couldn't talk you into a night on the
town in Seattle right now, we'd dress up, anyway, and eat
our dinner as guests of the—" he coughed, his eyes twinkling with humor "—Sutherland Cruise Lines."

The *Water Nymph* gently rose and fell on the clear water.
With its soft lining of mauve and purple cushions, it reminded Justine of an elegant gondola, poised to sail over a
mythical inland sea to an enchanted isle. She loved to be
surprised and had always wished that the men in her life
could've been a little bit more creative, more adventurous.
Blair was certainly making up for the unimaginative men
she'd dated in the past—in one fell swoop!

"Come on," said Blair, "or we'll miss the floor show."

He nodded toward the sky, which was streaked with colored ribbons of rose and persimmon. Another glorious Lake Shelby sunset had begun to unfold. Holding Justine's elbow, Blair helped her into the boat, set the picnic hamper in the stern, then stepped aboard himself.

A few minutes later Blair had rowed the boat out to the middle of the lake. He shipped the oars and glanced over at Justine, who was leaning back among the velvet cushions, feeling for all the world like a pampered Cleopatra on her royal barge. The lake was still and glassy around them.

"Oh, this is fantastic." She sighed, trailing one hand in the cool water. "I love the contrast," she added with a laugh. "I'll bet we're the only people who've ever rowed out to the middle of Lake Shelby in evening clothes."

She watched Blair light the candle and replace the globe over it. The amber glow cast a mellow pool of light onto the tablecloth. Then from out of the hamper behind him, Blair pulled dishes, silverware and a chilled bottle of champagne with two tulip-shaped crystal glasses. He smiled at Justine as he deftly released the cork so that the grand old bottle made the appropriate soft sigh. Then he poured the sparkling liquid into the glasses. Justine sat up and took her drink from his hand.

"We're celebrating tonight, Justine," he said as he raised his glass in salute.

"Oh? Celebrating what?"

"Several things. Here's to mission accomplished, for example. I was told when I got back to Seattle the other day that Eric Engoe, the Norwegian skiing star, might not be able to help launch our sale, after all. So I got on the phone and straightened out that mess. He'll be there." He lifted his glass higher. "So let's drink to Norwegian athletes and fast-talking businessmen everywhere."

They tapped their glasses together and drank.

Justine toyed with the fringe on one of the cushions and tried to keep the excitement out of her voice. "What else are we celebrating?" she asked.

Blair regarded her across the table and paused before answering. "Well," he said, "there's always your beauty."

"Oh, come on, be serious." She laughed.

"I am. You're lovely. Very, very lovely."

Her cheeks grew warm at his compliment. "It's . . . it's sweet of you to say that," she said softly.

His mood suddenly became brisk, and Justine had the fleeting impression that he was avoiding telling her something. He set his glass down and again reached behind him.

"Further toasts of celebration can wait until later," he said. "First, let's eat. I've brought Seattle to you, Justine." He glanced at her as he took a container out of the hamper and placed it on the table. "Now don't look so skeptical," he added.

"You, uh, have Seattle in that little box?"

"Perhaps I should amend that. I've brought you some of the best *tastes* from the Emerald City." He opened the lid of the box. "Voilà."

Fascinated, Justine leaned forward and peered into the container. Nestled on a bed of crushed ice were a dozen fresh oysters on the half shell. Feeling rather tentative, she looked up at Blair.

"This must be the fragile cargo you mentioned on the phone," she commented.

"That's right." He chuckled. "Need some encouragement?" He handed her a large linen napkin, which she spread across her lap.

"I'm afraid so," she said. "I've always meant to try raw oysters, but I've never gotten around to it."

"You're going to love them," he said. "Watch me."

He squeezed a little juice from a wedge of lemon onto one of the oysters. Then he plucked the small bivalve out of its pearly shell with a tiny fork and put the oyster into his mouth. He closed his eyes in obvious ecstasy as he chewed. Then he swallowed, opened his eyes and smiled over at her.

"Fresh and sweet and mild," he said. "And these were picked this morning, right out of Puget Sound. Nowhere else in the world can you get oysters that taste like this." He nodded toward the bed of ice. "Go ahead, try one."

Justine placed one of the small morsels into her mouth and was delighted to discover that it was exactly as Blair had described. In fact, it was delicious!

"These are fantastic," she said as she plucked another oyster from its shell. "I thought I'd object to the texture, but they're very firm." She chewed and swallowed. "Oh, these are wonderful. I could eat an entire meal of nothing but these little darlings."

Blair quirked one brow at her, his eyes teasing. "That would be most unwise."

"Oh? Why?"

"Oysters are supposed to be an aphrodisiac. You should limit yourself to about six, or you might not be able to control your passion." A wicked smile slowly spread across his handsome face. "On second thought, that's not such a bad idea. Maybe I should've brought several dozen with me."

"No, no," Justine said with a laugh. "I'll take your word for it." She paused as she concentrated on the last oyster. "Besides, you don't really believe in that old superstition, do you?"

"Well, I didn't until tonight," he said. "But I suddenly have the urge to grab you and . . ."

In a low voice he described some of the delicious things he wanted to do to her, and Justine felt herself grow warm as she listened to his vivid imagery. Then she laid down her fork and shook her head at him in mock rebuke.

"We'd better not try any of that out here," she said, "or we'll have to explain to the town sheriff why we went swimming in our evening clothes."

They laughed together, their eyes locked in playful conspiracy.

The next hour passed like a dream. The *Water Nymph* drifted slowly on the glistening lake as night fell in the valley. Soon the blackened sky was ablaze with stars, the Milky Way cutting a brilliant swath across the heavens. Then the moon rose, glazing the water with platinum and lighting the valley and the surrounding hills with its cool magic. Justine felt that she and a fairy prince were gliding on a sea of enchantment. Her heart brimmed over with rapture.

The meal was delicious. Blair had assembled the elegant picnic from the stalls and delicatessens in the Pike Place Market, and each item tasted better than the last. True to his word, he had indeed brought some of Seattle's best tastes to Justine, and the effort he'd expended in order to please her touched her heart. She savored the sweet, moist salmon and the lovely vegetables and crusty French bread. Her favorite turned out to be the pickled chanterelles, the wild golden mushrooms that are plucked each fall from the rainy western slopes of the Cascades. The final course was fresh fruit and a creamy cheese. As an extra fillip Blair produced a thermos of hot coffee and a bottle of fine old brandy.

Throughout the meal Justine kept wondering when Blair was going to tell her what was on his mind. As they relaxed with their brandy, he looked over at her, and she thought that he was going to return to the subject of what they were celebrating. Instead, he asked her to catch him up on the news in Shelby. What had happened while he'd been gone? he wanted to know. Justine told him about the happy development in Myra's life, and he reacted with pleasure upon learning that Myra was picking up the threads of her career. Of course, Ellen and Caroline were by now settled in at their campus dorm at the University of Washington.

Justine had received a surprising bit of news the day before, she told him. Ursula Pennington was leaving Shelby to spend the winter with her sister in Florida. Her doctor's opinion that her rheumatism wouldn't stand another Shelby winter had finally given the older woman the excuse she needed to visit the East Coast. While there, Ursula had told Justine, she planned to fly up to Baltimore to visit her old haunts. It would be a trip down memory lane, she'd said. Shelby would see her return in the spring when the apple trees were in bloom.

"Oh," added Justine, "I almost forgot the biggest news of all. Leonard and Mrs. Berwick are getting married."

"You don't say. That's great."

She smiled. "I'm so pleased for both of them. They've decided to live in her house, which thrills me because Leonard will be right next door to Lilac House. He's grown very attached to the park and wants to finish the restoration project, then maintain the place. He's amazing."

"Well, good for him and good for Mrs. Berwick. Bluebell and those crullers must've done the trick."

They laughed together at the memory of a cat playing Cupid. There was a long, easy silence as they sipped their brandy. The candle in its amber globe cast a molten glow over the little table and the surrounding cushions. The only sounds were the gentle slapping of water on the bow and the distant cry of a night bird.

"Thank you very much," Justine said to Blair. "The meal was incredible. Everything about tonight has been wonderful."

Blair gazed thoughtfully at her as he slowly revolved his brandy glass in his hand. "It was my pleasure," he said. "I wanted to make this evening special." He cleared his throat. "Which leads me into the other reason why we're celebrating. My goal here has been accomplished, thanks to you."

"Oh?"

"Yes, when I got back to Seattle, I looked through my notes and found that we'd covered more ground than I'd remembered. The time here has really flown. You've been a terrific help to me, and I'm now ready to start interviewing writers for the project. In fact, I made a few calls yesterday and lined up some people who want to come in and talk about my plan." He paused. "I wanted tonight to be perfect because it's my last one here. I'm leaving tomorrow, Justine."

All of a sudden it felt to Justine as if a fist were squeezing her heart. She set down her brandy glass and told herself that there mustn't be a tearful scene—not here, not now. She'd had plenty of time to prepare for this moment, and she'd known all along that it was coming. Somehow, reminding herself of this fact didn't comfort her, she noticed. She felt as if the wind had been knocked out of her.

"I'm not looking forward to leaving," Blair added quietly. He was watching her closely. "But my time here is up. There's the sale to think about, writers to interview—I've got a million things to take care of back in Seattle."

"Yes, of course," Justine said in a small voice. Then she mustered a smile. "I'm happy for you, Blair. I'm glad that your project is off and running, and I'm pleased that I was of some help to you."

Her mood had turned bleak, and then she recalled the phone message from Noel. How could she have forgotten that? A smile spread across her face. She felt a bit lightheaded as she remembered her ebullience at learning from Noel that Blair was buying property and that—gleaned from Mr. Gordon—someone from the coast was developing a piece of land in Shelby. She'd put two and two together and come up with four—Blair could be expanding his business in this area. She realized that she'd been clinging to this thread of hope throughout their meal. Now she was almost afraid to ask him about it, but she had to know. Were her deductions correct? Was he really making a major move in her direction, a move that could bring their lives together?

She cleared her throat and looked across at him. "Your friend Noel called me this afternoon," she began.

A look of surprise crossed Blair's face. "Really?"

"Yes, he'd been trying to reach you and wanted me to give you a message."

"Oh? What message?"

She took a deep breath. Here goes. "He, uh, asked me to tell you that the property you wanted to buy is available, at the price you'd offered."

She bit her bottom lip as she waited for his response. Maybe she'd jumped the gun. Perhaps Blair would've wanted to spring this surprise about property on her himself.

"Great," he said with feeling, "I'll drink to that." He sipped his brandy. "I really wanted that piece of real estate. It's a prime location on Capitol Hill."

Justine clutched the edge of the table, and her body tensed. She must've heard wrong.

"Capitol Hill?" she echoed.

"Yes, I want to open an annex to my Seattle store. I've found out that Seattle people are big buyers of recreational equipment. My business is already having growing pains."

"But...Capitol Hill. Where is Capitol Hill?" Justine said in a whispery voice. She already knew where it was but had to hear it from his lips. She felt like a drowning woman.

"It's a few blocks up from downtown Seattle," said Blair. "Why?" A look of concern crossed his face. He leaned forward a little. "Say, are you all right? You seem a little pale."

She tried to relax against the cushions as she laughed ruefully. "Oh, I'm okay." Feeling very foolish, she went on. "I, uh, thought that the property you were buying was over here." She explained how she'd come to that conclusion.

"But I told you that I don't think my business would do well on this side of the mountains," he reminded her.

"Yes, I know." Her embarrassment was acute. "I just thought that..."

She couldn't bring herself to go on. She hoped that in the dim candlelight Blair wouldn't be able to see the hurt and disappointment that surely must be showing in her eyes. She fiddled with her napkin.

Blair reached over and laid his hand on hers, stilling the nervous gestures. "Oh, Justine," he said softly.

At that moment Justine knew that she was going to lose every bit of her self-control if she didn't quickly shift the topic of conversation. She looked over at Blair. "I have something to celebrate, too. I haven't told you my big news yet."

Blair withdrew his hand and sat back. There was a look on his face that Justine couldn't interpret. Around the edges of his sober expression lurked a hint of the vulnerability that lay within him. Still, she might've only imagined seeing this glimpse of the hidden side of him.

"What's your news?" he asked.

"I'm buying some property, too. Mr. Gordon, my real-estate agent, found a storefront on the main street. And, as I told you, he says that there's a bit of a boom on the way because of that builder from the coast." She paused and took a deep breath. "So it looks like my timing's great for starting up my business here. I'm signing the earnest money agreement tomorrow."

She was anxious to hear Blair's reaction. In the back of her mind, she knew she was hoping that he'd say the one thing that could change everything. Her heart beat with such love for him at that moment, she felt a sweet yearning blossom in her heart. If only he'd say that he loved her...

But he didn't. Instead, he said, "Congratulations."

Behind the forced good humor in his voice, Justine thought she detected something else. Could it be disappointment? Resignation?

He continued. "You're getting what you want, and I'm happy for you. Now you can really put down your roots here, set up your bookstore and live in Lilac House. I'm sure you must be very happy."

Perhaps it was only the reflection of the flickering candle, but Justine thought she saw a flinty look enter Blair's eyes. His jaw stiffened, as if he were waging an inner battle. It was so difficult sometimes to read his moods. If only he'd speak up and tell her what was on his mind. Then she reminded herself that maybe he wasn't keeping any deep feelings hidden from her at all. He was probably looking forward to returning to the city routine, where he could once again immerse himself in the creative challenge of making money. And yet he'd indicated that leaving there wasn't going to be easy for him, and Noel had said that Blair's attachment to Shelby had surprised him. If only Blair would speak up...

Then the thought occurred to her that maybe *she* should speak up. She recalled Myra's words—perhaps Blair was waiting for her to make the first move. He knew that she was very independent; maybe he was reluctant to risk being rejected by her. Perhaps he was in love with her but was unsure of her feelings for him.

"I'm going to miss you, Blair," said Justine as a tentative beginning.

"I'm going to miss you, too." Then his face brightened. "But you're coming over in the spring, I hope. I'll look forward to that. In the meantime, it sounds like you'll have a lot here to keep you busy."

Justine's feeling of bravery faded as she listened to his words. It was obvious that he was willing to leave things as they were. He must know that a long-distance romance wouldn't work out. The miles separating them would be a strong deterrent against keeping alive the mutual attraction that had flared between them. As the awful truth dawned on her—that Blair probably thought of her as a summer romance, after all—the bleakness inside her intensified until she thought she might suffocate. At that moment a cold wind blew from the direction of the mountains. She shivered and reached for her wrap. Suddenly all she wanted to do was curl up into a ball in her big bed at Lilac House and escape into a dreamless sleep.

Blair slipped the oars into the water. "I think fall just arrived in earnest," he said. "I'll bet there'll be frost on the ground tonight. We'd better get to shore."

They traveled back to the dock in silence. Blair had extinguished the candle, for which Justine was thankful. She hoped that the moonlight was insufficient to illuminate the look of disappointment on her face. She'd never felt this let down in her life.

When they arrived at Lilac House, the grounds and building were dark. The moon's glow filtered through the massive tree branches, dappling the drive and porch with pools of silver. On the lake the lunar light had been magical, suffusing the landscape with an appealing unreality; now it seemed cold and uncaring. Justine shivered again as she and Blair walked up the wide steps to the porch. She

opened the door and switched on the porch light. Blair
looked tired, his eyes cast in shadows, his face drawn and
tense. She could see that the unpleasant end to their other-
wise perfect evening had taken its toll on him, as well.

"Thanks again, Blair," said Justine. "Would you like to
step in for some coffee..."

Her voice trailed off. She knew that she was inviting him
in out of politeness only. What she really wanted was to
vanish inside and fall, dazed and emotionally exhausted,
into her bed and sleep for twelve hours.

Maybe Blair read her mind, or perhaps he felt the same
way. "No, that's okay," he said. "I think I'll take a rain
check on it." He grinned briefly and nodded over her
shoulder. "I'll take a rain check on that little demonstra-
tion on the hall carpet, too," he added. His voice held a
poignant note.

Justine's heart suddenly welled up with love for him, as
she'd felt it do several times on the *Water Nymph*. She flung
herself into his arms and clung to him. He immediately
wrapped his arms around her and held her tightly to him. By
a supreme force of will, she kept back the tears that were
stinging her eyes. She wanted no heavy emotional scenes just
as they were saying good-night.

"Hey," Blair said softly against her hair, "does this mean
that you like me?"

There was humor in his voice, plus that same vulnerability that had touched Justine's heart before. She forced herself to sound light and cheerful as she stepped back and
looked up at him. She smiled.

"Yes," she said, "I like you, Blair. Very much."

She stopped herself before the rest of her feelings poured
out. It wouldn't be right to put Blair on the spot. He mustn't
be made to feel any pressure to say things that he didn't
really mean.

He kissed her on the forehead. "Will you see me off tomorrow?" he asked.

She swallowed hard. "All right." Then a thought occurred to her. "I'm going to release Aldora in the morning. Would you like to do that with me before you leave?"

He squeezed her shoulders. "Yes, I would. I've grown attached to her myself. Let's give her a grand send-off together."

They agreed to drive up separately and meet early the next morning in the same field where they'd first encountered one another high above Lake Shelby. Justine knew that the next day she'd need that time alone to compose herself for two very difficult goodbyes. Then they said their goodnights, and Blair stepped off the porch, where the shadows closed around him. His leave-taking had such a grim flavor of finality to it that Justine closed the door quickly as if she could shut out the sensation. But the impression persisted. As she wearily climbed the stairs to her bedroom, a fist of pain clutched her heart; the next day Blair really would walk out of her life.

Later, unable to sleep, Justine lay in the darkness and listened to the radio beside her bed. Soft music played, providing the soothing background that she needed if she ever hoped to fall asleep that night. Staring into the shadows, she reflected on recent events. She felt a curious sensation of having been abandoned. Many of the people who meant something to her were leaving. Parker was en route to the Southwest, Myra was returning to L.A. and Ursula would soon depart for Florida. Why, even Ellen and Caroline, two sprites who'd graced the summer with their laughter, were gone. Thinking about all this, Justine felt a little like the bird that is left behind in the fall when the rest of the flock flies south. She imagined that a grand and exciting migration was taking place and that she was the only one not taking part in it.

Tears welled up in her eyes and slid down her cheeks. The most painful departures were happening tomorrow. The day that she'd been dreading was arriving at last, the day when she'd cast Aldora into the air for the final time so that she could rejoin her wild cousins. Perhaps Aldora would find a

mate; Justine hoped so. She was thankful that Blair would
be with her as she released the falcon, for she knew that the
parting wouldn't be easy. It had been a rare privilege to bond
with a wild creature who had learned to trust her. Aldora
had never been her pet, but she was her friend.

And then she'd say goodbye to Blair. The long months
without him stretched ahead of her like a series of silent,
empty rooms. Once she started working on her store, she'd
be too busy to dwell on Blair, she tried to console herself.
And in the spring, well, maybe they could pick up the
threads of their relationship. That is, if Blair wanted to.

She closed her eyes against these depressing thoughts and
concentrated on the music that was playing on the radio. A
woman's voice was singing a sad song about two lovers saying goodbye to each other. How appropriate, thought Justine grimly, her hands clutching the bedclothes. As the
poignant strains unraveled in the darkened room, she recalled how many times she'd said goodbye in her life. Her
parents had died, then her grandparents. Now half of Shelby
seemed to be leaving. And tomorrow she'd lose her falcon
and her love.

She was crying hard now, her face crumpled in pain. The
sounds of her sobbing mingled with the dying notes of the
song and seemed to echo in the large, silent house standing
among the trees. In all her life Justine had never felt so
alone. How, she wondered, was she going to remain composed and dry-eyed the next day when she saw Blair for the
last time?

Chapter Twelve

The next morning Justine was jarred abruptly awake by her alarm clock. She turned off the annoying sound and lay still for a few minutes, staring at the ceiling. The light seeping into her bedroom was thin and pale, not the rich, warm gold of a summer morning. This dawn told her that the season was winding down at last.

She'd slept badly. After crying herself to sleep, she'd fallen into an unconsciousness that was neither forgetful nor rest-giving. Her dreams had bordered on the nightmarish and were peopled with amorphous figures that were vaguely threatening. Now her eyes felt tired and puffy, and her muscles ached. At first she wondered if she were coming down with a cold, then she realized that her body was simply reacting to the stress of emotional conflict. There was no cold remedy in existence that would ease this pain, she thought grimly as she hauled herself out of bed.

Walking to the French doors, she flung them open and stepped out onto the balcony. She immediately hugged her arms around her, for there was an unmistakable nip in the air. She looked down at the park and discovered that Blair's prediction last night had been accurate: ice crystals glittered in the shadows. The first frost of fall had silently crept in as she'd slept, leaving a promise of more to come.

She glanced toward the Cascades and saw that an early snowfall had arrived, as well. The upper slopes of the mountains were dusted with a pristine coating of white. The peaks seemed to taunt her, thrusting their pale, frigid crags at her—like accusing fingers. They reminded her cruelly that the winter mountains would soon all but close her off from the rest of the world. She shivered, not so much from the crisp chill in the air, as from an unnameable dread that seemed to embrace her in its icy mantle. She went back inside and firmly closed the doors behind her.

Later, as she drove her Jeep beside the lake, she noticed that harvest time had arrived in the valley. The limbs of the apple trees were heavy with red ripe fruit. Apple bins had been placed between the rows, ready to receive the season's bounty. Several of the orchards had Pickers Wanted signs nailed at their entrances. Everyone was revving up for the short but intense harvest. Soon the trees would be stripped of their fruit, then the leaves would shrivel and fall off. Justine could imagine the bare, twisted branches poking up like bony hands against the dull gray sky of winter.

By the time Justine had reached the upland field, the sun had melted the frost between the furrows and warmed the air. She walked out to a grassy knoll, where she waited for about fifteen minutes. Blair was late for their rendezvous. She bit her lip and glanced at the dirt road that snaked its way up to the field. There was no sign of his approaching vehicle. It wasn't like him to be late; she wondered what was keeping him.

Aldora stirred on Justine's arm, her bells tinkling softly in the still air. Justine stroked the falcon's breast feathers and murmured to the peregrine. She was actually glad that Blair hadn't arrived yet; his tardiness was giving her more time with Aldora. It seemed like only yesterday that she'd been handed the starving falcon. The bird had been so weak then she'd barely been able to hold up her head. Now look at her, Justine thought proudly. Good care and the falcon's own fighting spirit had turned the situation around. This magnificent creature shifting restlessly on her arm bore little resemblance to the pitiful starveling she'd adopted.

The purr of an engine broke into Justine's recollections. She turned to look at the road and saw Blair's truck bounding up the hill, a giant cloud of dust churning out behind it. Suddenly her throat constricted, and her lips began to tremble. The moment that she'd secretly wished would never occur had arrived, and there was no escaping it now. In a few minutes she'd say goodbye to Aldora, the creature that had graced the past few weeks with so many hours of pleasure. Vicariously flying with Aldora had taken Justine away from her worries. Although it wouldn't be easy, she would soon repay her friend with the gift of freedom. She took a couple of deep breaths to calm herself, determined to put on a brave face.

Blair was out of breath by the time he'd hurried across the field and reached Justine. He wore a brown suede bombardier jacket, blue jeans and dark glasses. When he took off his glasses and folded them into his pocket, Justine noticed that his eyes looked tired and his face was drawn. She wondered if something had disturbed his sleep, as well.

"Sorry I'm late," he said, raking his hair back from his forehead. "I, uh, I had some things to take care of."

The look on his face told Justine that he was uncomfortable and that he was purposely being vague. He'd probably been packing for his trip back to Seattle, she thought sadly. She stuck out her chin and forced her voice to sound light.

"No problem," she said with a shrug. "It gave me more time with Aldora."

"I guess you're not exactly looking forward to letting her go, are you?"

Justine's emotions were so close to the surface she knew that she'd have trouble discussing her feelings for Aldora without breaking down. Fortunately, she didn't have to an-

swer Blair's question because just then a harsh whistle
pierced the air above them.

Justine and Blair looked up. A red-tailed hawk circled on
a thermal. It called again, then adjusted its wings slightly
and slid across the sky, riding the air toward the wheat lands
south of the Columbia River. Aldora had also heard the
cries of the wild hawk, judging by the way she cocked her
head and caused the little plumes on her hood to tremble.
She twittered softly and tightened her grip on Justine's arm.

Blair laid a gentle hand on Justine's shoulder. "I think it's
time," he said softly. "She wants to fly."

"I know," said Justine, her voice a whisper.

With trembling fingers she unsnapped the clip that held
the falcon to her leash. Then she tried to loosen the leather
jesses that trailed from Aldora's ankles. When she fumbled, Blair reached over to assist her.

"Here, let me help," he said.

Soon the jesses were off, and there was nothing holding
the falcon to her human perch except force of habit and the
fact that she was still hooded. Justine reached up to remove
the hood, then withdrew her hand.

"You can do it," encouraged Blair from close beside her.
"It's the right thing."

"I know." There was a catch in her voice. "It's just
that... Oh, Blair, it's so hard. I didn't think it would be this
hard."

She wished that she could sidestep her feelings and simply get this unpleasant event behind her. Be brave, she told
herself. Releasing Aldora had always been her goal; why was
she so hesitant now?

In her heart she knew the answer. Letting go of Aldora
had come to mean letting go of Blair, as well. Helping her
release the falcon was Blair's final task there. As soon as
that was accomplished, he would also disappear over the far
horizon, out of sight and out of her life.

Gathering her courage, Justine took a deep breath and
removed Aldora's hood. The falcon blinked her black eyes
and swiveled her head to look around. She leaned forward

and shook out her feathers, their rustling sound as soft as the murmur of wind in leaves.

Justine's eyes grew misty as she leaned close to Aldora and whispered, "Goodbye, dear friend. I'm going to miss you. Good luck." She tensed her arm and added softly, her voice breaking with emotion, "Now go and chase the wind." Then she cast the peregrine into the air and dropped her arms to her sides.

Aldora flew rapidly away from the two watching humans, as was her habit. Then she wheeled around, following her pattern of returning to the lure or to the fist. She made a swift pass near Justine and Blair, then veered off, circling wide to arrow in from another direction. When Justine still made no motion to call her in, Aldora flew higher, then dove in a magnificent stoop. Like a bullet, she plummeted toward earth, opening her wings and pulling up at the last moment. She seemed to be showing off her hunting prowess one final time, Justine thought as she watched the stunning display.

The falcon suddenly appeared to sense that she was no longer tied to the earth-bound creatures below her. She began flying away, following the path of the red-tailed hawk.

"She isn't coming back," said Justine in a dull voice. She watched Aldora become smaller and smaller. "I wish I could fly so that I could go with her," she murmured, half to herself. "I want to go with her."

Blair put his arm around her shoulder and gave her a hug. He was also watching the southern horizon, where Aldora was quickly becoming a tiny speck.

"You gave her a wonderful send-off," he said. "I know she'll be all right."

Then suddenly all of Justine's pent-up emotions burst inside her like a dam opening its floodgates. Blair gathered her into the circle of his strong arms and held her close as she sobbed out her sorrow.

"It's okay," he murmured against her temple. "Go ahead and let your feelings out. It'll do you good to cry." He

hugged her closer to him, and she felt the warmth of his
body enveloping hers like a soothing balm.

They stood pressed together on the little grassy knoll for
some time. The only sounds were Justine's sobbing and the
words of comfort that Blair whispered against her hair.
Later, when her feelings of misery had lost their sharp sting,
Justine stopped crying and wiped away her tears with the
handkerchief Blair had given to her.

"You were very brave to let Aldora go," said Blair. "I
know you're going to miss her."

Justine tilted her head back and looked up at him. "Yes,
I'll miss her," she said, her voice trembling.

But it's you I'm going to miss a hundred times more, she
added to herself. Oh, how she would miss him.

As if he sensed the emotions that were welling up inside
of her, Blair bent his head closer and gazed more deeply into
her eyes. His voice was also suddenly overladen with emotion as he spoke to her.

"Justine, darling Justine."

Then he clasped her to him in an embrace that took her
breath away. Their mouths came together in a wild crush of
lips and tongues. It was a kiss of such fierce intensity it ignited flames of desire in Justine's veins. She felt faint, and
her knees threatened to collapse beneath her. Twining her
arms around Blair, she clung to his solid back covered with
its soft layer of suede. All the passion that she'd ever felt for
him poured out of her in those few moments as their bodies
arched together with an aching hunger. With her lips, with
her hands, with her entire being, she wanted to reveal to
Blair the depth of her feelings for him. How she longed to
cry out, *I love you, I love you*.

But even as she felt the words bubbling up inside her, she
knew that she wouldn't utter them. Too many times in the
past she'd exposed her true feelings, only to have them return to haunt her, turning her joy into bitter regret. No, she
would neither cry out her heart's desire, nor put words into
Blair's mouth. She would instead accept that the only reality—the only past, present or future—was here and now.

With a heart that felt full to bursting with the love she had for Blair, she gave herself up to the moment. Believing that this might be the last time that they'd ever make love, she yielded completely to her impulses. Come what may, she would always have the treasured memory of her and Blair entwined on the grassy knoll high above the lake. With the pale blue sky as their only covering, it felt to Justine that she and Blair were on top of the world and that they were the only people in it.

Blair finally dragged his mouth from hers. Her lips were swollen with desire. She wanted more and, lips parted, she reached for him.

"What an exciting woman you are," Blair groaned against her mouth, his voice husky with emotion. "I've never seen such passion written on a woman's face. You make me feel like I'm on fire."

"I'm on fire, too." She gasped, clinging more tightly to him.

"I'm going to take you right here," he said. He held her face in his big hands. Their palms felt warm and rough against her skin. "I'm going to make you forget about everything but us. Help me do that, Justine." He smiled down at her, his eyes gleaming with ardor. "Come fly with me, sweetheart."

"Yes," she cried out, pressing herself against him.

Together they sank down onto the soft, sun-warmed grass and began pulling impatiently at each other's clothes. Justine wrested Blair's jacket and shirt off him as he removed her blouse and jeans and tossed them aside. A button from someone's clothing popped off, and both of them laughed at their fevered urgency. Blair, clad only in jeans, knelt beside Justine's supine form and paused to gaze at her. She wore nothing except her bra and panties. The two little scraps of silk and lace accentuated the fullness of her breasts and the hollows of her narrow waist and hips.

"I love your taste in underwear," breathed Blair, his voice ragged with desire. "I can't tell you how many times I've looked at you in jeans and a shirt and thought about your underwear beneath those casual clothes. It drives me crazy, knowing that you always have that sexy stuff next to your skin.''

His head swooped down, and his mouth touched the bare skin of her belly. He grasped her around the waist, his hands roving up and down her curves and valleys as his warm tongue wet her skin with teasing strokes. Wherever he touched her, Justine felt that he was leaving a scorching trail in his wake. Her body had never before felt this alive, this sensitive to pressure and touch and temperature. It was as if all the nerve endings in her body had rushed to the surface. The sensations that were coursing through her were building a desire that knew no bounds. Primal sounds poured from her throat as she yielded to her upwelling passion.

Blair dragged his mouth from her belly, where he'd been paying lusty tribute to her navel, circling it with his tongue and licking her flesh with increased fervor. He straddled her body and leaned down to gaze into her eyes, as if searching for signs of the effects of his lovemaking. He must've approved of what he read there, for a slow, languid smile spread across his face.

Justine arched her body beneath him, reveling in the sensual contrast of the roughness of his jeans against her naked skin. Blair placed his hands on her breasts, pressing into them the imprint of his warm palms, then curling his fingers to grasp the twin mounds that were now swollen with unbearable excitement. Justine thrust herself toward him, shamelessly showing him how much she wanted him. The faded fabric of his jeans stretched provocatively across his loins as he dipped his head. Their mouths met in another wild kiss of greedy abandon.

Never still, Blair's hands loosened the front clasp of Justine's bra and impatiently brushed the filmy garment aside. With a low moan he tore his mouth from hers and bent to capture one of her breasts. Justine closed her eyes and tossed her head back. She laced her fingers in his hair as he focused on his erotic task, first tonguing the sensitive skin around her nipple, then catching the erect bud between his teeth. Justine cried out with pleasure-pain as he became carried away and nipped too hard at the swollen tip. She felt a hasty apology whispered against her skin. Then his mouth rained soft kisses onto her breast, kisses that seemed to burn her with their fervor.

Justine splayed her hands across Blair's chest, reveling in the soft hair that curled there. She felt the thunder of his heartbeat beneath her exploring touch. As he turned his attention to her breast's twin, Justine lowered her hands to the waistband of his jeans. He moaned low in his throat, the sound vibrating erotically against her heated skin, then he shifted slightly in obvious invitation to her searching hand. He reached down, and with strong, sure fingers deftly loosened the fastenings of his jeans.

"Do it," he whispered against her breast. "Touch me, Justine."

The erotic abandon of his words sent a shaft of pure desire arrowing through Justine, and she reached farther with her questing hand. What her eager fingers found was a searing heat and a straining tumescence that made her pulse pound. She fondled and teased, her touch featherlight. Then she grasped him firmly, telling him with her more assertive touch that the fire in her veins leaped higher and higher with each stroke of her hand on his hard, smooth flesh.

"You're driving me crazy," Blair rasped against her breast, where his lips and tongue had been paying sweet homage.

With an urgency that left both of them panting, they removed the rest of their clothing and flung it aside. Then they were tumbling nude on the soft, fragrant grass, their arms and legs entangled in sweet confusion.

Blair seemed unaware of anything except her. The expression on his face told Justine that his full concentration was on her pleasure. His eyes were hooded, a fine sheen of perspiration glowed like dew on his skin and his mouth was partially open, the lips full and eager to please. He lay beside her, caressing her curves and valleys with his hand

and dipping to pull at her nipple with his greedy mouth.
Never in her life had Justine felt so wanted, so desirable, as
she read on Blair's face how full to overflowing he was with
the honeyed pleasures of her body.

He ran a possessive hand down to her belly, then nuzzled
his face against the hollow of her throat as he dipped his
hand even farther. Her legs parted willingly as he nudged his
knee between them. Then with his hand he toyed with her
senses, fanning the sparks that burned in her with an intimate touch that left her breathless and close to tears. All her
nerve endings seemed to have collected at the center of her
womanhood, sending paths of fire streaking out to her fingers and toes. Panting animal sounds began purling from
her throat and were captured by the soft breeze that rustled
among the grasses. Blair pushed her to the brink and let her
peek over it, then he chuckled softly and withdrew his hand.

Justine cried out, "Don't stop, Blair. Please, please don't
stop. I can't stand it."

"I have a better idea." His voice was husky in anticipation of the pleasures he had in mind.

With the grace of an athlete, Blair caught her in his arms
and raised her so that she was straddling him as he lay on the
ground. Justine gazed down on the man who'd tapped her
hidden fountains of ecstasy, which she'd never even known
existed. She felt deeply grateful. For many years she'd believed that she'd already seen the face of passion. Now she
marveled to herself that she'd actually been waiting for this
wondrous lover who'd unleashed her erotic persona. She
would never have believed that she could fling herself into
lovemaking with such fervor or uninhibited abandon.

"You seem awfully pleased with yourself," breathed Blair
up at her. "I hope that I can take some of the credit for the
look that's written all over your face."

He reached up to touch her hair, which Justine could feel
was in wild disarray from their exertions. She swooped
down to kiss him, her lips parted, her tongue seeking and
hungry.

"You may take all the credit," she murmured. She ground her hips against his loins, causing him to moan. "It's your fault that I act this way," she added, "and I love it."

Grasping her by the waist, Blair raised her a little, then entered her with a long, smooth thrust. She cried out with the keenest of pleasure as he filled her with a shaft of heat that seemed to pierce her soul. With a small cry she flung herself onto his chest, her mouth open on his skin, her hands clutching his arms. With the sensitivity of an experienced lover, Blair paused as if to let them savor the bliss of being joined at last in the ultimate act of love. His breath rasped against Justine's hair, and she could feel the racing of his pulse in his neck. When he began moving inside her, she huddled against him, her legs bent and pressed to his sides. They rocked in each other's arms, trying now this rhythm, now that tempo, until they blended their strokes into a primal ballet.

Justine felt herself being pulled again toward that lovely, beckoning chasm where she could free-fall into perfect bliss. As she thrust against Blair's body, fingers of fire danced along her inner thighs, up through her chest and along her arms. Every pore of her body, every cell, seemed poised for that dazzling plummet, and she panted in sweet anticipation of tumbling off the brink. She was surprised to feel Blair work one of his hands between their fused bodies. Her surprise turned to delight as she guessed his intention. Shifting slightly, Justine soon felt Blair giving her special, intimate caresses where their bodies were joined. This fillip was new to her, but then, no lover had ever worked so hard to give her pleasure.

Blair's masterful lovemaking quickly brought Justine to the apex of ecstasy, where she hung for a delicious span of timelessness. She savored those moments of teetering on the brink, then she tossed her head back, clutching Blair's shoulders and bucking her body against his as she drew from their connection every last bit of sensual delight. She barely heard the raw animal sounds that ripped from her throat as fireworks exploded behind her closed eyelids. The waves of her release pounded hard and fast through her loins, rippling out to shudder along her arms and legs. *Come fly with me,* Blair had said. And now she was flying as her passion soared, and she floated weightless somewhere above the earth.

At that moment Blair's own shattering release gripped him in its throes. He pulled Justine down onto him one last time and called her name. His strong hands grasped her hips as the frenzied explosion claimed him. He shuddered over and over, and through her own dreamy haze Justine could tell that he, too, had been flung into another sphere. Like lovers everywhere, their ecstasy had sent them spinning into a different dimension, where nothing existed except the sensations of two bodies performing the ancient rituals of passion.

Justine collapsed onto Blair's chest, her breathing rapid and shallow. They lay still for some time. Gradually Justine could hear that Blair's heart no longer hammered inside his rib cage. With a feeling of drugged languor, she slid off his body and sprawled beside him in the grass. He reached for her, and they entwined their fingers. Blair squeezed her hand, telling her with his touch that their lovemaking had moved him as powerfully as it had her.

The piercing cry of a flicker split the air, and Justine shivered. As reality began filtering back into her befogged brain, she unsuccessfully tried to beat it back. Her body shook again.

Blair spoke. "Are you cold?"

"A little," she lied. Her sadness over his leaving was slowly returning. She cast about for a safer topic. "And I'm . . . I'm thinking about Aldora." She sat up and began reaching for her clothes.

"Are you worried about her?" asked Blair. He also sat up and began dressing.

"Yes, I guess I am," she said, relieved that she could hide her true feelings behind the lesser sorrow of giving up her falcon.

"I have an idea," said Blair, buttoning his shirt. "Why don't you come up in my plane with me, and we'll try to find her. If you could see that she's doing fine on her own, you'd feel reassured, right?"

"Yes, I would," said Justine as she pulled on her jeans and snapped them closed. "That's a wonderful idea, but..." She hesitated. "Do you have the time to do that for me? I mean, you're leaving today for Seattle, and—"

"I can certainly spare time for this," he said, shrugging into his jacket. "Come on."

He grabbed her hand, and they started walking across the field toward their two vehicles, which were parked side by side beneath some pine trees. Justine felt a sharp pang of wistfulness cut through her as she noted Blair's nonchalant attitude about his imminent departure. It was as if his leaving had no special significance whatsoever. Well, she thought with a wrenching poignancy, it probably didn't to him. The realization made her want to squirm out of his grasp, but instead, she clung even more tenaciously to his hand. No other man in her life had ever given her so much joy, and she wanted to cling to him right to the very end.

Half an hour later Blair and Justine took off in his small plane from the Shelby airstrip. As the two-seater left the ground, Justine temporarily forgot her troubles and fell under the spell of flying. Only once before in her life, when she was about fourteen, had she flown in a plane this small. Now, like the young girl she'd once been, she was transported with delight.

Circling the lake, Blair skillfully maneuvered the plane as they climbed higher. Justine felt a thrill of excitement in the pit of her stomach. What incredible fun it was to fly! And how breathtaking it was to soar above the earth like a bird and gaze down upon the natural treasures of her beloved Shelby Valley. A couple of sailboats—white butterflies— skimmed across the glimmering lake. The lacy scallops around the blue water were sandy beaches. A yellow toy school bus crept along a dirt road, and a red tractor puffed smoke in a field.

Justine was fascinated by how different everything looked from up there. Farmhouses shrank to tiny miniatures, roads were narrow scratches on the earth and the apple orchards gave the cultivated acres a soft, quilted appearance. She couldn't see the fruit on the trees, but she knew that the branches hung heavy with snappy-crisp red and golden Delicious apples, the world's finest. She looked off toward the horizon, and her breath caught. The magnificent Cascade Mountains thrust upward, rocky sentinels against an endless sky. She'd never before seen them from this perspective—as if through the eyes of a soaring eagle—and the sight awed her.

She glanced at Blair, her heart brimming over with a mixture of exhilaration, deep wonder and a feeling of profound thankfulness that she was alive on this crystal-clear day. Blair squeezed her hand and returned her smile. It was obvious to Justine that he felt the same as she. Perhaps he experienced this joyful feeling of freedom and awe every time he took his plane up. By now she knew how deeply he felt things and how keenly aware he was of his surroundings. The realization made her heart suddenly leap with love for him. She turned away, afraid that he'd see the tears sparkling in the corners of her eyes.

Leaving the valley behind, Blair flew the little plane south beyond the golden hills. Below them flowed the mighty Columbia River, which looked like a shiny gray-blue snake twisting through the brown sage lands and irrigated fields.

"What a gorgeous day to fly," said Justine, finding her voice at last. She was searching for Aldora as she admired the misty horizon and the stark grandeur of the terrain.

"Yes, it is," agreed Blair. He nodded toward some cliffs. "I'll swing by those rocks for a closer look."

He banked the plane into a turn and flew over the basalt outcropping.

"There she is!" exclaimed Justine, pressing her forehead against the window. "Can you fly by again so that I can be sure?"

"You bet."

On the next pass Justine was positive that the peregrine falcon perched on a rocky ledge below was Aldora, who was distinctive because of a light patch of feathers on her right shoulder. Justine noticed with satisfaction that she was feeding on a dead rock dove, prey that she'd obviously caught herself. There was no longer any reason for Justine to worry about the bird's ability to fend for herself. She smiled down at Aldora.

"Goodbye," she mouthed silently, and this time her happiness for the falcon was untainted by sadness.

Justine turned to look at Blair. "She's fine," she said. "Thank you very much for taking me up to check on her."

He smiled. "My pleasure."

They flew on for several minutes in silence. Blair seemed to be as lost in thought as Justine was as he glanced down at the passing scenery. Justine knew that she should tell him to turn around and head back to Shelby so that he could drop her off and begin the long flight to Seattle. Yet something held her back. She tried to relax and enjoy the beautiful eastern Washington landscape as she analyzed her feelings.

It was a sad and bitter truth that she'd fallen deeply in love with Blair and that she was about to say goodbye to him. How had events come to such a state? When she'd first met Blair, she'd been convinced that he was exactly the wrong kind of man for her. As time passed, however, she'd come to feel that just the opposite was true. Instead of the shallow, uncaring person she'd feared he was, he had slowly revealed himself to her as deeply caring, warmly reassuring and touchingly vulnerable. She admired him as she had admired no other person in her life. He had struggled against terrific odds and fought his way to the top of the business ladder. And he seemed to care for her, too. So what held him

back from proclaiming his love for her if, in fact, he felt that
way?

Then she recalled Myra's words again. Blair might be
waiting for a sign that Justine could love him on his own
terms. An irony dawned on her—perhaps both of them were
waiting for the other to speak up first. She knew that she
needed to hear him express his love for her in words that
clearly revealed his commitment to her. For his part, perhaps her fierce independence made him shy away from
committing himself because he feared her rejection. After
all, he'd grown up pretty much on his own, fighting his
battles with no family or support group to help him when
the going got tough. Maybe, deep down, he believed that
being alone was better than depending on another person
for emotional support. Why stick your neck out, just to risk
losing your head?

Loving Blair on his own terms... She recalled the reasons why she'd fled the city hassles and retreated to the
quiet, safe countryside. Her rejection of cities had been
complete until Blair had helped her see that she had overreacted out of empathy for her sister. She chuckled ruefully
to herself. Her total rejection of city life now seemed irrel-
evant and almost trivial. Why, if things were different, she
would even go to live in Seattle. If... if Blair loved her. She
realized with piercing clarity that she could live anywhere on
the face of the planet as long as she had Blair by her side.

She had the sudden impulse to tell him what was on her
mind. She cast a secret glance in his direction. He was staring straight ahead, a nerve twitching in his jaw. His brows
were knit into a frown, and he was gripping the steering
wheel hard. Justine placed her hand on his arm and was
surprised to discover that his muscles felt as tight and tense
as iron bands. He responded to her touch by turning to regard her. Justine saw such heart-wrenching emotion flicker
across his face, she felt her eyes mist over.

"What is it, Justine?" he asked.

Do it now, a little voice inside her said. *One of you has to
speak up. Do it now.* Myra had the right idea. You had to

take risks in life. A wild idea had been teasing around the edges of Justine's mind. Before she could lose her nerve, she blurted it out. It was now or never.

"Take me to Seattle with you," she said.

A look of astonishment crossed Blair's face. "What did you say?"

"I want to go to Seattle with you today, right now. Will you take me with you?"

Slowly he shook his head, a broad grin spreading across his face. "Come on, did you peek or what?"

His response confused her. What did he mean? "Did I . . . did I peek? Peek at what? I don't understand."

He jerked his thumb toward the area right behind their seats. "Look under that tarp, and you'll see what I mean."

She reached around and did as he'd told her. Beneath the tarp she recognized several pieces of her luggage mixed in with suitcases that must belong to Blair. Her knees suddenly felt weak, but she was still perplexed. She looked back at Blair and laughed nervously.

"I'm afraid you're going to have to tell me what this is all about," she said.

"I've been sitting over here trying to figure out exactly how I was going to break the news to you, but you've made it a lot easier for me, Justine." He took her hand and brought it to his lips, where he planted a couple of soft kisses on her fingers.

"What news? Blair, don't keep me in suspense," said Justine, her heart hammering in her chest.

"Last night, when I left you at your house, I'd pretty much accepted that you were determined to stay in Shelby and start up your new bookstore. I tried to tell myself that it didn't matter and that I could wait until next spring to see you again." He glanced at her, and his eyes told her volumes about the inner turmoil that he'd gone through. "As soon as I went to bed, I knew it wouldn't work. Long-distance romances are too chancy, Justine. So many things can happen when people live apart from each other. Why, you might even meet some rancher and fall in love with him and get married. Then I would've lost you forever. I couldn't let that happen.

"Sometime around midnight—I didn't sleep much last night—I came up with a plan. At first it seemed a little crazy, but then I figured that it was worth the risk. I had nothing to lose, I told myself." He looked meaningfully at her. "But I had everything to lose if I didn't try it.

"I was late meeting you this morning because I drove to your house first after I thought you'd be gone. I went to your bedroom and packed some of your clothes. Then I drove to the airstrip, stowed the stuff in the back of my plane and raced up to meet you in the field."

"You went to all that trouble...." Her mind was whirling.

"The way I felt last night, I was willing to walk through fire to get you to come with me." His voice was low and molten with meaning. "My original plan was to ask you about it as soon as we'd released Aldora." He quirked an amused smile at her. "Then you and I got a little carried away, and I decided to wait awhile."

His expression became sober. "To be honest with you, I wasn't sure exactly how you'd take to my idea. I mean, I was trying to make it easy for you to say yes, but I found myself sort of hanging back." He rubbed his thumb across his bottom lip. "I guess I was afraid you'd turn me down, and then I'd know that you didn't care."

"Oh, Blair," she said softly, squeezing his arm.

"Well, anyway, I was still trying to get up my courage when you mentioned how worried you still were about Aldora. Bingo, there was the perfect excuse I needed to get you up in my plane. From there I thought it'd be easy to talk you into going to Seattle with me." He shook his head slowly and added ruefully, "Like I said, I was sitting here trying to find the words when you brought up the subject yourself. It looks like you and I were on the same wavelength. Amazing, isn't it?"

"Yes," she breathed, close to tears, "amazing and wonderful."

"You know that piece of property I just bought in Seattle?"

"Yes."

"I got to thinking last night that it would be perfect for a bookstore. I thought I'd offer it to you as a sort of... incentive. Oh, and speaking of incentives, I've ordered a couple of tickets for *Throw Her a Kiss*, that musical you wanted to see."

"Oh, Blair—" she laughed "—I don't think I need any incentives."

"All the same, I'm giving that property to you. It really is in a terrific location. Best of all, it's only six blocks from my store. We could have lunch together, and—" There was an emotion-laden atmosphere in the little plane. He squeezed her hand. "We belong with each other, Justine. Think about what we did a few minutes ago, down there in the field. People who care that much for one another should be together, not separated by hundreds of miles and a mountain range. And it's not just the lovemaking. I realized last night that I'm not willing to let you go. I want you with me." He hesitated, then looked over at her. "Do I have to spell it out for you, sweetheart?" he asked softly.

The expression on her face must've told him all that he needed to know. A light came into his eyes. "I believe I do, don't I?"

There was a catch in Justine's voice. "I want to hear the words, dear Blair. I guess I'm a woman who needs to be told these things."

He kissed her fingertips. "The words don't come easily to me," he said quietly. "I've been on my own for so long I've never felt I could reach out to someone else and put my trust in them."

"Maybe you just need practice," she said. She held her breath, waiting for the only words that would make her happiness complete.

His eyes gleamed with fierce devotion, and he spoke slowly. "I am so in love with you, Justine, I am almost crazy from it. I don't know when I started loving you, but I feel as if it has been forever. For weeks I've tried to figure out how in the hell I was going to hang on to you. It has nearly driven me wild, thinking that I was about to lose you. That's why I did the crazy thing I did today—cramming your clothes into suitcases and practically kidnapping you." He paused. "I did all that because I thought, well, I thought that maybe you felt the same way about me."

With a sound of pure delight, Justine threw her arms around his neck. Wordlessly she kissed him everywhere her lips could reach—on his neck, on his cheek, on his hair. Her enthusiastic expressions of affection jarred Blair's arms, and the plane took a sudden shallow plunge.

"Hey—" he laughed as he leveled the craft out again "—watch out, or we'll make an unscheduled landing in a wheat field." He reached up and cupped the side of her head with one hand. His touch was infinitely tender.

"Blair, I do feel the same way about you," Justine said against his neck. "I've been wanting to tell you how much I love you, but I was afraid that you might not be in love with me."

He laughed briefly. "It sounds like you need some practice, too."

"Yes," she said, raising her head to look at him. "You're right, I guess I do." She smiled. "But something tells me that we're a couple of fast learners."

"I have an idea," he said, pressing her hand to his lips for another kiss. "What do you say we practice saying 'I love you' for the rest of our lives." He glanced at her, his eyes blazing with ardor and affection. "Will you marry me, Justine?"

Before she could respond, he quickly added, "Look, I know how attached you are to Shelby, and I think we can work out a compromise. Here's my plan: we'll spend part of the year in Seattle—maybe even get a place outside the city—and we can escape to Lilac House as often as you like." He smiled. "You know, you've helped me acquire a taste for country life, and I can't think of a retreat I'd rather escape to than lovely old Lilac House. If you like my idea, you can call your real-estate agent as soon as we land in Seattle and tell him that you've changed your mind. From what you told me, he won't have any problem selling that place to someone else." He paused, then his tone became more thoughtful. "So how about it, sweetheart? Will you marry me?"

Justine's heart overflowed at that moment with love and with the most intense happiness she'd ever known. "Dear Blair," she said with feeling, "of course I'll marry you. I love you so."

"Then you don't think that it'll bother you to spend part of the year in the city?"

"I'm looking forward to it," she said. "Besides, what would really bother me is not having you in my life. I don't care where I am, as long as you're there with me." Her eyes again blurred with tears of joy. "And now," she said softly, "would you mind flying us to Seattle? You see, I've got a date to see a musical there with the most wonderful man in the world, and I'd really hate to stand him up."

"You've got it, sweetheart," said Blair with a smile. "Next stop, the Emerald City."

Then he banked the plane and pointed it toward the mountains, and as he did so, Justine felt her heart chase the wind.

*   *   *   *   *

For the millions who can't read
Give the Gift of Literacy

One out of five adults in North America
cannot read or write well enough
to fill out a job application
or understand the directions on a bottle of medicine.

**You can change all this by joining the fight
against illiteracy.**

For more information write to:
Contact, Box 81826, Lincoln, Neb. 68501
In the United States, call toll free: 1-800-228-8813

**The only degree you need
is a degree of caring**

LIT-A-1R

Sarah

MAURA SEGER

Sarah wanted desperately to escape the clutches of her cruel father.
Philip needed a mother for his son, a mistress for his plantation.
It was a marriage of convenience.
Then it happened. The love they had tried to deny suddenly became a
blissful reality... only to be challenged by life's hardships and brutal
misfortunes.
